Sam's F

Phantom Ba⎯ ⎯⎯ MC

Book 4

Erin Osborne

Photographer: Reggie Deanching at RplusM Photography

Cover Model: Dixie Hartt

Editors: Full Bloom Editing – Courtney Lynn Rose and Rebecca Ernst Vazquez

Proofreader: Kim Richards

Sam's Playboy Blurb

Sam Hart

Growing up, I saw the evil of a man who wants to control a woman. I don't trust easily, and the only person I love is my son, Caleb. One chance meeting changes my entire life and world. I'm taken away from the life we've been existing in and given a chance to grow and get away from the abuse.

Now, I'm surrounded by people who care about my son and me. I'm just not sure if I can truly let them in. Especially Playboy. When our situation changes, I don't want to be in Benton Falls alone with his family. Playboy is the main reason I'm staying there and not leaving. Now, he's locked up and won't see or talk to me.

Can I let him in, or will he break my heart beyond repair?

Griffin 'Playboy' Busch

I grew up in the Phantom Bastards MC with my dad, Slim, being the President. I'm used to being alone and only using the house bunnies when I need to. At least now that I'm older. They don't call me Playboy for any other reason than I used to take whatever woman caught my eye.

That all stopped when one woman and her young son entered my life. Now, she's the one I want and the only one I won't be with because of her past. Until fate decides to step in and our lives change. I'm locked up and don't want her to see me as anything but who I am on the outside.

Can I win her back and then protect her when a new enemy poses a threat?

Dedication

This book is dedicated to Rebecca. One meeting at a signing and you've become not only a member of my team, but you're an awesome friend. Thank you for everything you've done to help me, listening when I need to talk, and helping with story ideas. And, for putting up with me adding a million- and one-story ideas to the line-up along with Courtney. You're amazing, and thank you will never be enough!

#BeckyChronicles

Character List

Strip Club – Allure
Nightclub – Phantom
Bar – Bottoms Up
Tattoo Parlor – Phantom Ink
Diner – BF Diner

Table of Contents

Prologue

Sam

WHEN YOU'RE YOUNG, you think you have it all figured out how your life is going to be. You know the kind of man you want to marry, what you're going to do for work, and there are people in your life you idolize and see as heroes because of the way they live their lives and treat others surrounding them.

I had my entire life planned out by the time I was ten years old. I wanted to be a nurse, just like my grandma. She lived her life the way she wanted to and always helped everyone out around her. Hell, even though she was alone after her and my grandfather split up, she showed more love on a daily basis than most people I know.

If my parents were going through a fight or just ran out on me, my grandma was always there to hold me, pick up the pieces of my broken heart, and support me no matter what. To her, I was 'Sam, the girl who could do no wrong. My grandma was always there for me until the day she passed away. I miss her every day of my life, and I want to make her proud, but life doesn't always work out the way we want it to.

I was sixteen the day my entire world shattered around me, and I lost the only person in my life who cared about me and loved me. My parents and other family members only cared what my grandma left them and how much money they were going to get from selling off her possessions. Including the house she left me. There was nothing I could do about any of it. Except for the trust she left me. No one could touch it.

After that, my life went on a downward spiral. See, my parents would fight and leave me for however long because they were both cheating on the other one. My dad is an alcoholic and used to leave us for weeks on end while he went out and got smashed and fucked around on my mom with his flavor of the week. At the same time, my mom would find her flavor of the day and either stay at his house or bring the man back to our home. It's not the best way to grow up.

When I turned eighteen, I moved out of the house and didn't let my parents know where I went. It's not like they really gave a damn or noticed anyway. Really, they're selfish and only care about what they're doing and what they want in life. I've always been an afterthought, and I don't know why they even had me.

I used some of the money from my trust to get my apartment and then more of it to go to school for nursing. It's at school where I met Carl. At first, he was a great guy, always there to walk me from classes, he took me out to lunch a few times, and offered to study with me even though we weren't in the same program.

Carl was slightly taller than me with sandy blond hair and blue eyes. Nothing other than his eyes ever really stood out to me. And the only reason his eyes did is that they weren't clear, startling, or a brilliant blue; they were a dull blue. He always dressed a little better than most of the other kids. While the rest of us were comfortable in jeans or sweats in class, Carl always wore khakis and polo shirts. I'm not sure who he was trying to impress.

A month after we met, Carl began staying at my apartment. I'm not sure exactly who initiated it because we weren't having sex. I just went with the flow because it was honestly nice to have someone else in the house with me. Instead of being alone and bored, there was someone there to talk to or have movie nights with. The simple things in life were what made us happy. At least that's what I thought at the time.

Over the course of the next few months, I started dating Carl. We were happy at first. Then things began to change. He would stay out all hours of the night, came home smelling of cheap perfume and having lipstick on his clothes, and he had blood on him more than once. Whenever I questioned him, I'd get ignored until the day he started hitting on me.

The first time Carl hit me, I was so shocked I didn't know what to do. He came home late again, and I was up studying for a test. When I asked where he was, he lost his shit on me and slapped me across the face. Immediately afterward, he went to bed and ignored me for the next two days. Finally, he apologized and told me it was the stress he was under at school. I hadn't seen him on campus in over two months, though. I wasn't about to bring that point up and have him get mad again.

After that, each time Carl lashed out at me was worse than the time before. Until I told him I was pregnant. At that point, everything stopped. Carl stayed home, didn't look in the direction of another woman, and was very attentive toward me.

I thought we were going to be happy and that he really loved me.

Instead, once I had my son Caleb, the beatings started once again. I'm not sure why I thought he'd stop, but I did. Thankfully, he never went after Caleb— it was just me. Carl started going out nightly again, coming home wasted and smelling of cheap perfume, and he was using drugs. I could tell just by looking at him. He blamed me for having a son when he wanted a daughter. I was shocked at his admission and began to worry about what he was doing when he was out.

I had already quit school to be a full-time mom to my son. He started bitching about money and how we didn't have any. I was constantly told if I wasn't going to be in school, I could get a damn job and pay my way. The apartment was mine, and I wasn't letting him touch what money I had left from my grandma. He didn't even know about it.

When I couldn't keep a job because I didn't have a reliable babysitter for Caleb, Carl did the one thing I never thought he'd do; he began pimping me out. It turns out, Carl was a pimp, and I was just another person he could use to make money. He was spending all the money the women and girls gave him on drugs and the woman he had seen behind my back. Caleb and I never saw a dime of it, and he never pitched in for bills or food.

When I was out 'working,' Caleb would be with one of the other girls. If I had a busy night, I would ask one of my neighbors to watch him overnight. She couldn't all the time because she worked early and her husband was only home on certain days because of his work. So, we made it work, and I was turned into a shell of my former self with each man Carl sent me out to.

The final straw for me was the day Carl came home and broke my son's arm because he was crying. Caleb wasn't feeling very good and was fussy all day. When Carl came home, high on whatever he's using, he snapped. I wasn't quick enough to get to my son because I had just given him more medicine and was taking care of the items I had out. If the house isn't kept clean, Carl also has a fit and beats me. He wants to be able to bring his side pieces here to fuck whenever he chooses.

He also beat me because I wasn't making Caleb stop crying. My son and I ended up in the hospital, so my son's arm could get fixed, and I met with Renee because CPS and the cops were called in. They were going to take my son from me, and Renee kept it from happening. That's how I ended up in Benton Falls.

The Wild Kings MC didn't have any houses available for a domestic violence victim, but one of the clubs they associate with did. So, we went and met Slim with the Phantom Bastards MC. I was leery about being away from Renee and my hometown, but Caleb and I needed a fresh start.

It's also where I met Playboy. He saw Caleb and I and started coming around the house. At first, it was just to make sure we didn't need anything, and then it turned into him spending time with us.

I was instantly attracted to him. Playboy is over six-foot-tall with long blond hair. He's got eyes almost a gray color, and tattoos cover his body. I've never seen a man with muscles who's also trim like a fighter in real life until I met him. Playboy is strong, but it's almost understated because he's not massive in size.

Playboy and I started hanging out more, and he became a man who touched me whenever we were close. Instead of being repulsed by his touch, I wanted more of it. But, he wouldn't go past a lingering graze here and there or a kiss on the top of my head now and then.

No matter how much I want it to go further, Playboy won't make a move on me, and I'm not sure what to do about it. Well, there was one night we were at the house and got drunk. That night we ended up having sex. Even drunk, it was the best I've ever had. Playboy made the night all about me, and I'll never forget it. Now, he won't mention it happened and hasn't made a further move on me. Maybe it wasn't as good for him as it was me. Or maybe he's disgusted he touched me since he knows about my past.

Chapter One

Playboy

IT'S BEEN A few days since I beat the shit out of a man who attacked Sam. He took her in broad daylight and ended up leaving a four-inch gash in her side. Doc looked her over and said it didn't need stitches because it wasn't that deep, but he put a few butterflies on it and put her on antibiotics to prevent her from getting an infection.

We still haven't heard anything from the cops about me killing a man in daylight and out in the open, but I'm not going to rest anytime soon. Most of the cops around here don't bother us because they know we do things to help victims of domestic violence, and we try to help out around the community. But, there are a few cops who have it out for us. I know it's just a matter of time before they get me and haul me off to jail.

In the meantime, I've been keeping a close eye on her wound to make sure we don't need to take her to the hospital, and so far, nothing has happened with the wound. So, I try not to worry about it. But, I can't help thinking of the terror and feeling of helplessness I felt when I pulled up on her and realized this man had taken her and was going to hurt her.

As far as I'm concerned, Sam is mine. She has been since Gage's club brought her here, and I laid eyes on her. Sam is short, not much over five-foot-tall. She's got short blonde hair and the brightest blue eyes. Unlike most women, she doesn't like to wear a lot of make-up. The one time I saw her with it on, she had smokey eye shadow on and mascara. Her lips were coated in lip gloss that made her lips look shiny. That's all she ever wears. And she dresses more for comfort than anything else. It's what attracted me to her; she doesn't care what anyone thinks about her.

Caleb, her young son, is amazing. You can tell he's seen some shit in his young life, and he constantly sits back and watches what's going on around him. He gets out and plays with other kids, but he's reserved. He saves his laughs, smiles, and happiness for his mom. And now, for me. I'm blessed to have them in my life.

Because of Sam's past, I haven't tried to push her beyond what she wants, but I want all of her. One night, I got my chance with her. We were drunk and ended up in bed together. I remember every single second, every sound, every taste of her. But, I won't talk about it, and I won't do it again until I know she's truly ready for what I want with her.

No, I'm not into bondage and all that shit. I just want more than a friend with benefits relationship with her. When it comes to Sam, I want her heart, body, and soul. I won't settle for anything less. So, I'm waiting on doing anything more with her until she gives me a sign she's ready. Until then, I have a hand, and I know how to take a damn cold shower. I won't touch a house bunny or any other woman. They aren't her, and they'll never measure up to her.

Today, the club is having a cookout at the clubhouse. The ol' ladies are going to be there, so I invited Sam and Caleb to come with me. I know she spends time with the other ol' ladies, but I want her to be around the club and know they have her back no matter what. To truly understand they'll help her out and make sure she's okay if something happens to me.

I get ready for the day at the clubhouse before heading over to pick up Sam and Caleb. As I leave my room, I see the house bunnies cleaning the clubhouse and preparing the food for the day. My dad and Hound are already out preparing the grills for the meat. There's a buzz of excitement in the air, and I know it's only going to grow as our friends and family show up for the day.

Grabbing the keys for one of the SUVs from my dad's office, I head out to get Sam. Before I get to the door, Whino stops me. He's got a new woman on his arm, and I know she'll be a new house bunny before too long.

The woman has tits almost as big as my damn head. She's skin and bones, barely wearing clothes considered decent considering kids and ol' ladies will be here today. Her face is coated in make-up, and she looks like she's been ridden hard and put up wet more than once. Yeah, I wouldn't touch the bitch with a ten-foot pole and someone else's cock.

"Where you headin'?" he asks.

"To get Sam and Caleb," I answer, my impatience showing.

"You ever gonna make her your ol' lady?" he asks as disappointment covers the woman's face.

"Not your concern," I answer, turning my back on the pair.

Continuing out the door of the clubhouse, I pull my hair back and secure it with a hair tie I keep on my wrist. Pulling my sunglasses out of my shirt, I place them on my head before getting into the SUV. As soon as I have it turned on, I roll the windows down and open the sunroof. *Read Me My Rights* by Brantley Gilbert blares from the speakers, and I begin to laugh. I'm not sure who was in the SUV last, but this song fits perfectly for my mood lately.

It doesn't take long to get to Sam's house. She's waiting outside on the porch with Caleb, and a few containers are on one of the small tables next to her. I pick them up before leaning down to kiss the top of her head.

Sam's wearing a pair of cutoff shorts today with a Phantom Bastards tank top. Flip flops cover her feet, and I can see a fine sheen of sweat already coating her body. Her short hair is tied back with a hair tie to keep it off her neck in the unusual heat we have today. She's got sunglasses on the top of her head, and a bag slung over her shoulder.

"You look good, babe," I tell Sam.

"Thank you," she says, blushing.

I've never seen a woman blush the way Sam does. It shows there's an innocence about her no one's breached yet no matter what her past is. Some days, I say outlandish things to her just to get her to blush and see how far down it goes. Today, it covers her chest, neck, and face. Before the end of the day, I'll have her turning red more than that. Being at the clubhouse, I'll be staking my claim, so no one gets any ideas they can talk to my woman.

"Playboy, I been waiting for you," Caleb says, drawing my attention to him.

"Oh yeah. You been good for your mama?" I ask him, holding out my fist for a fist bump from him.

"Yep."

Caleb jumps off the porch and waits for us to join him on the sidewalk. He's wearing a pair of shorts with a tank top. Little sneakers cover his feet, and I know they'll be off before too long. Caleb hates having his feet covered. Sam has to fight him daily to wear them outside to play.

"So, what did you bribe him with today?" I ask on a laugh.

"I told him we were going to the clubhouse, and he needed to wear them, or he couldn't go," she says.

A smile covers her face because Caleb loves being around the guys. He's gotten used to a few of us and knows we won't let anything happen to his mom or him. Going to the clubhouse is a treat he likes doing, and he won't jeopardize it for anything.

"Alright, bud, let's get in the SUV and get on the road," I tell him.

Caleb stays close to us as we make our way to the SUV. I set the containers in the back seat before helping Caleb inside. There's already a booster seat, and I place him in it before putting his seatbelt on. As soon as he's strapped in, I close his door and walk around to the driver's side. Getting in, I see Sam has one foot resting on the dash, her toenails painted red.

As soon as I have the SUV on, she pulls her phone out and hooks it up to the Bluetooth. She puts on *Love Me* by Aaron Lewis. It's a country song and not one I'd really listen to, but I deal with it because it's Sam. She listens to a little bit of everything and usually has music playing. When music is playing, Sam is relaxed and calm. It's one of the few things that calms her down and keeps her demons at bay.

Sam sings along to the song as I drive the short distance to the clubhouse. Pulling into the parking lot, it's packed. A lot of people have arrived since I left to get Sam and Caleb. I pull the SUV off to the side of the building where it won't be in the way of anyone else leaving and far away from the bikes filling the lot.

Looking at Sam, I see her body is tense. We all thought this was just going to be a family cookout today, and it seems as if we were wrong. I don't even know who the hell is here. Placing my hand on her thigh, I give her a gentle squeeze of reassurance before sliding out of the driver's side door.

Opening the back door, I unbuckle Caleb's seatbelt and then grab the containers of food Sam prepared at home. I told her she didn't have to, but I know the guys will appreciate her brownies with peanut butter and the salad she made. Sam makes the best pasta salad the guys have ever had, and they constantly beg her for it.

Sam finally gets out of the SUV, and we head toward the front door of the clubhouse. The door is propped open, and we can hear the music blaring from inside already. Right now, *Bad Boy* by Brantley Gilbert is playing. This tells me the ol' ladies are here and have taken control of the music. My guess is Shy. She's always changing the music up on us, and it drives everyone crazy. But, we love her, and we deal with it.

I place my hand on Sam's lower back as we walk through the crowds of people milling about the common room of the clubhouse. Caleb takes her hand and looks around at all the people inside. He's looking for my dad or any of the kids running about.

Caleb loves my dad and calls him Papi. He's the only one Caleb calls anything other than their road name, and I know my dad loves it. He's got a soft spot for all of the kids in the club, and Caleb is no different. Slim may be the President of the Phantom Bastards and a tough man when he has to be. Put him around the ol' ladies or kids and his soft sideshows. He doesn't give a fuck what anyone thinks about it, either.

"Papi!" Caleb suddenly yells out as he sees my dad walking toward us.

Caleb pulls his hand from his mother's and runs to my dad. He hands his beer off just before Caleb jumps into his arms. Yeah, Caleb's nervous as hell with so many other people here. If I'd known, I wouldn't have walked inside. Not that outside is going to be much better. People will be spilling out the back door and filling the backyard of the compound.

"How's my grandson doin' today?" Slim asks Caleb.

Yeah, he knows I want to claim Sam, but I'm waiting for her to be ready. Everyone in the club knows except for her. She has no clue how I truly feel about her, but today is the beginning of the end for her. She'll know before we leave here.

"I'm good. Ready to eat," Caleb tells my dad, as everyone around them laughs.

"You are? Well, let's see what we can do to make that happen," Slim says. "I got him."

Sam nods her head at him, and the two disappear. We'll be lucky to see Caleb again for the next hour. He'll be helping my dad at the grill, and it's going to be hot, so then he'll be in the hose or little kiddie pools we bought for today. I hope Sam brought him a change of clothes to have in case he doesn't dry off before she's ready to head home.

"You stay here. I'll be right back," I tell Sam. "Why don't you get us some drinks before we head out back."

"Okay. Beer?" she asks.

"Yeah."

I head to the kitchen and see Shy and Jennifer there. They're going through all the food to make sure it's ready to take outside.

"Hey, Playboy," Shy says, turning to kiss me on the cheek.

It's weird to think my stepmom is the same age as me. But, she makes my dad happy, and I couldn't think of anyone better for him. She's given me another sister, Rayven, and she truly cares about every member of this club. Including the house bunnies. Don't get me wrong; Shy will beat their asses if they need it. However, if she senses a problem with anyone, she's right there and doesn't leave until there's a solution.

"Hey, Shy. Jennifer," I greet both women.

"Where's Sam and Caleb?" Jennifer asks.

"Do you really have to ask where Caleb is?" I ask her.

"Nope. He's with his Papi," Shy says on a laugh.

"I should've known. What about Sam?" Jennifer asks.

"She's gettin' us some drinks so we can head outside. I'm sure she'll be in here soon to help you," I answer. "Who the hell all is here? I thought it was just gonna be family today."

"Butcher's club is here. I don't know what's going on. You'll have to ask Slim about that," Shy answers. "And some hang arounds are here too. Your dad decided to let them stay for a while to see what happens. They need to be able to party with the family and not just the house bunnies."

Nodding my head, I leave the containers in the kitchen and make my way back to the common room. I thought Sam would've been here by now, but she's not. Scanning the room as I go, I finally spot her in the corner of the room with a man standing in front of her. There's pure fear covering her face, and I rush to her side.

"What the fuck is goin' on here?" I roar out when I'm close to them.

The guy turns around, and I see he's nothing more than a hang around.

"She's not marked as anyone's so she's fair game. You know the rules, Playboy," he tells me, already sounding drunk.

"Not her. She's mine, and every fucker who comes to this clubhouse knows that. You can fuckin' leave. Now!" I yell at him, placing my body between his and Sam's.

She grips the tank top I'm wearing under my cut. I can feel her trembling. Looking up, I see Killer and Stryker heading my way. They're pissed as fuck, and I know this is about to get interesting. This hang around will no longer be welcome at the clubhouse.

"Got a problem here?" Killer asks.

"Yeah. This bitch thought he could corner Sam when I went to the kitchen," I answer him. "Keep an eye on her while I take out the fuckin' trash."

"No. I think I want to help take the trash out," Killer answers.

"I got her. I'll take her outback," Stryker answers.

I turn around and see Sam shaking against the wall with our drinks in her hands. Kissing her lightly on the mouth, I remove her hand from my tank top and bend down so I can look in her eyes.

"Go with Stryker, precious. I'll be right there," I tell her, giving her another kiss.

Sam goes to Stryker, and he puts an arm around her to make sure no one gets close to her on their way outside. If I didn't know he was head over heels in love with Sally, I'd be beating his ass next. But, I do know he is, and he's just trying to protect Sam from the rest of the assholes in here.

Turning my attention back toward the douche canoe in front of me, I see his eyes widen as I grab his shirt and haul his ass out the door.

"You don't ever fuckin' touch somethin' that's not yours!" I yell at him. "You're nothin' but a fuckin' hang around and don't even get to touch the house bunnies, so I don't know what you think gives you the right to touch Sam. To scare her to the point she was shakin' like a fuckin' leaf. Now, you'll deal with the consequences."

I don't waste another second. Balling up my fist, I land punch after punch on the asshole. There's a large crowd surrounding us, but no one tries to stop me. When the man goes down, I begin kicking him in the ribs before straddling his abdomen so I can land more punches to him. I'm not about kicking a man while he's down; I want to feel his bones crushing under my bare fists.

"Playboy, enough!" Slim yells. "Get him the fuck off him!"

Killer, Stryker, Wood, and Butcher pull me from the man lying at my feet in the parking lot. Before anyone can say or do anything else, I hear sirens approaching the gate. Today is the day I leave my family. They're here to take me in, and I already know it as I look at my dad.

"Get this piece of shit the fuck outta here. Now!" Slim yells.

Fox, Des, and Valor get rid of him. They carry him into the clubhouse, and I'm sure they'll stash him somewhere until the cops are gone. Fuck!

As the four cop cars come to a stop, I'm surrounded by Killer, Stryker, Wood, Boy Scout, Valor, Vault, Hitter, Des, and Slim. This is the last thing I want to happen right now, but with what I did, everyone knew it was coming.

While the cops are getting out of their cars, a hand wraps around my waist, and I look down into Sam's face. She's got tears streaming down her face. Behind the tears, I see something else, something she hasn't let me see until today. Sam loves me, and she's scared to say it. I get it; I'm scared of what I feel for her and Caleb too.

"It'll be okay, precious. I love you, and you're mine. Just remember that," I whisper to her.

Leaning down further, I place a kiss against her lips, and she instantly opens her mouth to me. I deepen the kiss, and the world around us disappears. It's just Sam and me, and we're going to get through this. If not, I hope someone in the club takes care of my woman and kid until I can finally make my way home to them.

"This is my fault," she tells me when I break the kiss.

"No, it's not. This is on me, and I'm ready to do my time for it," I tell her. "Stay with my dad for now until I'm gone. Then someone will take you home."

"Can I help you?" my dad's voice booms in my ears.

"We're here for a Griffin Busch," one of the cops says as I turn to face them.

They all have their hands on their weapons, ready to pull on us. I smile at them, and it's the evilest smile I can plaster on my face.

"What's this regarding?" my dad asks.

"A murder that occurred in town," the cop says.

I step forward after handing my dad my cut because this is what I have to do. When the cops turn me around to face the crowd now gathered outside, my eyes stay glued on Sam. She's wrapped her arms around her small body, and tears are still streaming down her beautiful face. My heart is breaking at the look on her face. Thankfully, Caleb isn't out here. It's bad enough Sam is seeing me with cuffs around my wrists while I'm being read my Miranda rights.

My dad and Shy are on either side of my woman with their arms wrapped around her. She's not seeking comfort from either of them, though. Sam is trying to appear strong even though I can see her breaking apart.

"Don't you say a word until our lawyer gets there," my dad says as Killer steps away to call him.

I nod my head and let the cops lead me to the back of one of the cars. There's no struggle on my part because Sam is here, and I'm not adding any charges to a fucking murder charge.

Once I'm in the backseat of the cruiser, I don't turn around to look at my family. I'll fucking break if I see Sam still crying. Or Caleb running around the building to figure out what's going on. The only way I'm going to get through this is by remaining facing forward. I have my memories of Sam, Caleb, and the rest of my family.

As the cruisers leave the clubhouse, I sit back and close my eyes. Visions of Sam and Caleb hit me. We've made memories since she came to

Benton Falls. I see flashes of laying on the couch with Sam, playing in the yard with Caleb, and eating dinner with both of them. These two people are going to be the only reason I make it through whatever happens to me now.

Chapter Two

Sam

WATCHING PLAYBOY BEING handcuffed and placed in the back of a cop car is the hardest thing I've ever had to watch. And that's saying something with the life I've led. My heart is breaking as he doesn't look back or say a single word after leaving my side.

I didn't even tell him I loved him when he told me. Tears fall faster and harder from my eyes as the cars begin to pull out of the parking lot in the clubhouse. Slim and Shy still have their arms around me as we all stand still and watch Playboy be taken away from us.

"This is all my fault. If I hadn't called him that day, he never would've been taken today," I cry out as the guys from Benton Falls surround us.

"Stop, Sam. This isn't your fault, and you're not gonna take the blame for this. Playboy did what he had to do to protect you," Slim tells me. "I'm gonna head down there and meet the lawyer there. Shy, take her and Caleb to the house for now. When I know anything, I'll fill you in."

Slim kisses Shy, and he walks to his bike. Several of the men follow him, but the rest remains because there are still a ton of people here for a party and cookout today. Shy leads me around the side of the clubhouse and to the house she shares with Slim and Rayven.

Shy's on her phone, and I'm sure she's texting someone to bring my son to me. While I don't want him to see my upset, he's going to find out about Playboy soon enough. It's best he hears it from me and not all of the gossiping men and women at the cookout. This is one piece of news I don't want to have to give my son. He worships the ground Playboy walks on and looks forward to seeing the man every single day. This is going to crush him.

"Killer is gonna bring Caleb over. Can I get you anything?" Shy asks me.

I shake my head as I sit down on the porch of her house. Right now, I want to see my son as soon as he gets close. Taking a few deep breaths, I try to calm myself down as I wipe the tears from my face. The less upset I am, the better right now.

"Mama!" Caleb yells out a few minutes later.

He comes running at me as I stand up and prepare to catch him in my arms. Caleb is a smart little boy and knows something is wrong.

I just realize I can no longer hear the music from the clubhouse, bikes are shaking the ground as large groups start up and leave the clubhouse, and women are walking toward their own homes close to Shy and Slim's. The party is effectively over.

"What's wrong, Mama?" Caleb asks me.

"Well, I have to talk to you about something," I begin, sitting down on the grass with him. "Do you remember a few days ago when mama was hurt, and Playboy helped save me?"

Caleb nods his head. He looks deep into my eyes, and I almost crumble.

"Well, because of that, Playboy had to go away for a while. I'm not sure when he'll be back," I tell him.

My son looks at me, and I can tell he's trying to be strong in front of Shy and Killer. He looks between the three of us, and I can see the questions in his eyes.

"He gonna be okay?" Caleb asks.

"Playboy is gonna be just fine, buddy," Killer tells him. "Your Papi is down there with him, and he's gonna get it all figured out so Playboy can come home to you and your mama."

Caleb nods his head and rests it on my shoulder. I feel the wetness hitting my neck and know he's crying. The dam breaks and I start crying all over again. Killer and Shy help me stand up with Caleb in my arms and lead us inside the house. Shy walks us directly to an empty room on the first floor, and I lay down in the bed with Caleb.

It's not long before my son goes limp in my arms, and I know he's fallen asleep. I let sleep claim me and dream of Playboy being led away in handcuffs. He's going to prison because he tried to save me. I'll never let go of the guilt I feel over this.

Waking up, I'm disoriented as I look around the room. The day's events surface in my mind, and I want to start crying all over again. This isn't fair, and there's nothing I can do until Slim gets back to let us know what's going on.

A thought suddenly pops into my head, and I gently untangle myself from Caleb's small body. He nestles back into the pillows, and I pull a blanket up to cover up him up. After making sure he's going to remain asleep, I leave the room and go in search of Shy or whoever else is in the house.

I find Slim, Killer, Shy, who's holding Rayven, and Stryker all sitting at the kitchen table. They stop talking when I walk into the room. Slim stands from his seat and makes his way over to me. He wraps his large arms around me and holds me against him for a minute. I soak up the strength and warmth because I'm going to need it for the next few minutes.

"What's going on with him?" I ask, pulling back and looking up into the eyes that remind me of Playboy's.

"I'm not sure right now. It's not lookin' good, though. Supposedly, they have a witness," Slim tells me as my eyes once again fill with tears. "Sam, I need to tell you somethin'."

"What?" I ask him.

"Playboy doesn't want to see you. He won't accept any visits from you at the jail," Slim tells me.

"What? Why?" I ask him, my voice rising several octaves.

"I'm not sure. He just asked me to tell you that," Slim answers. "I'll work on him about it, though. I promise."

"Slim, what if I went to the police and told them what happened? This is all because he was trying to save me. I can save him if I go there and tell them the man kidnapped me. They can pull the footage from the store and prove I'm telling the truth," I rush out.

"Not gonna happen, darlin'," Slim tells me. "You didn't go forward when it happened, and now it will look like you're just protectin' your man. The lawyer is gonna work on it and talk to the witness so he can get his story."

"But . . ." I begin as Shy comes to stand next to me.

"This isn't the club's first rodeo. Let them handle business. They're going to keep you out of it as much as possible," she tells me.

"Can I just go home, please?" I ask, suddenly completely drained and needing to be on my own with my son.

"Yeah. I'll take you," Killer tells me, leaving to go get the SUV after Shy hands him the keys.

"Can you get me the information I need so I can write to him at least?" I ask Slim.

"Yeah. I'll message you in a little while and give it to you. Let me go get Caleb and put him in the SUV," Slim answers.

Slim returns to the room, cradling a still sleeping Caleb to his massive chest. He's protecting my son, and I know he'll continue to do so no matter what happens with Playboy. My guilt ramps up again as I realize I just took a son from his father, stepmother, sister, another sister, niece, and nephews. Not to mention everyone in the club he considers his family.

I hang my head in shame as Killer walks back into the house. The compound is eerily quiet as we walk outside and get in the SUV. I hear Slim whisper something to my son and don't pay attention as I get in and fasten my seatbelt. Killer slides into the driver's side after talking to Slim for a minute and leaves the clubhouse.

The sky is gray and overcast as we head home. It looks exactly how I feel right now. No matter what I do, the club is going to shoot down any idea I have about making sure Playboy leaves jail and doesn't serve too much time. I stare out the window as I think of what I can do since he won't see me. I guess my only option is to write him a letter and hope he accepts that.

Killer pulls up in front of my house. He shuts the engine off and grabs Caleb from the backseat. Caleb still hasn't woken up, and I know the day is taking a toll on him. I walk in front of Killer and lead the way to the house. After unlocking the door, he walks inside and directly to Caleb's bedroom.

Our rooms are on the first floor of the house. There's three more bedrooms upstairs, but we don't use them. The first floor has two bedrooms, a kitchen, dining room, bathroom, laundry room, and living room. There's even a mudroom off the garage. Everything except for the hallway where the bedrooms are is an open floor plan. I can easily see from one side of the house to the other, and that's what I love. Caleb is never far from my sight unless he's in his room playing.

Killer walks back into the living room and looks at me. He wants to say something, it's written all over his face. Instead, he walks by me, places a hand on my shoulder for a minute, and then walks out the door. He remains on the porch until I follow him over and lock the door behind him.

Now, I'm at a loss. I'm not sure what I should be doing because, without Playboy, my life doesn't make sense. Not anymore.

So, I walk to my bedroom, leave the door open because of Caleb, and grab my notebook. Sitting on the bed, I quietly turn my phone on and pull up my music. I choose *Missed* by Ella Henderson.

Dear Playboy,

I'm so sorry you're going through this because of me. I should be the one sitting in there while you live your life with your family and club. Instead, you're paying the ultimate price for trying to protect me.

Before you left, you told me you love me. Well, I love you. I never thought I'd let anyone in again after Carl and the life he made me live for so long. But, you broke through all my walls and showed me not all men are the same.

I love you for the man you are. You're my friend, my son's hero, and an amazing man. There's no one in the world like you. I wish I could tell you how I felt about you. For now, I'll have to settle for writing it in this letter.

I'm not sure why you won't let me see you. I don't think any less of you, and I never will. You're a man who's not afraid to do whatever's necessary to protect those you care about. I hope you change your mind about letting me see you.

Caleb was told you weren't going to be around for a while. It broke his little heart, and I don't know what to do to take his pain away. I can't when my own heart is shattered now. You knew, though, didn't you? Why didn't you warn me? I would've spent every single second with you and kept you wrapped in my arms. You'd know how much you mean to me. To us.

If you can, listen to Love Me *by Aaron Lewis. That song is our song, and I'll never listen to it again without thinking of you. Because all you've done since I got here is try to show me you want more, and I never realized it until this minute.*

Love Always,

Sam

My tears are flowing, and they drip on the paper as I rip it from the notebook. I fold it and place it in the envelope before sealing it. Placing a kiss on the back of the envelope, my lip gloss leaves a mark because it lasts all day. There's a faint pink outline of my lips, and I smile because Playboy is always teasing me about it.

Setting the letter on the nightstand next to my bed, I walk through the house and make sure everything is locked up tight. I should get something to eat because I didn't get a chance at the clubhouse. Caleb ate before Killer brought him over to Slim and Shy's house. Unfortunately, I know I won't be able to keep any food down now.

My stomach is in knots, and I'm too upset to eat. The only thing I'll accomplish is getting sick, and that's the last thing I need right now. So, I take a glass down from the cupboard and fill it with cold water from the tap. After taking a few sips, I dump the rest down the drain. Even that seems to be too much for me right now.

Walking into Caleb's room, I cover him up again. My son kicks his blankets off all night long, and I usually check on him whenever I get up and cover him back up. I kiss him on the forehead and brush his hair back from his face. Then, I go back into my room, slide my shorts from my body, and take my shirt off.

Climbing into bed, I pull the covers up and check my phone. Slim has sent me a message with the information I need to send Playboy a letter. I pull the envelope to me and fill it out before placing it back on the nightstand. Laying down in bed, I pull my phone back over to me and pull up my reading app. I'm currently reading an MC novel, and I'm completely in love with the characters.

I read until I fall asleep with my phone on the charger. Playboy fills my dreams, and he's pissed at me. He hates being in jail because of me, and I don't blame him one bit. I toss and turn as the dream plays on a loop in my mind.

Chapter Three

Playboy

I'VE BEEN IN this hellhole for two days now. Instead of going to the yard for rec or hanging out with the other inmates, I stay in my cell. I've gotten a pad and pen and spend my time writing to Sam. I've written a letter for both days I've been here.

My thoughts remain on Sam and Caleb. I had every intention of making her mine at the cookout. And those plans went out the window when the cops showed up to arrest me for murder.

As soon as I got to the police department, the cops took me into an interrogation room. They questioned me and tried to get me to talk for over an hour before the club's lawyer got there. He answered their questions for me and told them I wouldn't be saying a word until he saw the evidence against me and had a chance to find out more about the witness.

So, here I sit in the county jail awaiting trial. I've had no contact with the lawyer since I was transferred, but I know he'll show up when he needs to. It's the way he works, and he's gotten more than one of us out of jams we manage to find ourselves in more than once over the years. He's good at what he does, and the club pays him well to do his job.

"Busch got a visitor," one of the guards tells me.

I stand from my bunk and turn my back to the guard. He places the cuffs on me before leading me to the visiting room.

"You got twenty minutes with no camera on. Make it count," the guard tells me.

Yeah, we have guards in our pocket. It pays to have friends on the inside.

"Is it a woman?" I ask, walking down the hall.

"No. It's your dad," he answers, opening the door for me.

I walk in and take a seat at the table. He lets me know he'll be outside the door and lets it shut behind me. Taking my seat, I look across the table at my father and club President. He stares at me with a blank expression on his face, so I have no clue what's going through his mind right now.

"Did you tell Sam not to visit me?" I ask him, needing to break the silence.

"I did. Broke her fuckin' heart when I did too," he responds. "Playboy, she doesn't understand why you won't see her. Hell, she's ready to go to the cops and let them know what happened to her."

"You better talk her outta that, Dad. I don't want her involved in this, and I'll be damned if she's dragged into this shit. Sam's been through enough," I tell him.

"You love her," my dad states. "So, tell me why you won't see her."

"I don't want her to see me this way. I'm a fuckin' caged animal in here, and that's not the image I want in her head," I tell him. "I won't be acceptin' her letters or calls either. Let her know that for me."

My dad shakes his head. He doesn't understand how hard this is for me. Hearing her melodic voice will kill me. Seeing her words written on a piece of paper will gut me. I can't reach out and touch her, pull her into my arms, or comfort her the way I want to. Doesn't he understand that?

"Would you want Shy to see you in here?" I ask him trying to make him understand.

"No, I wouldn't. But, I wouldn't completely shut her the fuck out either. You've been the one person she's let all the way in since comin' here. Now, who knows what the fuck is gonna happen. I don't know if she'll see any of us. Then where's that gonna leave her?" he asks me.

"It's gonna leave her to live her life with Caleb. That little boy and woman mean the absolute fuckin' world to me. I'll do anythin' to keep them safe and protect them from everythin' I can. Includin' me," I tell my dad.

"Son, I don't think this is the way to do that. Those two are in a world of pain right now, and you're the only one who will be able to help them," he tells me.

I shake my head at him. It kills me to hear they're in so much pain. There's nothing I can do about it while I'm in here, though. I can't take them in my arms or reassure them I'm okay and I'll be home as soon as possible. No, I don't know if I'm coming back home. Ever. If I'm lucky, I won't get life. If I'm not, Sam and Caleb need to forget about me and move the hell on with their lives.

My dad lets me know what's going on with the club. Then he tells me Anderson, our lawyer, will be going over everything he has on my case and will come to see me soon. Then he lets me know about Rayven and her latest antics. She's crawling all over the place, and he thinks it won't be long until she's walking. My little sister is smart as hell, and she knows it too.

Rayven is a perfect mixture of my dad and Shy. She's got Shy's blonde hair and my dad's eyes. She's going to be a beautiful woman when she gets older, and my dad will have his work cut out for him. We all will because none of the club's Princess's will ever date. I feel bad for them, but no one will be good enough for any of them.

"Son, I love you. I'm goin' to head home. I want you to think about Sam and lettin' her in while you're in here. It could help make your time go by faster until you come home," he tells me.

"Dad, we both know the chances of that happenin' are slim to none," I tell him. "I love you. Give Shy and Rayven my love. Please don't tell Maddie what's goin' on either. She'll lose her fuckin' mind and come here. With or without Tank."

My dad nods his head because he knows it's the truth. Maddie has gotten very confident and doesn't let anyone stand in her way when she wants to do something. If she finds out I'm locked up—she'll be in Benton Falls quicker than hell and try to fix the situation. There's nothing she can do to help me. My only form of help will be coming in Anderson.

Dad hugs me before leaving the room. Yeah, he's not supposed to, but we don't give a fuck about rules and regulations. We live our lives the way we want and don't give a fuck about what anyone thinks about us. Now, I don't have my freedom, and I'm on someone else's timetable.

I watch as my dad leaves the room before I turn to face the guard who will walk me back to my cell. He opens the door and lets me get in front of him before we make the short trip back. Once I'm in my cell, he uncuffs me and goes about his business.

Sitting on my bunk, I pull out the paper and pen I have. It's time to let Sam know why I can't see her, talk to her, or read her letters. Not that she'll get it because I don't see myself sending any of these letters to her. I'll probably keep them with me and give them to her if I ever get outta here.

Dear Sam,

I love you more than I could ever tell you or show you. Caleb is my son, and if I ever get the hell out of here, I'm going to make you both mine. You'll be my ol' lady, and we'll do what we have to do for me to adopt Caleb. I hate bein' away from you both, and I wish I were there with you.

That being said, I don't regret the choices I've made. I'd make them all over again and do the same thing. This isn't on you, and I don't want to hear you're shoulderin' the blame for what I've done.

Sam, you're an amazin' woman, and I'll never be able to tell you all the reasons I say that. You're an amazin' mom, you're my best friend, my woman, and I love you. Caleb is smart as hell, he's

*crazy, amazin', and makes everyone around him
laugh. He sits back and accesses every single
situation before he makes a choice and will be a
great man when he gets older.*

*There are reasons I can't see you. I can't
see you and not be able to touch you, hold you, or
kiss you. I'll want to pull you in my arms and never
let you go. If I hear your voice, I'll want to keep
you on the phone, and that's not possible. Finally,
if I see your words on paper, I'll want to be there
with you. I'll see the tears you're cryin' on the
paper, and it will kill me. So, please, let me have
this.*

*Another reason is I don't want you to see
me like a caged animal. That's what I am right
now. I'm an animal, and if I see you, I'll be
handcuffed the entire time, and we won't be able to
touch or get close. Your memories of me need to be
filled with me on the outside. Memories we made at
your house and the clubhouse. Or anywhere else
we've ever been.*

Love You Always,

Playboy

I fold the letter and put it in the box I have
with the other two letters. Lying back on the bunk, I
place my hands under my head and let thoughts of
my family fill my head. Not my club family; Sam
and Caleb. They're my family, and I'm going to do
whatever I can to keep them with me unless I'm
stuck in here for the rest of my life. I won't hold
either one of them back from living their lives.
They both deserve to live, love, and have chances
they wouldn't normally have with me in the picture.

Those thoughts are still swirling through my head as I close my eyes and let sleep claim me. I take cat naps in here because you never know what's going to happen. I'm never fully asleep as things can happen in the blink of an eye. I'm going to need to sleep for a week straight once I get out of here.

If I get out of here.

Chapter Four

Sam

IT'S BEEN ALMOST a week since Playboy was arrested. My letter was sent back to me. Unopened. So, not only is he not going to see me, but he's not going to call me or accept my letters. When I got it, I cried my heart out on the front porch. Caleb was in my arms to comfort me, and he cried right along with me. He doesn't understand what's going on.

Caleb asks about Playboy every single day. Then he asks about Papi and the rest of the guys from the club. There's no way I can explain he can't see Playboy anytime soon. I've tried. When anyone from the club has stopped by, and they do daily, I ignore the door and take Caleb to my room. It hurts too much to see them right now. I'll face them soon, just not yet.

Waking up, I run to the bathroom once again. For the last three days, I've been waking up and getting sick. I have a feeling I know what's going on, but I don't want to acknowledge it right now. Not when Playboy isn't here with me.

As soon as I'm done getting sick, I flush the toilet and brush my teeth. I splash cold water on my face and run a brush through my hair so I can throw it up in a messy bun. Once I'm as presentable as I'm going to get, I walk in my room and throw a pair of shorts on with a tank top. I walk into Caleb's room and wake him up before heading to the kitchen to start making breakfast.

I'm mixing the pancake batter when Caleb comes walking out. He's already dressed in a pair of shorts, and one of the Phantom Bastards support shirts Playboy got him. All week he's worn anything he can to think of the man got him. He's only played with the toys bought by Playboy, and he's drawn several pictures for him. Those are all being stored in my nightstand, where they're safe and sound.

I pour the batter onto the griddle, and there's a knock on the door. Before I can stop him, Caleb is running for the door, and he opens it to Slim, Shy, and Killer. Shy's holding Rayven, and they're all looking at me expectantly.

Fuck my life!

"Come in," I tell them as I turn my back on them to rescue the pancakes before they burn. "You guys want breakfast?"

"Yeah, we'll eat with you guys," Slim answers me.

"Papi, you're here," Caleb says, running to him.

Caleb sits down on Slim's lap and wraps his arms around him. I've separated them, and my heart breaks as I watch him soak up the attention. It's not long before he's walking over to Shy so he can see baby Rayven.

"Need to talk," Slim tells me, as I continue to make breakfast for everyone.

"What's going on?" I ask, keeping my back to the table, so I don't have to look at anyone.

"Playboy may be in jail right now, but that doesn't mean you get to push the rest of us away. I know why he won't see you," Slim says. "Saw him a few days ago, and he doesn't want you to see him that way. Doesn't want you to be there and not be able to be in his arms or anythin' like that."

"What about the letter, then?" I ask, tears beginning to form in my eyes.

"What do you mean?" Shy asks me softly.

"I wrote him a letter, and it got sent back, unopened. He won't even accept that," I tell them.

I pull the pancakes from the griddle and put more batter on to cook. Once they're on, I grab the eggs to make scrambled eggs and the sausage links I pulled out when I started making breakfast. Shy comes over to me and helps me cook breakfast while the guys and Caleb sit at the table.

In no time at all, breakfast is made and served. I grab orange juice for the table and hope no one wants coffee. I'm not really in the mood to run to the bathroom again right now.

"Give him some time," Killer tells me before taking a bite of his food. "He may change his mind about seein' you. Probably not little man here, but that's no place for him to go."

I nod my head and force myself to eat the food in front of me. Everyone else eats their breakfast.

"Papi, want a ride," Caleb suddenly says.

"On my bike?" Slim asks him.

"Yeah," he answers, trying to make himself appear taller and bigger.

"When you get a little older, you can go for a ride on my bike," he tells him.

Caleb pouts and slumps down in his seat. It's something Playboy had planned to do, and now I'm not sure he'll be able to. I want to break down and cry again. It seems that's all I've been doing for the last week, though. Now, there's an even bigger problem I'll have to face. Alone.

"So, is there any particular reason you guys stopped by?" I ask.

"Wanted to check on you. Know you been avoidin' us," Slim answers. "Not gonna let you hideout, though."

"It's not that I'm hiding from you guys. I'm just not good company right now. And I feel as if this is my fault. I've got a lot going on, and I'm trying to figure everything out," I respond.

"Well, we're here to help you with all that," Killer tells me. "You may not be claimed officially by Playboy, but you and Caleb are family. We're here for you as we've always been here."

Killer doesn't usually talk much. Today is honestly the most I've ever heard the man talk. He's more the silent, brooding type who only has eyes for Gwen. Well, when he's not fucking the house bunnies. But, that's his deal and not mine.

"I appreciate it, but I need to stand on my own two feet. I get people in trouble and locked up when I'm around," I tell the people around the table.

"Look, what if this had happened when you were rescued instead of now. Would you be holdin' this much guilt about it?" Slim asks me.

"Yes, I would. No one deserves to be in prison because of me. Or because they helped me. I'm not good enough for that," I respond honestly.

"You sayin' my son ain't good enough for you?" Slim asks.

"Not at all. What I'm saying is I'm not good enough for him. I've had more men than he's had women. I can guarantee that. I've got a child, and I'm living in a home belonging to your club. I don't have a job or anything else. So, I'm not good enough for Playboy," I say on a sob. "I love that man with everything in me, and I know I need to let him go. That's what I'm going to try to do. He deserves someone clean and without a tainted past like mine."

"Fuck that!" Killer explodes, leaving the table and house.

"I didn't mean to upset him, but it's the truth. Playboy may have blood on his hands, but I'm way dirtier than he'll ever be."

"You truly believe that, don't you?" Shy asks me.

Nodding my head, I finish my breakfast and begin to clean up. Slim and Shy stay for a few more minutes until Caleb's done eating. They let me know they'll be back and won't accept me hiding out from them anymore. Slim kisses me on the top of my head, and they leave.

Once I have everything cleaned up and put away, I grab my purse, and we walk to the garage. Caleb and I get in the car, and I fasten him in before opening the door and heading for the pharmacy. I need to grab a few things and then start looking for a job. It would be easier if I didn't have my son with me, but that can't be helped right now. I would've asked Gwen, but not after the way Killer stormed out of my house.

It takes minutes to get to the middle of town and the pharmacy. I park the car alongside the row in parking spots. Caleb and I get out, and we head inside. The front clerk greets me before she goes back to stocking the shelves.

I wander around the store, so I don't head directly to the pregnancy tests and grab a few other items, including a few little toys for Caleb. I don't have much, but Playboy made sure I have money in an account. I'll take forty dollars out of it since I've never touched it before. At this point, I don't even know how much money is in there. I won't touch it, though. I've got some saved up, and that will have to last us for a little while.

Finally, I grab a few different tests, and we make our way to the register at the front of the store. Once I've paid for our purchase, Caleb and I walk down the street. I stop in several stores and ask for an application. Out of the stores I go in, I walk out with only two applications. This isn't looking good. And, I'm not about to go to the club for a job. I'm not a stripper, and I don't know what else they have going on. But, with what I suspect, I'm not sure I'll be around here much longer.

I feel defeated as Caleb, and I walk back to the car. We get in and head back home where I can look over the applications I have and take the pregnancy tests that seem to be burning a hole in the bag holding them. At a stop sign, I look at the bag, and I don't want to find the results out. I have no choice, though.

"Mama, I play?" Caleb asks from the back seat as I pull into the driveway.

"In your room, for now, honey. We'll come outside in a little while," I tell him.

"Okay," he tells me.

We get into the house, and Caleb makes his way to his bedroom. I follow him and hand over the three little toys I got him at the pharmacy. When he's distracted and playing with them on his bedroom floor, I make my way to the bathroom and close the door behind me.

Taking a deep breath, I pull the boxes from the bag and open the first one. Sitting down on the toilet, I do my business with two out of the four tests I bought. I place them on the empty boxes on the counter in the bathroom and wash my hands. While I'm waiting, I clean the bathroom a little bit.

My hands are trembling as I try to wipe down the wall of the shower. I can feel my heart racing in my chest, and my breathing is picking up. If I don't get myself under control, I'll have a full-blown panic attack. So, I look down at the tests and see both of them are positive. I'm pregnant with Playboy's baby, and he's currently sitting in a jail cell because of me.

I let a few tears slip free before I throw the evidence away and tie off the bag so I can throw it in the garbage. If anyone else from the club comes over, I don't need them seeing that I'm pregnant. Right now, I don't want anyone to know I'm pregnant. If Playboy can't find out, no one else deserves to know. He's the father and deserves to know before anyone else.

After taking the garbage out and placing it in the garbage can, I go back inside and sit down at the kitchen table. Looking over the applications, I already know I won't be getting hired at either of these stores. They're looking for a college education, and I didn't graduate. I don't think going for partial nursing degree counts.

Despair fills me, and I try to think of something I can do while looking for a job. Maybe I can work at the fast-food place on the outskirts of town. That's about the only thing I'm qualified for. And it won't provide much of a future for Caleb much less a new baby. I'm royally fucked.

The rest of the day I spend with Caleb. I push thoughts of a new baby out of my mind. It's not easy because it's all I can think about. But, Caleb deserves my full attention as we play in the yard, and I hear the rumble of bikes passing every so often. I know it's the members of the club riding by to make sure we're okay. My heart breaks a little every time I hear a bike. Caleb gets so excited and wants to run to meet Playboy. I have to tell him it's not Playboy coming to see us. Then he's defeated, and it hurts even more.

I've messed everything up.

Later on, when Caleb is asleep in my bed because he didn't want to be alone tonight, I pull out my notebook and pen. I write a letter to Playboy and tell him about the baby, how I'm scared to be pregnant and alone. My fears of the baby growing up without a father or anyone in the club in his or her life. Then, I tell him about my plan to leave town. If he can't know about the baby, no else can either. It's not fair or right.

After writing the letter to him, I set everything aside and lay down. Caleb cuddles me in his sleep as I shut the lights and TV off. The dark consumes me, and my thoughts are of Playboy. He's the only thing I think of when I fall asleep these days. I can't push him out of my mind, and that's what makes this so hard.

Chapter Five

Playboy

THE DAYS ALL blend together. Spending time in my cell, the only thing I do is think of Caleb and Sam. They're the only thing on my mind from the time I get up until the time I go to sleep. Even then, they're in my dreams, and I can't get away from them. Not that I want to.

Images of Sam with tears streaming down her face and her arms wrapped around her body in defeat and guilt fill my mind. That's never a way I wanted to see her. She takes the blame for me being locked up, and she shouldn't. Sam didn't kidnap her fucking self and then call me. A madman kidnapped her, and she got rescued because she needed it.

The only time I leave my cell is when my father or another club member comes to see me or when it's time to eat. Everyone leaves me the fuck alone because my dad made sure I'd be protected in here. Yeah, we have it like that, and it's just a fact. We'd do it for any club member locked up.

One of the guards has tried to give me another letter from Sam, and I send it back with him unopened. It breaks my heart, and I hate myself for not reading it, but to keep my sanity, it's what I have to do.

I haven't seen my lawyer since the day I got arrested. So, I've been in here three weeks now, and he hasn't done a damn thing to get me out or to a hearing before trial. I'm pissed about it, and my dad knows. He keeps trying to reassure me the lawyer is working his magic, and he'll let me know when he has something. Until then, I'm supposed to just sit tight and not think about it.

How the fuck am I supposed to not think about it?

When I'm in my cell, I use my time to do push-ups, sit-ups, and any other workout I can without going to the yard. Yeah, I could be networking and shit while I'm in here, but that doesn't interest me. At least not right now. Maybe once my fate is sealed, and I know what's going to happen to me, I'll feel more like networking and things.

"Busch, time for lunch," the guard calls out.

Getting off my bunk, I head out of the cell and join the line with the rest of the men I'm in jail with. We're all heading to the cafeteria when a fight breaks out. I'm not sure who's involved in it, but my goal is to stay away from the mess. The last thing I need is more charges added on to what I'm already facing.

The fight seems to drag on and on, while more inmates join in. You can barely tell who's fighting and who's not as bodies are flung around, and fists are being thrown in every direction. Looking around, I see several men trying to get against the closest wall to show they're not involved in this mess. I'm included in this, but it seems the fighting surrounds me. What a clusterfuck.

Guards charge into the room, and as I try to get against the wall. Before I can place my chest to the wall, I'm sucker punched by one of the men in the fight. I have to fight every single instinct in me to retaliate. But, I do, and I can already feel the pain radiating in my face. My jaw is aching, and I know there's gonna be a nasty bruise. Fucking great!

When they finally get the inmates involved in the fight taken out of the room, we're all taken back to our cells. It's not like I enjoy the food they serve us. Or what they call food. But, I'm hungry, and now we won't get to eat until dinner time.

Once I'm back in my cell, I collapse on my bunk and wait to see what else today is going to bring.

It's not long before I'm being called by a guard again. This time, I have a visitor.

Walking into the room, I see Shy sitting at the table waiting for me. What the hell is she doing here?

"Sit down, Playboy," she tells me.

"What are you doin' here?" I ask, not bothering with the pleasantries.

"Need to talk to you. Now, sit down and listen before you lose the best thing to ever happen in your life," Shy tells me.

"What are you talkin' about?" I ask, finally sitting down. "Where's Sam and Caleb?"

"They're still here for now. I'm not sure how long she'll stay here, though. With the way you're acting right now, she doesn't think she has anything left to stay here for. Hell, any of us can hardly get in the door to spend time with them these days. She's pushing us away because as far as she's concerned, we're your family and only accepted her because she came to us as a domestic violence victim," she tells me.

"And she's told you all this?" I question.

'No. I can see it in her eyes. She's taking everything on her shoulders, and she's gonna break. And, she's hiding something from us," she answers. "It was so bad; Killer left the house without a word last week and hasn't been back since. Said she wasn't good enough for you. You're not helping the situation."

"Fuck!" I yell out.

"Yeah. And what happened to your face?" she suddenly asks.

"Nothin'. Somethin' happened just before you showed up for a visit," I tell her. "What am I supposed to do, Shy?"

"What do you mean?" she asks me, placing her hands on the table as she waits for me to answer.

"I don't want her to see me like this. I'm a caged fuckin' animal in here. If I hear her voice or see her tears stainin' the paper of her letters, I'm gonna break and want her to come here. Do you know what I've been doin' for the last three weeks? I've been writing her a letter every single day. And I don't send a single one of them to her. They sit in a box in my cell. Because I don't want her to see my words when I'm not there to hold her or comfort her," I tell her. "So, I ask again, what am I supposed to do."

"Then either send her a fucking letter or let her come see you once so you can explain this shit to her, Griffin. She deserves so much better than what you're doing to her now," Shy says.

"I can't do it. I want to be with them so bad, and it's not meant to be right now. Shy, I don't know what the future holds for me, but I know what it has in store for Sam and Caleb. She's goin' to move on with her life and finish school. That's what I want for her; to finish nursin' school and follow her dreams. Caleb will benefit from her doin' that. she's got money in her account from me, and she's not touchin' a dime of it. You tell her I want her to use that money to go to school and make somethin' of herself.

If I don't get the fuck outta here, then I want you to make sure she moves on with her life. Sam needs to forget about me if I'm goin' to spend my life here. I love that woman and little boy with my entire heart, and I'll do anythin' for them. Now, there isn't a fuckin' thing I can do for them in here."

Shy takes a minute to think about everything I've said. Instead of understanding where I'm coming from, she shakes her head, and a tear slips free from her eye. If my dad finds out I made her cry, he'll whoop my ass if I ever see the outside of these walls.

"Playboy, I love you. But, you're making the biggest mistake of your life. Sam won't be here *when* you get outta here. Because mark my words, you will be walking free. Are you ready to throw her away because you don't think she can handle seeing you in here?" she asks me. "Think about that shit because that's what's going to happen. Sooner than you think. I'm going to see her, and I'll let her know what you said, but I'm not going to make her stay here if that's not what she wants."

I nod my head and stand up. Shy remains sitting as I leave the visiting room. I don't look back at her because I know she's telling me the truth. I'll be very surprised if Sam and Caleb are still here if I ever get out of here.

Lying down on my bunk, I place my hands behind my head and think of what Shy said to me. I sit up and grab a pen and paper to write her another letter. Hopefully, she gets to read it one day.

Chapter Six

Sam

FOR THE LAST week I've been putting applications in to find a job. There's nothing in Benton Falls for me. I don't have any qualifications, and my unfinished college education isn't good enough. Even the hospital won't hire me for a janitor position or deliver supplies and linen to the different floors of the hospital. There truly is nothing in Benton Falls for me anymore.

Playboy was my reason for staying, but he won't have any contact with me anymore. I'm not sure what's running through his mind, but I know what's going through mine. It's not good, and there's nothing I can do to stop the thoughts racing when I have nothing to occupy me.

It's even worse when Slim and Shy or one of the other club members make an appearance at the house. I visit, and I talk with them, but they're painful reminders that they have contact with the man I love, and I don't. Even Shy's been to see him. She'll be here soon, and I know she's going to talk about him. I'm not looking forward to hearing anything about him. My heart will just break even more.

I'm sitting at the table with a glass of water in front of me, trying to decide what I'm going to do. Caleb is playing in his room. He's been quiet today, and I know it's because he can sense I'm going through something. Caleb's a smart kid like that.

"Sam, I'm here," Shy says, walking in the door.

"In the kitchen," I respond.

Shy walks into the room, and Caleb comes running out of his room. He almost seems to deflate as he doesn't see Slim with her. Or Rayven.

"Hi Shy," he says, walking up to me.

"Hey, buddy. I'm sorry Papi isn't with me today," she says, knowing he loves seeing Playboy's dad.

"I like you too," he tells her, leaning into my side.

"Well, that's good because I like you too, honey," Shy tells him, leaning over to ruffle his hair.

Caleb makes a funny face at her and runs away to his room. We laugh at him because I'm pretty sure he has a little crush on Shy. He's always trying to be around her, but he doesn't want his Papi to know. Slim knows.

One day a few months ago, we were going to the clubhouse with Playboy, and Caleb picked the flowers I had just planted outside the house. Playboy sat down with him and asked him where he was taking the flowers. Caleb told him he was taking them to Shy because every pretty woman deserves to have flowers to make her happy.

I was eavesdropping on the conversation and shed a tear or two. I've always tried to teach my son to be a decent boy and then man when he gets older. Honestly, I'm wasn't sure if he was listening to me as I talked to him, but apparently, he was. Caleb makes me so proud, and I'm so lucky to have had him. He's the only bright spot in my life right now. Well, along with the baby, I'm keeping a secret from everyone.

"How is he?" I ask when I can't stand the silence any longer.

"Not good, sweetheart. He's so freaking torn about what to do with you. Playboy loves you so much, and he wants to be able to hold you and comfort you. He doesn't want you seeing him like a caged animal. That's where his head's at," she tells me.

I can't help the tears from falling. I'm so tired of crying every single day. Never once did I believe he felt that way. Playboy is the best man I know, and I'd never view him as anything other than that. He's a great man and for him to believe otherwise is absolutely ridiculous.

"Shy, he's the best man I know. I don't want him thinking that of himself in that way. I'll leave him alone and not do anything to make him feel like that again," I say, my heart breaking.

"Honey, it's his issue, not yours. You keep doing what you're doing, and we'll be here for you. No matter what," she says, placing her hand over mine on the table.

"I still won't do anything to hurt him more than I already have. This is my fault, and no matter what you guys say, I know it's my fault," I tell her.

"Playboy said a few more things. The first is he loves you both. He wants you both in his life, no matter what. Secondly, he wants you to use the money you've been ignoring in the account from him to finish schooling," she says matter-of-factly.

"That's his money, not mine. I've touched very little of it for something, and I'm going to pay him back for it," I tell her. "Here, take this."

Getting up from the table, I walk over to my purse on the counter and grab my wallet. Pulling out the card Playboy gave me, I walk back to her and hand it over. Shy looks from the card to me and back. She's not sure what to do, and I'm not going to take it back. That's Playboy's money, and I'm not going to use it; not anymore.

"I'm not giving this to him," Shy says.

"Then give it to Slim and have him give it back to him," I say, not backing down from this. "Please don't leave this with me anymore."

Shy puts the card in her pocket, but she's not happy. The look on her face is one of censure and her being upset. There's nothing I can do about that. I've made a few decisions, and there's nothing anyone is going to do to change my mind.

"Can you do me a favor?" she questions as she stands up.

"What's that?" I ask in return.

"Don't give up on him and don't make any moves without really thinking hard about it," Shy tells me.

"All I've been doing is thinking. And it's hard not to give on him when it seems as if he's already given up on Caleb and me," I say honestly. "You have no clue what's been running through my head and what I've been thinking about."

"Well, don't make any decisions without talking to someone first," she says.

Shy pulls me in for a hug and holds onto me for a few extra minutes. It's almost as if she knows what I'm about to do. I don't think she truly knows, though, because I'm not even sure what's going on just yet. We'll just see what's going on in the next few days as I continue to decide things.

After she leaves, I begin packing the few belongings Caleb and I have. I'm not taking anything Playboy bought me. I'll take the toys he bought my son, but that's for my son because I know if he doesn't have them, he'll be even more upset than he already is about not seeing Playboy.

Within two hours, all of our things are packed. I sit down to write one last letter while I'm here. Well, two letters. I'll write one to Playboy and one to whoever is the next one to come to the house to 'check' on me. They'll find it and know I don't want to leave, but I have no choice at this point.

I've done a lot of thinking, and if Playboy doesn't know I'm pregnant, I don't want anyone else here to know either. I'll start showing sooner or later, and then I won't be able to hide it anymore. I'm not going to flaunt my pregnancy while Playboy is in there and wants nothing to do with me. So, my only option is to move away. If I hear he's gotten released, I'll let him know what's going on. Or, I'll say something to his dad once I've left Benton Falls behind.

"Mama, we leaving?" Caleb asks me.

"Yeah, honey, we are," I answer him.

Caleb slinks back to his room, and I know this is going to hit him hard. I pick the pen up and write the letter to whoever comes here. I'll write Playboy's when Caleb and I stop for the night. It will give me something else to focus on. For now, I just need to get out of here and help Caleb deal with all the feelings he has running through him right now.

My heart breaks because I don't know if this is the right decision to make or not. Deep in my gut, I feel as if it's the best solution for now. Things may be different when Playboy gets released because I have to believe he will. If I think of him spending the rest of his life behind bars, my heart shatters, and I can't breathe. This isn't what I want for him.

When I'm done writing the letter, I get Caleb and pack up the remaining toys he has in his room and grab the bag with some clothes and other necessities in it for us. Once we're in the car, I turn on the music, and *Best I Ever Had* by State of Shock is playing. Instead of connecting my phone for music, I leave the song playing because Playboy is the best man I know, and we could have made something amazing together. We have made something amazing together.

Leaving our little home, I keep glancing in the rearview mirror until it disappears from my sight. Tears silently fall as I think of everything we're giving up by leaving. Maybe we'll be back one day. That's my hope, at least.

Chapter Seven

Playboy

IT'S BEEN A few days since my visit with Shy. There's still been no word from anyone else, including Anderson. I'm getting pissed because there should be some news by now, and he either has nothing, or he doesn't feel like sharing it with me. And, I'm a little surprised no one from the club has come to see me. They try to make it here every few days.

The only thing I've been doing is working out in my cell and writing letters to Sam. I've even included a few to Caleb, so he has something. I'm still not going to send them, though. I don't want my pain to shine through the letters and not be there for my woman and son. That's the last thing I want to happen.

Then my thoughts turn to what Shy said to me. Maybe I should send one of the letters to Sam. Or have my dad take it back to her. If he ever comes to see me. The last thing I want is Sam to breakdown because I haven't talked to her or let her see me. It's not my intention for that to happen, but I don't want her to see me like this.

I've also been thinking about what Shy meant when she said she thinks Sam is hiding something. If someone were going to the house and bothering her, Fox would know about it. There's security out the ass on the house, and he can see inside at any point in time. Plus, he's got alarms around the perimeter in case someone wants to try looking in the windows or breaking in.

If it's not someone bothering her, I don't know what else it could be. During the day when I'm working out or thinking about writing her a letter, I try to think of all the things she could be hiding. The worst one is something being wrong with either Caleb or her. I know I won't be able to handle it if something happens to one of them.

"Busch, you got a visitor," a guard says, walking to the door of my cell.

"Who is it?" I ask, getting up and turning around for the handcuffs to be placed on my wrists.

"Lawyer. And your cuffs go in the front," he tells me.

Turning back around, I let him place the cuffs on me, and we walk down the hall to the visiting room. As soon as I'm in the room, the guard leaves us, and I take my seat across from Anderson. For the first few minutes, I simply stare him down. Most men cower when I stare at them this way or shift with their unease. Anderson merely sits there and shuffles through the papers in front of him.

"What have you been doin'?" I ask him.

"Tryin' to figure out which one of the residents of the street the incident happened on is. I still don't know which one and no one's talking. They're keeping it close to their vests, and I have the right to question this person. Unfortunately, they're not making it easy on me," he tells me.

"Then talk to my dad or someone in the club. Have them help you out," I tell him.

"No. They need to steer clear of this so no one can say they were intimidated or anything else," Anderson says.

"Fine. Why haven't I at least had a hearin' yet?" I question.

"They're taking you straight to trial," Anderson answers. "I think we've got a date for trial in two weeks. Are you sure there's nothing else I need to know about what happened that day?"

"Nothin' at all. What are you askin' me, Anderson?" I ask him right back.

"I just don't think you were the only one there that day. Playboy, if you're covering for someone, I need to know," he says, releasing a breath which tells me he's frustrated.

"No one else was there. You know what you need to do, and that's all I'm saying," I tell him.

"Fine. We'll leave it as is. I'm gonna go see if I can talk to the witness or the Prosecutor on the case," Anderson says, putting the papers back in his briefcase.

"Come back when you got somethin'," I tell him, standing from the table and going to the door so I can go back to my cell.

The meeting with Anderson was absolutely pointless. He has nothing to tell me, and he's not doing shit to get me out of here until the trial. Maybe it's time we talk as a club about getting a different fucking lawyer. One who can make things happen and do their damn job.

Yeah, I know I'm probably just frustrated I'm still in here. But, I'm itching or a fight now, and I can't afford to have more charges added on to me. I want to go to Sam and find out what's going on. So, once the guard removes the cuffs, I sit down and write her another letter.

This one is talking about not being free and with her and Caleb. About how I'd be holding her in my arms and make sure nothing could touch her. I want that more than anything in this world, and I can't have it right now.

Lying down on my bunk, I let images of Sam fill my head. Sliding my hand down my pants, I slide it up and down my cock. I picture her on her knees in front of me with my cock in her mouth. She's sucking me off fast and hard, her hand moving down to roll my balls in her hand. Before I know it, I can feel the tingling start, and I know I'm about to cum.

Picturing her swallowing me down is all it takes for me to cum all over my hand and stomach. It's not the way I want it to happen, but it's the only option I have right now.

Waking up today, I find I finally have a visit from someone in the club. My dad is here to see me. Maybe he can shed some light on a few damn things for me, like Anderson and Sam.

"It's good to see you, son," my dad says as I walk in the room and sit down across from him.

"Yeah, why have you been away? Everythin' good with the club?" I ask him.

"Yeah, we're good. Anderson been in to see you?" he questions.

"He was here. Waste of time if you ask me. Maybe we should start lookin' for a new lawyer," I tell him honestly.

"What's goin' on?" my dad asks, sitting up straight in the metal chair he's sitting in.

"There's a witness, and he can't find out a fuckin' thing about him to talk to the person or anythin'. Apparently, the Prosecutor is keepin' it close to the vest on this case," I respond.

"I see. I'll get ahold of him and see what's goin' on. What about gettin' you out before trial?" he asks.

"Not gonna happen, I guess. I don't know any more after talkin' to him then I did when I came in here. It's fuckin' insane," I tell him. "What's goin' on with Sam and Caleb? Have you seen them?"

"Haven't seen them in a few days. It's hittin' her hard, though. She's takin' it all on her shoulders, doesn't think she's good enough for you, and I don't know what else is goin' on. Somethin' else is hittin' her hard, but Fox hasn't gotten any hits on security. And you know he won't look inside the house because he doesn't want to invade her privacy," Dad answers.

"I need to know what she's hidin'. What if she's hurt or sick and doesn't know what to do? Or what if somethin' is wrong with Caleb?" I question, worry, and dread filling me.

"I'll stop over on my way back to the clubhouse. Shy went over yesterday and said she didn't answer the door. Didn't hear shit comin' from inside either. I know she's been lookin' for a job because we've got a few hits of her turnin' in her applications. No one's gonna hire her, though," he informs me, regret, and sadness on her behalf filling his face. "I don't know what to do to help her. And, she gave Shy your card back the last time she went to see them."

"The card to the account I put money in for her?" I question.

"That's the one," he tells me.

"She's gonna run," I tell him flatly. "Don't let her leave, Dad. I'm beggin' you."

"Fuck!" my dad growls out. "I'll leave now and get over there. Someone will be here in a few days to see you. You need anythin' while I'm here?"

"No. I just need to know Sam's okay. I'll call the clubhouse later."

Standing up, I leave the room with the guard. I can't believe Sam's gonna leave Benton Falls. If she didn't give my card back, I never would've known what she has planned. That told me all I need to know, though. Now, I have to get out of here. There's no way in hell I can be in here and let her and Caleb go off on their own without the protection of the club.

I'm not saying Sam and Caleb are in any danger, but they don't need to leave the family either. Sam and Caleb have been adopted into the family, whether they like it or not. They quickly went from victims of abuse to two people we all love and care about. Especially Gwen. Gwen loves Sam and Caleb. And Sam loves Gwen too. She's sees a lot of herself in the younger woman and wants to help her do what she wants to do to live her life.

I start forming a plan in my mind. The next time Killer comes in to see me, I'm going to have to talk to him about having Gwen go over and spend some quality time with Sam and Caleb. If anyone can figure out what's going on with her, Gwen can. She's so innocent and sweet you can't help but open up and talk to her.

Gwen will also be the one to make Sam understand she's perfect for me. I'm definitely not good enough for her, but I'm a selfish fuck, and I'm going to take what I want; Sam and Caleb are the only two I want.

With a plan in place in my mind, I pull my shirt off and begin my daily workout from the inside of my cell. It's the only thing that even remotely makes me feel calm and not want to find someone to beat the shit out of while I'm in here. It would be too easy to get caught up with more charges because I let the anger and rage I feel prompt me into beating the fuck outta someone.

Chapter Eight

Sam

IT DIDN'T TAKE me long to figure out Caleb and I weren't gonna be able to get very far from Benton Falls. I don't have the money to do much of anything, and Caleb hates being in the car for extended periods now. This really started once he started seeing the guys on the motorcycles. Now, that's what he wants to do.

We managed to make it four hours from Benton Falls when Caleb was getting too wound up to be in the car. So, I got off the highway and drove until I found a truck stop. As soon as I was parked, Caleb unfastened his seatbelt and waits for me to open the door.

"I'm hungry," he tells me.

"I know, baby. We're gonna get something to eat right now," I answer, grabbing my purse and getting out.

Opening up Caleb's door, I stretch and try to relax the muscles in my aching body. I grab his hand and close his door before we head to the restaurant in the truck stop. First, we'll be hitting the bathroom because I'm in dire need of it. Hopefully, they have a family one we can use.

A man coming out of the building holds the door open, and I see a cut on his body. Instantly, I tense up because I don't know if anyone in the club knows we're gone yet. He doesn't even look at us as we brush past him.

"Thank you," I tell him on our way past.

"You're welcome, ma'am," he responds, a southern drawl to his deep voice.

Once we're through the doors, I look around and see a store on the right of us, the restaurant on the left of us, and straight back is the bathrooms and a game room. I know we'll be making a stop in there before we head back out on the road because Caleb will need something to do before getting back in the car.

Caleb and I head into the family bathroom, and he keeps his face buried in my phone as I head behind the short wall to take care of business. We quickly head out, and I direct him toward the restaurant as he keeps glancing behind us toward the room filled with games. Honestly, I just want to sit down and rest. I don't want to drive anymore or play games. But that's now how life works.

There's a sign at the entrance of the restaurant saying to seat yourself. So, I lead Caleb toward the back of the area designated as the diner. We take seats in a booth where the backs are high, and no one can see in. I place Caleb in the seat with his back toward the entrance of the truck stop while I face the same area. If anyone did find us in here, he'd yell out to whoever he saw come in. Not exactly what I need to happen when I don't want to see them.

"Welcome to Torrino's. Do you know what you'd like?" an elderly waitress asks, walking up to the table.

"Um, no, we haven't had a chance to look at the menu yet," I respond.

"Are you okay, honey?" the woman asks me.

"Just tired," I respond automatically.

"How about I bring you over milk for the little man here and a coffee for you if you have more traveling to do?" she questions me again.

"Oh, um, well, I can't have coffee right now," I tell her.

"Gotcha. Are you just passing through or hanging around for a bit?" she asks.

"I'm not sure yet. Don't really know where we're heading," I respond.

"Are you running from someone?"

"No, ma'am. Just need a change of scenery. Just been on the road a few hours, and my son was getting antsy in the car, so we stopped," I say.

"Well, if you have no destination in mind, I know we're looking for help here. The money isn't too bad, but it's not great either. Enough to pay the bills, I suppose. Carson has an apartment for rent. He's been looking forever for someone to take it," she says. "Carson is the boss man here while I'm just the waitress. My name is Edna, by the way."

"It's nice to meet you, Edna. I'm Sam, and this is my son, Caleb. Maybe I will talk to Carson about the apartment and the job. I don't have any experience, though," I warn her.

"Oh honey, that's not a problem," she assures me. "I'll grab some milk and water for you while you look over the menu. And I'll get Carson to come out and talk to you."

"Thank you."

Edna walks away, and I take a deep breath. Maybe this is our starting over point. I pick up the menu from the stand at the back of the table and look over the food. It all sounds so good, but I better stick to something cheap for me, and I'll make sure Caleb has a good meal. I need to save money if I'm going to get this apartment and buy things we need for it.

I settle on chicken fingers, french fries, and apple sauce for Caleb and grilled cheese for me. It's not much, but it will hold me over for now. Placing the menu back in it's stand, and I look at my son. He's got the crayons from the cup on the table and is coloring on one of the placemats.

Caleb is concentrating on his drawing. There's a crease in his forehead, and his eyes are zoned in on the paper in front of him. His little hand is moving with deliberate movements, and I want to take a picture of the moment. So, I pick up my phone and capture Caleb as he colors furiously. He doesn't even look up or anything when I snap a few pictures of him.

When Edna comes back over to the table, there's an older gentleman following her. He's wiping his hands on a towel, and I'm guessing this is Carson. The man is smiling in our direction, and it fills his entire face, including his eyes.

"Carson, this is Sam. She's looking for a job and a place to stay," Edna says, introducing us.

"Nice to meet you, Sam," Carson says. "Have you ever waitressed before?"

"No, I haven't. We were just leaving Benton Falls and looking for somewhere to start over. Four hours in a car was enough for my son," I answer honestly.

"That's not a problem. Any reason you can't be on the books?" he asks me.

"No."

"Alright. I'm gonna hand the keys over to Edna. When you guys are done eating, she can show you the apartment. It's just down the road from here. Not even a half-mile," Carson says. "It may not look the best, but it's warm and will put a roof over your head."

"Thank you so much," I tell him.

"One last thing. You'll start the day after tomorrow so you can get settled in. I'll put you on opposite shifts of Edna if you want to talk to her about watching your son for you," Carson tells me.

Carson tells me what the monthly rent is, and my mouth drops at how low it seems to be. I have more than enough in my purse for the rent and down payment. Plus, I'll have money for food and anything else Caleb and I may need. He lets me know if I want it, just to give Edna the money, and he'll go over the lease with me when I come in for my first shift.

I nod my head and wipe away the stray tears. These people don't even know me and yet they're willing to take a chance and offer me a place to live and a job. That's more than I got from the applications I submitted in Benton Falls. No one would even talk to me because they knew I lived in a home owned by the Phantom Bastards and believed I was one of their whores so I could work for them.

Edna takes me to the apartment once Carson and I are done eating. It's a small house, smaller than where we were in Benton Falls. I guess this is why they call it an apartment. There's only one story, and it doesn't look like much from the outside. The paint is peeling, and the shutters are missing from the windows.

There's a small lawn that's mowed and looks as if it's taken care of regularly. I look around and can easily envision Caleb and the new baby playing out here and having a good time. The only person missing is Playboy.

"Let's take a look around the inside," Edna says as I grab Caleb's hand.

I nod my head, and we follow her up the three stairs leading to the small porch. She unlocks the door and lets us step inside before her. We walk into the living room, and there's a full set of furniture and a TV already in the room. I pass the room and head to the kitchen that's separated by a low wall. It's got a stove, refrigerator, and dining table already in the room. There's even dishes and glasses in the cupboards when Edna opens them up for me to see.

"There's two bedrooms down this hall over here," she tells me, pointing to the left of the kitchen.

I walk down the hallway and peek into the open doors. Both rooms are clean but on the small side. I'm not worried about the size of the rooms, though. As long as we have somewhere to lay our head at night, Caleb and I will be good. We're not picky, and we don't need much in our life to make us happy.

Walking back to Edna in the living room, she points out the laundry room and bathroom off to the right of the living room. After looking at the rooms, I decide we'll take the place.

"I'll take it," I tell her.

"Are you sure? I'm sure you could find someplace better than this," Edna tells me.

"I'm sure. There's things I can't do, but there's things I can to make improvements if Carson doesn't mind," I respond.

"I don't think he will. He just doesn't have the time to get here to work on the place. Between the restaurant and other places, this one has just kind of fallen to the background," Edna tells me.

Looking around again, there's peeling paint and wallpaper has been ripped in places too. There's a small hole in the wall toward the laundry room as if someone ran into it with a washer or dryer as they were moving it in. There are stains in the carpet, and a few spots where it's fraying and holes are starting to appear. The house definitely isn't much, but it's better than nothing. Nothing in this house can't be fixed.

"Okay, well, I'll take the money back to Carson and let him know you're staying here. There's a grocery store right down the road so you can get some things. A larger store is about twenty minutes away. We can go one day if you want to," Edna says as I hand over the money to her.

"I'd like that," I tell her honestly. "Thank you for everything."

"You're welcome, honey. Welcome to Torrino," Edna says as she hands me over the key and leaves the house.

Once she's gone, I bring all the bags into the house and see what all I need to get when Caleb and I go to the store. So far, it appears we need to get towels, food, and storage containers. I'll also need to get cleaning supplies while we're shopping too.

With my list in hand, Caleb and I head out to get our things so we can head home and I can make us some dinner. It's been a long day and I'm more than ready to lay down and go to sleep. Hopefully, Caleb will go to sleep easy tonight and won't want to be up half the night because he's not worn out.

Chapter Nine

Playboy

TODAY I'M ON my way down for another visit with my dad. Killer came with him this time, so I can put my plan in motion regarding Gwen and Sam. I'm just hoping the damn plan works and we find out what's going on with my woman. Even if it's not official, Sam is mine and so isn't Caleb.

The guard leaves me in the room and I take a seat across from my father and Killer. Neither one says a damn word for a few minutes and it's making me uneasy. Especially not knowing what's been going on with the club.

"What's goin' on?" I ask them, looking between the two men.

"Well, not much with the club. How are you doin' in here?" my dad asks me.

"I've been goin' crazy tryin' to figure out what's goin' on with Sam. Have you guys heard anythin'?" I question.

Killer and my dad look at each other before turning their attention back toward me. They're not telling me something and I want to know what it is. My gut tells me it's about Sam and I'm going to have to pry it out of them.

"So, I've been thinkin' about things," I begin when it's clear they're not going to answer me. "Killer, can you get Gwen over to Sam's? I want her to talk to her and see if she can figure out what's goin' on with her."

"Well, there's a problem with that," Killer begins. "Sam's not at the house. We're not sure when she left, but she's gone. No one knows where she is right now."

"What the fuck?" I yell out, pain swallowing me whole as I realize she took off like I knew she was going to. "Why hasn't Fox tracked her phone or car?"

"He never put a tracker on her car and her phone's off. The last time he got a hit was just outside of town. It turned on a while later but not long enough for him to get anythin' on where she is," my dad tells me.

"So, she's just gone. Vanished without a trace and no one knows where she is?" I question, my voice rising with each word slipping past my lips.

I slam my hands down on the table in front of me. The chain on the cuffs rattles as I pull my hands back ready to hit the table again. Rage boils in my veins and if I thought I was looking for a fight before now, that has been blown out of the water. I want to beat the shit out of someone to calm down and get this rage back under control.

A red haze fills my vision and I can't see much more than that at the moment. I'm ready to break the fuck out of here and find Sam and Caleb myself. Before I can do anything else, my dad puts his hand on top of mine. I look up into his eyes and see him silently telling me to calm down before the guards come in and take me out of here. So, I take a deep breath and release it.

"Son, she'll be in touch. There's a reason she chose to leave and there's a reason she'll come back. Sam will come back when you're out and free. For now, she's got to live life on her own and find her own path," my dad says.

"Considerin' we don't know what's goin' on with her, or Caleb, I want her found. Now!" I tell them, looking from one man to the other.

"What are you talkin' about?" Killer asks me.

"Shy told me she felt as if Sam's hidin' somethin'. I'm not sure what, but just after that, Sam gave her my card for the account I put her name on and now she's gone. Somethin' happened to her or Caleb and now she's gone," I inform them.

"I'll look into it," my dad responds. "You have my word I'll find out what's goin' on and where she is."

"Thank you. I need to get out of here," I tell them, my voice almost pleading with my dad and Killer.

"I'll get with Anderson and see what he has to say. Dependin' on what he says, I'll look into gettin' a new lawyer. Might not happen for your case though, Playboy," my dad says.

"Let me know when you find her. Please," I beg him, not caring what anyone thinks of me right now.

This isn't about me, it's about Sam and Caleb. I need to know what's going on and that they're okay. If I don't, I'll go fucking crazy in here and I'll end up with more damn charges than I have right now.

"We're gonna head out. I'll get with Fox and have him look over the footage at the house and then we'll figure out where to go from there," my dad says.

I nod my head and stand from the table. Turning my back on my dad and Killer, I walk to the door and the guard opens it for me. We head back to my cell and my mind is reeling with the thought of Sam being gone. What would make her leave with no word to anyone about why?

Once I'm back in my cell with the handcuffs off me, I pick up the letter I started to Sam this morning. Ripping it from the notebook, I ball it up and toss it on the bunk next to me. This is one letter Sam's going to get somehow. I'm not sure how yet, but I'll get it to her.

Dear Sam,

I know something is going on with you. You ran from Benton Hills with no warning or letting anyone know where you are. What's going on to make you run like that? Are you and Caleb okay?

Sam, we used to talk about everything and now things are so fucked up with me being in here. I want to be the man you confide in and the man you lean on for strength. The man Caleb turns to when he has a problem you can't solve for him.

I want to be your best friend, your lover, and your protector. I'll be a mentor, friend and father to Caleb. The only thing I want is to love you and whoever joins our family along the way.

When I told you I loved you, I meant it with every bone and fiber of my being. I have never once said those words to another soul and I never will. Sam, you came in and burrowed your way into my heart. I can't imagine a day without you and Caleb and I don't want to begin to try.

Please, I'm begging you, let someone know where you are and if you're okay. You have an entire club at your back and they'll help you out in any situation you find yourself in. If something is wrong with Caleb, your family, the Phantom Bastards will help you get him better. Or just be there for you until I can get the hell out of here.

I wish nothing but the best for you and our son. When I get home, we're going to have a long talk about what that means, including you going back to school to finish your degree. And we're going to talk about why you gave Shy my card when that money is for you and Caleb to use. You know this and still haven't touched a penny of it. Well, other than the money for the pharmacy.

I love you a million times over. Until I take my last breath, I'll love you.

Love Always,

Playboy

Setting the pad and pen next to me, I slump back against the wall and let my thoughts tumble free. All thoughts regarding Sam and Caleb. They're always on my mind and I know they'll never be out of my head. Even when I'm dead and buried in the ground, Sam and Caleb will be protected and watched over by me.

"Dinner," one of the guards says as they pass my cell.

Getting up, I head out to join the line of inmates and make my way to the mess hall. Just before we get there, one of the other inmates brushes up against my side and I feel a stinging sensation. Looking down, I see blood seeping through my shirt. What the actual fuck?

"You okay, Busch?" the guard asks me.

"No, I'm not," I reply, lifting my shirt.

"Infirmary. Now," the guard tells me. "The rest of you, figure out who the hell is responsible for this."

The guard leads me to the infirmary and leaves me once the nurse on staff begins taking care of me. She cleans the wound in my side and checks to determine if I'll need stitches or not. After examining it, she decides I don't need stitches and just puts a few butterfly stitches on it.

"You should be good to go. Just make sure you keep it clean. Come back and see me if you need *anything*," the nurse says to me.

"Excuse me?" I ask.

"What?" she questions, trying to feign innocence.

"You don't have anythin' I want. I have a woman and you're not her. I suggest you worry about doin' your damn job and not about fuckin' an inmate," I growl out.

She looks away from me as another inmate begins laughing his ass off.

"You're not the first one she's used that line on. And you won't be the last. She'll take any cock she can get," the inmate tells me.

"Not mine. Not cheatin' on my ol' lady," I respond.

Getting up, I leave the infirmary and find the guard waiting outside the room for me. He lifts an eyebrow in question at me and I shake my head.

"Might want to keep an eye on that nurse though. Likes inmate cock," I tell him.

"Will do," he says.

"Only sayin' somethin' cause I've heard the stories of bitches gettin' in over their head and windin' up dead or tryin' to help an ass escape," I say, not wanting anyone to think I'm a fucking rat because I'm not.

He walks me to the mess hall and I grab the shit they pass off as food. Once I sit down at a table alone, I eat my meal so I can get back to my cell. No one comes close to me and no one tries to talk to me.

The second I'm done eating, I stand up and take care of my trash. On the way back to my cell, I ask the guard if they caught who got me. He shakes his head and I head into my cell so I don't say or do anything I'll end up regretting.

I lay down and let images of my family consume me. Especially of the night Sam and I spent together. I can't get that night out of my head and I want to repeat it. There's not a single time I'll ever not want to be with Sam. She's perfectly imperfect, which makes her perfect for me.

Chapter Ten

Sam

I'VE BEEN IN Torrino for a week now. I'm settling in at the truck stop nicely and Caleb absolutely loves Edna. They play, watch movies, and he helps her make dinner. When I get home and Caleb and I wake up the next morning, he goes on and on about what they did the night before. It's the most he's ever talked before and I'm loving the change in him.

Today, Edna and I both have off from the truck stop. It works out amazing because I have a doctor's appointment. Caleb doesn't need to go to that because I'm not sure what they're going to do. Plus, I doubt he'll be able to sit down while we're in the exam room and behave while I'm being examined.

It's actually my first day off from the truck stop since I started a week ago. Carson made me take the day off because I've been covering other people's shifts and picking up shifts when we're busy. I stay late if we're busy and the waitresses taking over need help. Carson doesn't care unless it gets to the point it affects your health or something. He pays us for all the overtime too.

"So, is this your first appointment?" Edna asks when she gets to the house.

"Yeah. I found out just before I moved here," I reply.

"How's your morning sickness?" she asks.

"It hasn't been too bad," I tell her, but that can all change. "I was the same way with Caleb. It didn't hit until I was about four months pregnant or so."

"How far along are you?" she asks.

"I'm not sure. Things have been kind of crazy," I answer honestly.

"Well, you head out and we'll be here when you get back," Edna says, shooing me out of the house.

"I'm going," I respond.

Leaving the house, I get in my car and make my way to the doctor's office. The one good thing about Torrino is everything is close by. It doesn't take long to get anywhere in town and I'm thankful for it. Other than being tired, I haven't been feeling too bad.

My thoughts drift to work. I've been taking every shift I can take because I need the money and it keeps me busy. There's not much I can do at the house because I can't paint and I can't replace the carpets alone. I don't have the money for someone to come in to replace them for me.

Carson doesn't care about what I do to the house. As far as he's concerned, any repairs I do will be bettering the place. So, he's approved everything and will take the money off the rent. About the only thing I've done so far is patch the hole in the wall by the laundry room. And it looks horrible because I can't paint over it.

Which is what's on my mind because a few of the women are coming down today. I broke down and called Gwen a few days ago. She told me everyone is worried about me and wants to make sure I'm okay. Since I'm not showing yet, I decided they could come down. The house isn't going to be what any of them are used to, but there's nothing I can do with it.

The women will just have to accept this is my life and I'll make an excuse as to why I haven't been able to make repairs or paint like I should. No one will know I'm pregnant when they leave here. I can't let it happen. They'll tell the guys in the club who will tell Playboy. That's not how he's going to find out.

If I've learned anything being around the Phantom Bastards or the Wild Kings, it's that the men gossip in those clubs worse than any female I know. They'll run to Playboy in jail and tell him about the baby the first chance they get. I'll be the one to tell him about the baby and that's the final decision.

Pulling into the parking lot, I park as close to the building as I can. I get out and lock my car before heading inside. On the way, I pull out my license and insurance card. I know I'm going to be flagged by Fox if he's tracking me and I can't do anything about it. There's no money to pay for the appointment, but the women already know so I don't have to worry about him tracking my location anymore.

"Can I help you?" the receptionist asks.

"Yes, Sam Hart with a ten o'clock appointment," I answer, handing over my things.

She scans my license and insurance card before handing me a stack of papers to fill out. I take a seat next to the door I'm guessing leads back to the exam rooms. Taking the paperwork, I begin to fill it out with all of my information. I'm not exactly sure about all of Playboy's so those sections are left blank. It kills me that he's not here with me for this appointment. That we can't share in this excitement together. Hell, I'm not even sure if he'd be happy about the baby.

I get called back and the nurse takes my weight and vitals before sending me in to leave a specimen for them to test. The same thing I remember doing when I was pregnant with Caleb.

"What brings you in today?" she asks when we get in the exam room.

"Before I moved here, I took a home pregnancy test and it came up positive," I answer honestly.

"Okay. Doctor Manning will be in shortly to see you. I'm not sure what she'll want to do today, possibly an ultrasound," the nurse tells me.

"Thank you."

Once she leaves the room, I get undressed and put on the uncomfortable paper gown and sit down on the exam table. I place the sheet over my lap for a sense of modesty and wait for the doctor to come in and see me.

This is the part I hate, waiting. I'd rather be doing something than sitting still and waiting for someone to come in and see me. Instead, I'm sitting here, almost completely naked, waiting on a doctor I don't know. But, doctors are busy and I know waiting is a part of the process. So, I suck it up and get as comfortable as I can.

It's not long before Doctor Manning comes in. She's a woman who appears to be in her early forties and greets me with a smile.

"Hello Sam, I'm Doctor Manning. It's nice to meet you," she tells me. "Looking over your results, you're definitely pregnant. When was your last period?"

"I'm honestly not sure. I've never been regular and sometimes go months without having one," I tell her. "It's how I've always been."

"Okay. Well, we'll do an ultrasound today. I'll have her start with an external one and see what it shows," the doctor tells me.

I nod my head as the doctor does her exam of me. This is definitely something I could do without, but it's part of being pregnant and being a woman. As soon as she's done, she lets me get dressed while I wait for the ultrasound technician to come in.

She comes in just after I get dressed and I pull my shirt up and my pants down. The technician puts the gel on my stomach and turns the machine on so we can see the baby. Once everything is ready to go, I relax back and wait to see what's about to happen.

All of a sudden, I hear the whooshing sound of the baby's heartbeat. A smile fills my face and I close my eyes to take in the sound. At the same time, a tear slips free because Playboy is missing this. He's not here to listen to the sound of our child nestled protectively in me.

"Ready to see your baby?" she asks me.

"I am," I respond.

Turning my head, I look at the screen and wait for the image to become unblurry. When it comes into focus, the technician and I are both flabbergasted. Instead of one baby on the screen, there are two.

"Well, it appears you'll be having twins, Miss Hart. Do they run on either side of the family?" the technician asks.

"Not in mine. I'm not sure about the father's family," I tell her.

"Alright. Well, regardless, you're having twins," she tells me, a smile on her face as she looks in my direction.

I keep my eyes glued to the screen as she takes measurements and does whatever else she has to do. At the end, she prints me out a few pictures and labels them 'Baby A' and 'Baby B.' With them in my possession, I wipe the gel off my stomach while she cleans up her equipment.

"You're going to make an appointment for a month from now. You'll have another ultrasound and the doctor will check you over. You're approximately four months pregnant based on the looks of things," the technician tells me before leaving the room.

I've been back home for a while now. Edna stayed for lunch and then went off to enjoy her day off. Caleb and I cleaned the house up the best we could and I tried to hide most of the damaged area, not that they look much better now. He's excited the girls are coming for a visit and made sure his room was especially clean for them to see.

Now, I'm just waiting and thinking. I can't believe I'm having twins or that I'm four months pregnant. It seems like a lifetime ago that Playboy and I shared a night together. Usually, if he stays the night with me, we sleep and that's it. One night is all it took for his supersonic sperm to not only get me pregnant but have me pregnant with twins. This is an entirely new ballgame for me. I have no clue what to do with twins.

Hearing a car pull up, I quickly stuff the ultrasound pictures in my purse and take it to my room. On my way back to the front door, I double-check everything and make sure there's nothing out of place. It's not like we have many possessions to our name anyway. Most everything in our small home belongs to Carson and I'm thankful we have it.

Caleb runs past me and stops at the door. He looks back at me and I nod my head for him to open the door. My son unlocks it and flings it open before beaming up at Gwen, Shy, Jennifer, and Kim.

"Hey girls," Caleb says, letting them in the house.

The four women look around the house and I can almost see the disgust on their faces. Well, all except for Gwen. She stares at me and I swear the girl is looking straight into my soul. It's unnerving and a little scary because she'd be the one out of the women currently standing in my house to figure out the secret before Playboy knows what's going on.

"How have you guys been?" I ask, placing my hand on Caleb's shoulder as he stands in front of me.

"Worried about you," Shy says, not holding back her anger or sadness.

"Look, it's nothing personal. This is the best thing for Caleb and I right now. We need a change of scenery and to live our life without the thought of . . . well, you know," I say, not wanting to mention Playboy's name in front of him.

"He's pissed as hell and worried about you. We all know something is going on. Why aren't you talking to us about it?" Kim asks another one to never hold back what she's feeling.

"Because I can't. Look, Caleb and I are okay. No one's after us, we just need a break. Playboy doesn't want to see me or have anything to do with us. So, I'm trying to live my life without him," I say, tears forming in my eyes.

"What about us? We're your family too," Gwen says, tears pooling in her own eyes.

"You're right, you are. But, I don't want you to choose between Playboy and me. And it seems as if I'm the only one he doesn't want to see. So, for now, I need time and space away from all the reminders of him," I respond, heading to the small kitchen. "At least this way, he can come home and not have to worry about him telling me he loved me or anything else."

"What are you talking about?" Shy asks me.

"Right before they handcuffed him, he told me he loves me. Yet, he won't see, won't call me, and he sends my letters back unopened. That's not love," I reply, letting my anger out slightly. "This is his way of brushing me off. So when he finally gets out and comes home, he doesn't have to worry about me being there and expecting anything from him."

"You're dumber than I thought," Kim suddenly blurts out.

"I'm not dumb. I'm just not going to stay where I'm not wanted. And, there's other factors which helped me make my decision. Look, I have a job here, Caleb and I are okay. I've got a friend who helps me with him while I'm working, and everything is super close by. Caleb and I will be fine here. Please, let me have this," I plead with them, looking at each one in turn.

Shy finally nods her head and lets the subject drop. I know they're going to let the guys know what's going on here, but there's nothing I can do about it. I'm given a quick break when Caleb speaks up and offers to show them around the house. Gwen looks at me because they all know he barely speaks, so this is a rare occurrence for him. One they all love.

While Caleb shows them around the house, I pull out drinks for everyone and a few snacks. We sit at the table and talk. I'm told stories of the kids and the trouble they're causing around the clubhouse. Rayven is the spoiled club Princess and everyone takes her from Slim and Shy as soon as she shows up. But, all the kids are feeling the loss of Uncle Playboy being there. He's got a way about him with the kids. He has no problem getting down and playing with them or making sure they have the good snacks their parents don't normally let them have.

"Are you really okay here?" Shy asks as I let my thoughts wander to all the things Playboy used to do with the kids.

"Yeah. Just got lost in thought for a minute there," I respond, forcing a smile on my face as I look up.

"Mama, I'm gonna play," Caleb says, tired of us talking already.

"Okay, baby boy. I'm here if you need me," I tell him.

"What are you hiding from us?" Shy asks once he's gone.

"Nothing."

"You're lying. It's bad enough Playboy wanted Gwen to visit with you alone because even he knows something is going on. He also knows she's the only one you'll tell," Shy says.

"Look, things are going on, but I can't talk about them right now. When I can talk about them, you'll all be the first to know," I respond, looking at each woman around the table.

"Why don't you just tell us now, so you don't have to live like this," Kim says.

"Guys, leave her alone. She has her reasons and let her do what she feels is best right now," Gwen says, standing up for me.

"We just care about you, Sam. If something is going on, we want to know so we can help you with it," Shy says.

"I know you guys do and I love you for it. But, you'll understand why when I can finally let you all in on what's going on. Trust me, I would if I could," I say.

"Fine. We'll drop it for now. We're not going to let you put us off forever, though," Kim tells me.

The rest of the day, we talk, laugh, and make dinner together. I'm grateful I went grocery shopping and they don't have anything else bad to say about where I'm living when they get back to the clubhouse.

All in all, the day is amazing and I truly miss the women of the club. I miss the men too, but I can't be there right now. It's bad enough I know what I've said today is going to get back to Playboy and that's the last thing I need right now. Oh well, too late for things to change now. I'll have to see how it plays out.

Caleb comes out of his room to spend more time with the women. He ends up falling asleep in Gwen's lap and she puts him to bed for me. I really don't need to be carrying him at this point, but I would have if it had just been us.

Once they leave, I clean up the house and make my way to bed. I cry for the loss of Playboy as I look at the pictures from today's ultrasound. This is crazy to think I'm having his babies and he has no clue. I want him to know but there's no way I can tell him when he won't have anything to do with me.

"We'll be okay little ones. I'll love you more than enough for your daddy and me," I say, rubbing my hand on my still flat stomach.

It's not long before sleep claims me and dreams of Playboy and the life we could have had play. I dream of him playing and laughing with our children and being the amazing father I know he'd be. If he would have anything to do with me. With us.

Chapter Eleven

Playboy

THINGS HAVE BEEN calm since I was sliced on the way to the mess hall last week. I haven't seen the lawyer again since he came to visit me the last time. Hell, my dad hasn't even heard from him since our visit after I saw Anderson last. My dad is as pissed as I am right now.

Yesterday the women went down to see Sam and Caleb. She called Gwen and they talked for a little bit. Shy found out and showed up while they were still on the phone. Gwen had already worked her magic and found out where she was staying. Somewhere in the small town of Torrino. I don't even know where the hell that is.

I'm waiting for my dad to visit today because I have trial this afternoon and Shy got me some clothes around, so I'm not wearing these jail clothes. The only thing I won't be wearing is my cut. I feel naked without the thing, but there's nothing I can do until I get the fuck out of here.

"Busch, visitor," the guard tells me.

I stand up and place my hands in front of me. He cuffs me and we walk down the hall to the visiting rooms. My dad is sitting there waiting for me and he looks as if he's aged since the last time I saw him. I hate this shit because I know this is taking its toll on him. He hates to see any of us on the inside, but I'm his only son and the Vice

President of the club. He's been grooming me for longer than I can remember to take his spot at the head of the club.

"You ready for today?" he asks as I sit down.

"As ready as I can be without knowin' what the fuck is goin' on," I respond.

"I know. I'm not sure what the fuck is goin' on with Anderson. Hopefully, he's on point today. That's the only thing I care about. You comin' home is the most important thing to me. To us," he says. "The guards got your clothes. Said they'd bring them to you when it was time."

"I know, Dad. So, what's goin' on with Sam?" I ask, needing to know about my girl.

"Well, she's workin' at a truck stop. And, from what Shy says, she's livin' in a complete hell hole. Worn out carpet, walls need to be painted and wallpapered again. There's a hole in the wall by the laundry room. Everythin' is just plain worn out and Sam doesn't seem to mind one bit. Neither does Caleb. They're just livin' life the best they can," he answers me, waiting for me to blow up.

"What the fuck?" I explode. "Why would she live like that?"

"I don't know. They tried to get out of her what's goin' on and she won't say a word. Only thing she said is she wants you to come home and not have to worry about seein' her because of you havin' nothing' to do with her while you've been in here," he says. "Said you don't love her because you won't talk to her, let her see you, or read her letters. Her head is completely fucked because of this shit, Playboy."

I hang my head. Not in shame, I hang it in guilt. I've got my reasons for not wanting to see her or anything else, ones I've explained to the guys when they come visit me. Hell, I even explained it to Shy when she came to see me. I don't imagine that helped the situation because I saw her and I won't see Sam.

How many more ways can I fuck this up with her?

"So, no one knows what's goin' on with her still?" I ask to be clear.

"Nope. She refuses to say a word. Just that when she can talk about it, she will," my dad answers. "I'm gonna keep this short, so you can get ready for trial. We'll all be there."

"No, you won't. Sam won't be there," I respond, standing from my seat and making my way to the door. "Oh, any news on the fucker who tried to stab me?"

"None yet. Got the guards lookin' into it. They'll have somethin' soon. Even if you aren't in here, we'll make sure it's taken care of. Won't happen again either," he tells me as I step through the door.

The guard leads me back to my cell, my home for the time being. Hopefully, not after today, though. I want to go the fuck home so I can find Sam and Caleb to bring them home where they belong.

I've changed clothes into the dark wash jeans and the button-down grey shirt Shy picked out for me to wear today. She sent a tie too, but I'm not going to wear that shit. I have my new pair of boots on my feet and my long, dirty blonde hair is pulled back in a man bun because I need to keep it out of my damn eyes.

"Busch, let's head out," the guard tells me.

This time I turn around so he can place the cuffs on me. I'll be leaving jail so they have to go behind my back. I'm fine with it as long as it means I don't have to come back here for very long. We head out of jail and he leads me to the cruiser. Because I'm the only one heading to court today, we're traveling in a cruiser instead of the jail van.

It doesn't take us long to pull up to the courthouse. The parking lot is filled with every member of the club, the ol' ladies, and Gwen and Kim. I don't know why the fuck Fox hasn't claimed that woman yet. He better get his head out of his ass before he ends up like me.

Even though I know she's not going to be here, my eyes still scan the parking lot for Sam. My heart breaks as I realize I've pushed her so far away by not talking to her or seeing her that she hasn't come on the one day she could see me. I shake my head as my dad steps forward. No, as Slim steps forward. He's not my dad today; today he's Slim, President of the Phantom Bastards MC.

"Let's go, Busch," the guard says, leading me past my family on the way into the courthouse.

We walk into the room reserved for me while any other cases are going on. I take a seat, and the guard switches my handcuffs to the front of my body instead of leaving them behind my back. Once he's done, I sit in the chair, and it's not long before Anderson comes into the room.

"How are you doing today, Playboy?" he asks me.

"I'd be better if I knew what the fuck was goin' on with the case," I reply, staring the man in his eyes.

"Not much to tell. I'll know more once we get into the courtroom. Shouldn't be long now, the judge is almost finished with the current case, and then you're up," Anderson tells me.

"Look, you get paid damn good money by the club. Why does it seem as if you've dropped the fuckin' ball on my case? Who's ridin' your ass, Anderson?" I ask, letting my anger out in full force before we get in the courtroom.

"Playboy, I'm doing my damn job. As far as I can tell, there's no damn evidence against you and there's only one witness. We just need to see how reliable the witness is before we make our case that your innocent," Anderson says, completely ignoring my outburst.

Yeah, it's time for us to get a new damn lawyer. Anderson isn't worth the money we pay him these days. At least, not in my opinion. I'd rather have someone who's not afraid to step on toes and will do the work necessary to find out exactly who we're dealing with. Not taking a chance he'll see something in the courtroom no one else does.

Before I can say another word, the court clerk comes in to get us. I'm lead to the courtroom and Anderson and I take our seats while the

Prosecutor takes her seat across from us. I don't look at anyone as we wait for the judge to enter the room. He must have left after the last case for a break. I don't care as long as I get this shit sorted out today. Hopefully, this trial doesn't drag out, but I don't think it will with no evidence and only one witness.

"Please rise for the honorable Judge Norse," the clerk says as everyone in attendance stands while the judge gets to his seat.

"All take a seat," he says. "We're here today for the trial of the state versus Griffin Busch on the charge of murder. Miss Landry, you may speak first."

The Prosecutor stands up and outlines the supposed crime I committed to the jury.

"This man, Mr. Busch, murdered a man in cold blood in broad daylight. There is no remorse from the defendant and he hasn't said a word to anyone about the events of the day. The only thing we know for sure is that Mr. Martinez was beaten to death outside of a vehicle. This happened in a neighborhood filled with homes. We have a witness who saw Mr. Busch commit this crime," Miss Landry says, never once looking in my direction. "Mr. Busch is a member of the Phantom Bastards motorcycle gang and as you can all see, they're in attendance today. These criminals are hoping for a not guilty charge and are here to intimidate you into pleading their way."

"I object," Anderson says, standing up from his seat.

"Miss Landry, you're walking a fine line here. The entire club is not on trial here today, one person is," Judge Norse says.

"Nothing further at this time," Miss Landry says, walking to her seat.

Now, it's Anderson's time to speak. Let's see what the fucker has to say in his defense of me.

"Ladies and gentlemen of the jury, we're here today to determine if my client, Mr. Busch, committed a murder. There is no evidence against my client. The cops can't even find the body of the supposed deceased. Miss Landry has one witness to this supposed crime and that's all her case is based on," Anderson says. "Yes, Mr. Busch is a member of the Phantom Bastards motorcycle *club,* and they are all in attendance today. They are a family and help out this community more than Miss Landry would like to admit. Listen to the facts presented to you and only those facts. Make your decision based on what you hear as fact and not Miss Landry's obviously biased opinion.

"And let it also be said, my client has been sitting in jail for multiple weeks awaiting trial without even a hearing for bail. That's not how the judicial system is supposed to work ladies and gentlemen. He should have had a day in front of the judge with the opportunity to be released until today."

Anderson sits back down and for the first time since I got arrested, my entire body calms down. I relax in my seat and put my trust in Anderson to do his job. Maybe he's done more than we realize. But, I still think we need to bring someone else in to help him or something.

"Miss Landry, bring in your witness so we can move this along. And, I'm going to remind you to stick strictly to the facts of the case," Judge Norse says.

"Yes, your honor," Miss Landry says, standing up once again. "I'd like to call Mr. Gentry to the stand."

The clerk brings in Mr. Gentry. He has him swear in before taking his seat in the witness stand.

I look at the man before us, and I know how Anderson is going to play this. Mr. Gentry is an elderly man, who can't be younger than seventy years old. He's got thick glasses on his face and at least one hearing aid in his ear. I'm not sure about the other ear because I can't see it with the way he's sitting.

"Mr. Gentry, can you please tell us what you were doing the afternoon of the day in question?" Miss Landry asks.

"Yes, ma'am. I had just made a ham sandwich with some potato chips for lunch before going back to my living room to eat. I was sitting in my chair watching TV as I ate. Just before the weather came on, I heard a scuffle outside and got up to look out my window," Mr. Gentry says.

"What did you see when you looked out the window?" Miss Landry asks him.

"I saw a man standing outside of an SUV with a phone to his ear," Mr. Gentry answers.

"Is that all you saw?" she asks him.

"No, I saw a pair of feet sticking out of the front of the vehicle," Mr. Gentry answers.

"That's all you saw?" she asks him again.

"Yes, ma'am," he responds.

"No further questions," Miss Landry says, walking back to her seat with a smirk on her face.

I don't see what she's so happy about. Him seeing a set of feet sticking out from the front of the SUV doesn't prove a damn thing. At least not to me.

"Mr. Gentry, how are you today?" Anderson asks, standing up from his seat.

"I'm doing okay. Thank you," Mr. Gentry answers.

"So, you didn't see a fight or anything take place after getting out of your chair?" he questions.

"No, sir."

"Is it possible they had car trouble and the feet you saw on the ground were simply a man looking under the SUV to try to diagnose the problem?" Anderson asks.

"Well, I suppose that could have been the case," Mr. Gentry says.

"Now, Mr. Gentry, I see you wear glasses. Did you have them on when you looked out your window?" Anderson asks him.

"Yes, sir I was."

"Thank you. Do you see the man standing by the SUV on the phone in this courtroom today?" Anderson asks him.

Mr. Gentry looks around the courtroom for several minutes. He looks right past me at least two or three times before turning his attention back toward Anderson.

"No, sir, I don't see him," Mr. Gentry answers.

Everyone is so quiet; you can hear a pin drop. I look over toward Miss Landry and she's pissed. Her face is beat red and I can see a vein pulsing in her neck. I smirk in her direction before facing forward again.

"Now, you recall what you had for lunch and that the weather hadn't yet come on the news. Are you sure you don't see the man from that day in the courtroom?" Anderson asks him.

The man once again looks around the courtroom and his gaze stops on someone from the club, but it's not me. I don't even turn around to see who he's looking at. Anderson does, though. So doesn't the judge. If anything out of the ordinary were occurring, the judge would be speaking up right now.

"No, sir. I don't see him in the room today," Mr. Gentry once again tells Anderson.

"Thank you, Mr. Gentry," Anderson says, turning to walk back to the table I'm sitting at. "Your honor, I'd like to call a mistrial. The Prosecution has no evidence and no witness to put him at the scene of the supposed crime. There isn't even a body of Mr. Martinez, so we don't even know if the victim in question is deceased or not."

For a few minutes, the judge says nothing. He steeples his hands and rests his chin on them. Miss Landry is steaming mad and I know it's because she just lost this case. We're just waiting on the judge to make the final call.

"Mr. Gentry, you may step down. Thank you," Judge Norse says.

Everyone waits as Mr. Gentry steps down from the witness stand and the clerk leads him from the room. Once he's gone, the judge looks directly at me.

"Mr. Busch, I'm sorry you've been in jail for so long while the Prosecutor was trying to find evidence against you. That should have never once happened. It won't happen again in the future," Judge Norse says, looking at Miss Landry. "Due to the fact there's no evidence of a murder even taking place, Mr. Busch, you're free to go. You'll go back to jail, collect your personal belongings, and then be released.

"Ladies and gentlemen of the jury, thank you for your time today. You're dismissed."

Judge Norse slams his gavel down and stands from his seat. He leaves the courtroom as my family explodes in applause and joy. Miss Landry stands from her seat and casts a heated look in my direction. She's pissed as fuck, and I'm about to hear it from her.

"You may have gotten off today, but you won't in the future. I'm making it my mission to put every single one of you behind bars. For life," she says before picking up her briefcase and stalking from the room.

"Well, I guess we've been put on notice," I say to Anderson. "You might want to do somethin' about that."

"I'll take care of it," Anderson says, picking the papers up in front of him and placing them in his briefcase.

"Son, we'll meet you at the jail. I'll have your cut and bike there waiting for you," my dad says as the guard from the jail leads me from the courtroom.

We head back to jail, and I smile the entire way. I'm finally fucking free and can go home. I can get my girl and son back home where they belong. Knowing I'll never have to worry about this shit again is a relief, and a load lifted off my shoulders. Now the only thing I have to worry about is getting Sam and Caleb home where they belong.

Chapter Twelve

Sam

GOING IN TO work today, I decide it's time to talk to Carson about my pregnancy. Since the girls left yesterday, I've been getting sick. Morning sickness is now in full effect, and I spend more time in the bathroom than doing anything else. Even Caleb is worried about me, and I can't tell him what's going on because he'll let it slip with the girls.

When I first got to work, Carson wasn't here. He has an appointment, so I force it to the back of my mind and get busy waiting on the tables in my section. It's not long before I have to run to the bathroom, though. I get there just in time to lose the little I managed to eat this morning before coming here.

I go back to my section once I've washed up and used the mouthwash I carry with me. No one seems effected by my sudden disappearance in the least. So, I work until it's time for me to take a quick break. The smells of the food and coffee have me constantly feeling sick to my stomach, and I know I need to let Carson know what's going on. So, instead of getting something to eat, I head to his office.

"Carson, do you have a minute?" I ask from outside the door.

"Sure, sweetheart. What can I do for you?" he asks, setting his paperwork aside and giving me his full attention.

"Well, I need to let you know I'm pregnant. I found out yesterday I'm about four months along with twins," I tell him, wringing my hands in front of me.

"That's why you keep disappearing today then?" he questions gently.

"Yeah. I'm sorry about it. Just the smells of the food and coffee are getting to me," I tell him honestly.

"Nothing to be sorry about. Where's the children's father while you're here busting your ass and raising that little boy?" Carson asks me.

"Well, last I knew, he was in jail. He got arrested for protecting me when I was being kidnapped," I answer.

"Does he know where you are?" my boss asks.

"No, he doesn't. He wouldn't see me or talk to me. No one from home knows I'm pregnant because when he finds out I'm pregnant, I'll be the one to tell him," I say, standing up straight.

"What the fuck, Sam? This man wouldn't have anything to do with you because he's in jail. He has no clue what's going on with you and that you need help right now?" Carson bellows out.

"No, he doesn't," I respond, not afraid of the man before me.

Carson is mad on my behalf. He's not mad at me, and that's why I'm not afraid of him. My boss treats every single one of his employees as if we're his family. So, I don't expect him to be any less pissed than he is right now. I've been pissed about the situation, but there's nothing that can be done about it.

"What do you need from me?" Carson asks, standing up and walking over to me.

"I just wanted to let you know in case customers or other employees started complaining about me disappearing regularly. I'm hoping the morning sickness won't last long, but I'm not sure because of having twins this time. It's all-new for me," I tell him.

"Okay. Well, if you need anything, you let me know, and we'll do what we can to make sure you get it. For now, take it easy, and I'm going to limit the overtime you work," he informs me.

"No, please don't do that, Carson. I need all the money I can get— at least, until I can talk to the baby's father and let him know what's going on. I need to be able to get what Caleb and I need and then what I need for the babies when they get here, too," I plead with him.

After a few minutes, Carson finally nods his approval for me to continue picking up extra shifts and working later. He does tell me to take extra breaks when I can and not to overwork myself. I hug him before returning to the floor. Vanessa, the other waitress on shift with me, glares at me as I return to my section to check on the tables.

Vanessa and I have had a love to hate relationship since I started working here. Part of it's because Edna and I are close and become closer on a daily basis. The other part of it is because Carson gave me the small house Caleb and I live in. She's had her eye on it for a friend, and he refused to rent to the friend. I'm not sure why; it's not my business. So, she's always being pissy with me, and I just ignore her.

"Are you okay, honey?" one of the truck drivers asks me as I bring coffee around for refills.

"Yeah. I'm not sick or anything, so nothing will happen to you," I assure him.

"Not worried about that, darlin'. Worried about you. You're very pale and look about dead on your feet. First trimester?" he asks me.

"Oh, well. No, I just found out I'm four months with twins," I answer him.

"Ah. No wonder you're pale and look ready for a long nap," he responds. "My wife was the same way when our twins were born."

"I have a son, and I was never this tired from that pregnancy," I say with a laugh.

"Well, you take it easy and don't work too hard," the customer says as I refill his cup. "And don't let that other bitch keep trying to steal your tips. She goes behind you when she thinks you're not paying attention."

"Thanks for the heads up," I say. "I'll make sure to keep an eye on her better from now on."

I go about the rest of my shift with a smile on my face and pain in my back and feet. This is only going to get worse the further along I get in my pregnancy. Nothing new, and definitely things I'll be dealing with from now on.

Just before the end of my shift, I catch Vanessa trying to get my tips from the tables as I walk through my section.

"Can I help you?" I ask, turning around to face her.

"Not at all," she replies with an attitude.

"Good. Then I suggest you get out of my section and leave my tables alone," I tell her, placing my hands on my hips. "You're done taking my money from me."

"What's going on out here?" Carson asks.

I just stare at Vanessa for a minute, waiting to see what she's going to do. When she stomps off in the direction of her section, Carson puts a hand on my shoulder.

"You don't gotta say a word. Had a customer plant a bug in my ear, and then I started watching the security footage. Vanessa won't be here any longer. She's being terminated for theft," he tells me.

"Well, I don't know that she deserves that," I tell him.

"Yes, she does. I'm not going to have an employee stealing from another one because she's got a bug up her ass," he says, turning to let me finish my shift.

Once my section is cleaned, and Riley is here to relieve me, I head to the back to grab my purse. I've been keeping my phone off because I don't want to talk to anyone. I'm so afraid I'm going to let something about the babies slip, and I don't want to. Plus, I honestly don't want to hear anything about Playboy. He made his choice, and it's time to move on.

"Carson, you can't fucking do this to me!" I hear Vanessa yell. "That bitch is the one stealing, not me."

"Vanessa, we have footage of you doing it. And, a customer told me he watched you walk behind her, taking her tips. So, collect your things and get out of my restaurant," Carson tells him.

"Fuck you, Carson! Keep this shit in mind when you realize I'm the best waitress you've *ever* fucking had in this dump," Vanessa screams.

As she leaves Carson's office, she literally slams into me. I catch myself on the counter behind me as pain shoots through my back.

"This is all your fucking fault, bitch," Vanessa shouts at me. "I'll get my payback on your ass too."

Vanessa storms from the truck stop, and I know she means every single word she's spewing at me. Now, on top of everything else I have going on, I'll have to watch out for Vanessa or one of her lackeys coming after me. Just fucking great.

"Are you okay?" Carson asks, rushing from his office.

"I'm okay. A little pain in my back, but it's okay," I answer him.

"Tyler, walk Sam to her car. Make sure Vanessa doesn't follow her," Carson orders the night manager.

Tyler walks me to my car and waits outside until I'm out of the parking lot. I don't watch him go back inside the truck stop or anything else. The only thing I'm concerned with right now is getting home so Edna can get home. She has to be up early for her shift, and I'm sure she's going to ask what happened tonight. Carson has more than likely already called her.

Sure enough, as soon as I walk through the door, Edna is on her feet and holding me back from her. She inspects me from head to toe and then motions for me to turn around. I do, and she lifts my shirt. Edna gasps, and I can only imagine the bruise I'm sporting from crashing into the counter behind me earlier.

"That dumb bitch!" Edna growls out. She reminds me of Playboy right now.

"It's over, Edna. I just want to go to bed and forget about tonight at all," I respond to her.

"What exactly happened?" Edna asks.

"Vanessa has apparently been stealing my tips when I wasn't paying attention. A customer brought it to my attention and then to Carson's. When I was checking out my section before Riley got there to relieve me, I caught her following me through my tables and looking for my tips. Then, Carson fired her," I say, giving her the short version of tonight's events.

"I've never known Vanessa to be such a bitch. I wonder what the hell is going on with her," Edna says.

"I don't know. You know she's never liked me since I started working here though," I say. "Apparently, we just rubbed one another the wrong way."

Edna leaves, and I walk through the house. After checking to make sure all the windows and the door is locked, I make my way to Caleb's room. He's sound asleep, and I cover him back up before walking into my room. I undress and get ready for bed. My back is now killing me as I try to find a comfortable place when I lay down. It's not easy, and it takes me a long time to get comfortable enough to let sleep finally claim me.

Chapter Thirteen

Playboy

I'VE BEEN OUT of jail for two days now. I spend my time getting caught up on club business and trying to get a hold of Sam. She's not answering any of my messages, and when I try to call her, it goes straight to voicemail. Now I'm not only worried about my family, but I'm pissed the fuck off. Why the hell doesn't she have her fucking phone on?

Today, the club is properly welcoming me home with a huge ass party. I don't want to be here for it. What I want to be doing is out looking for Sam and Caleb. Instead, I've been stuck here at the clubhouse, and I'm dealing with everything here.

We've had several sessions of church to get me caught up on things, and I've talked to Fox about tracking her whereabouts. He can't find her no matter what he does. Other than knowing she's working at a truck stop and that she has her own place. Well, she's renting it. I also know one of the other waitresses watches Caleb for her. That information came from Shy.

Yeah, I've been finding out everything I can from the women. What I'm hearing, I don't like one bit. Sam is struggling to make ends meet, and she's living in a shit hole. She doesn't need to be doing that, yet she is. And it's my fault because I couldn't see past my own ass to let her see me.

"Hey, Playboy. You're looking a little tense," one of the house bunnies says, running her hand down my chest.

"Get the fuck off me," I growl out as I make my way to the bar.

"Don't be like that. You know I could give you the relief you need. No one has to know," she says, following me. "Besides, it's not like that bitch is here to take care of your needs."

"Don't you *ever* fuckin' talk about my woman again. You do, and I'll toss your ass outta here. Permanently. Got me, bitch," I yell, getting in the house bunnies' face.

She turns on her heels and runs from me. I can hear the fake as shit tears she's crying to get sympathy from someone else here at the club. Trust me, we've seen it all, and nothing these bitches do phase us anymore. Especially not some fake ass tears.

"Did you have to be that harsh?" Shy asks, walking toward me.

"Yeah, I did. No one's gonna talk shit about Sam and get away with it," I answer.

"She'll be back, Playboy. I know she will," she says, sitting down next to me with Rayven in her arms.

I grab my little sister from her and rest her against my chest. Rayven is a beautiful little girl, and my dad is going to have his hands full with her as she gets older. I don't envy him at all.

"Shy, are you sure she didn't say anythin' to you about why she left?" I ask her, looking her straight on as I wait for her answer.

"I'd tell you if I knew. I'm not sure what's going on with her. Or why she chose to leave here. Other than what she told me and you already know that," she responds. "Why?"

"I've been tryin' to call and message her, and I'm gettin' nothin' back. Her phone goes straight to voicemail. Why wouldn't she have her phone on?" I ask, not expecting an answer.

"I'm not sure about that. We've taken care of the bill while you were inside, just like you asked us to. So, her service is on," Shy says as my dad walks in the room.

"I see you've already kidnapped my baby girl," he says on a laugh.

"Damn straight, I did. When's everyone supposed to get here?" I question.

"Should be any time now," he informs me.

"Okay. I'm gonna take a shower and get ready then. I'll be back for my baby sister later on," I say, reluctantly handing her back over.

Standing up, I grab my beer and head to my room here at the clubhouse. I do have a place built here on the compound now, but I refuse to stay there without Sam and Caleb. It's our home, and that's what it will always be. So, I refuse to be there without my family in our home. Right now, it's just a pile of wood and the other shit making up a building.

As I enter my room, I try to shut the door only to have it stopped. Standing outside in the hall is the same house bunny who tried to get me to fuck her less than an hour ago. Her eyes look up at me, and I groan.

"Not doin' this with you. Thought you would've gotten the message earlier. There will be plenty of biker cock here for you in a little bit. For now, get the fuck away from me," I growl out, not giving a shit about her feelings.

She stomps her foot like a petulant child and walks down the hall toward the common room. It's not like she'll be out and about while the ol' ladies are around the clubhouse; house bunnies aren't allowed out until later at night when the families go home. It makes all of our lives easier.

I finally slam my door shut and make sure it's locked before stripping out of my clothes. Once my cut is hung on the back of my door, I head into the bathroom and turn the shower on. Maybe the hot water will help me ease the tension from my body.

The party is in full swing. Everyone from the Phantom Bastards MC, Wild Kings MC, and Satan's Anarchy MC are here to welcome me home. We're all outside, and I'm sitting with my dad and Shy when I realize I better make the rounds. Standing up, the first people I meet are Grim, Bailey, Skylar, and Cage. Joker is around here somewhere. He's never far from his woman's side.

"How you doin'?" Grim asks me, pulling me in for a man hug.

"Been better. Lots goin' on right now," I answer him, turning to my attention to Cage. "How have things been with you guys?"

"Same ol' shit just a different damn day," Cage responds.

"Heard about Sam taking off," Bailey says. "Everything okay there?"

"I have no clue. I haven't been able to get ahold of her since I got released. As far as I know, she doesn't even know I'm home and don't have to worry about this shit again," I answer her, pulling her in for a hug. "Anyone seen my sister around here?"

"Yeah, she's with Tank and Joker over by the food," Skylar answers as I pull her in for a hug next.

"Thank you. I'm gonna go say hi before they decide to find a private corner," I tell them, earning laughs all around because we know it's true.

Walking through the crowded yard out behind the clubhouse, I stop and talk to men and women as I pass. Kids run through everyone, though there's not as many as there used to be. Most of them are getting to be teenagers and living their own lives.

Finally, I get to my sister and Tank. Tank's facing me, and I place my fingers against my lips so I can sneak up behind Maddie. She's been dying to see me, and I've purposely put it off because I know she's going to give me shit about Sam and Caleb leaving here. Yeah, she already knows because everyone in these clubs talks and nothing is a secret.

I pick Maddie up around her waist and spin her around. She screams and tries to hit out at me as Tank, Joker, Pops, my dad, and Shy all laugh their asses off at us. When I finally set her down on her feet, I keep a hand on her elbow to make sure she doesn't fall to her ass after spinning her around so many times. I'm a little damn dizzy myself.

"Playboy! You scared the shit outta me," she yells, throwing herself back in my arms. "How you doing?"

"Not good. But I suspect you already know that," I tell her honestly as I pull Tank in for a man hug. "Good to see you, man."

"You too. You need any help, let me know, and we'll be there," he says.

"Mad, have you been able to get ahold of Sam?" I ask, wondering if she's tried to reach out to her.

"No. I haven't talked to her since the last time we were all together," she tells me. "I feel horrible because we've been busy, and I haven't made time to check on her. Especially once dad let me know what was going on with you. You know I would've been here if I could've been."

"I know, Mad. We all have lives though, and it's okay. I just can't get a hold of her. She's got her phone off, and if she's turned it on, she's not responding to me," I inform her.

"I'm here no matter what, brother. We love you and want to see her home where she belongs," she tells me, grabbing me a plate of food.

I nod my head and go off in search of a table to sit at. Across the way, I see Renegade, Psycho, and their ol' ladies sitting together, so I head in their direction. It's been a while since I've seen them too. Not since the last time we were all together.

"Mind if I have a seat?" I ask, looking at everyone.

"Not at all, man," Psycho answers. "Good to see you home."

"Thanks. It's good to be home," I respond before taking a bite of my burger.

"Where's Sam?" Hadliegh asks. "I haven't seen her at all since we got here."

"I don't know. All I know is she's in Torrino. Got a job there and a small house. Took off while I was inside," I tell her honestly.

"What did you do?" Natasha asks me as Renegade growls at her.

"Don't worry about it, Renegade. This fuck up is all on me. I wouldn't see her or talk to her while I was inside. Hell, I sent the one letter she tried to send me back without reading the damn thing. She took that to mean I want nothin' to do with her," I say, letting the small group know as Smokey comes over to join us.

"If I pulled that shit, Had would have my balls in her hands," Psycho says as the women glare at me.

"Why the fuck wouldn't you see her? Or at the very least talk to her on the phone?" Hadliegh asks, her anger filling her voice.

"Because I'd want to be with her to comfort her. She already blames herself for me being locked up. If I couldn't comfort her, I couldn't handle hearin' her voice. Or seein' her," I answer them honestly, digging into my food.

No one says anything for a few minutes. They either stare at me or drink their beer. The women are still glaring at me, though. It's insane, and I don't think I deserve to be glared at, but I realize I was a complete asshole to her.

"I get where you're coming from," Natasha says. "But, you handled the situation wrong. Instead of letting her know what was going through your head personally, you had Shy, and everyone else, deliver your message. Didn't you?"

"Yeah, I did. I figured they could tell her in a way I wouldn't be able to," I say.

"What now?" Hadliegh asks.

"I have no fuckin' clue," I answer. "She's not answerin' her phone, and none of the women here have heard from her since they went to visit her."

"We'll try calling her," she tells me, pulling her phone out of her pocket.

"Thank you. I'm gonna make rounds before the house bunnies come out to play. I don't want to be near them," I say, standing up and grabbing my now empty plate.

"We'll catch up soon," Renegade says, giving me a chin lift as I leave.

For the rest of the night, I catch up with most everyone here. All of the ol' ladies let me know they'll keep trying to get a hold of Sam for me. So far, they're all getting the same thing I am; voicemail or no response to a text message. This is so fucked up.

I keep alternating between anger and worry about Sam and Caleb. I'm not sure where I'm going to land when I finally get a hold of her, but the image of putting her over my knee comes to mind. Hell, that image has my cock hard as a rock, and I adjust myself as I make my way to my father.

"Dad, I'm headin' in. Want to be gone by the time the house bunnies come out. One bitch is already pushin' my buttons," I tell him.

"Okay, son. I'll see you tomorrow. And stop worryin' about Sam. We'll see her soon," he tells me cryptically.

I give Maddie and Shy hugs before heading into the clubhouse. As I walk in, all the house bunnies are milling about waiting for their time to head outside and find their cock for the night. A few eye me up and down, and I blatantly ignore them so I can get to my room. Not a single house bunny here, or any other woman, holds a candle to Sam, and they never will.

Chapter Fourteen

Sam

MY LIFE SEEMS to be falling apart. I'm working more than ever with Vanessa being fired. Carson hasn't been able to find a replacement who will work more than a shift or two. If they make it that damn long here. And I don't understand why they all leave because Carson is amazing to work for, and the customers are great. Well, for the most part.

Caleb has been acting up. He hasn't been his usual cheerful self, and I'm not sure why. The only thing I can think of is he's missing the men and women from back home. I am too, but I can't go back.

I went from having virtually no sign of being pregnant to being sick from the time I get up until the time I fall asleep. And, I'm now sporting a large, round stomach showcasing the fact I'm very pregnant. Well, I'm not quite five months, and it looks as if I'm almost nine. I'm as huge as a damn house.

I'm tired as hell, and I know it's only going to get worse the farther along I get. But I have to keep moving. There's no way I can stop working, stop being there for my son, or stop trying to make our house a home. I have so many plans, and I've been putting away a little money now that I'm actually getting all of my tips.

To top everything else off, I seem to have lost my cell phone. I got a cheap one the guys in the club would call a burner phone. That's just so Carson and Edna can contact me. If it weren't for them, I wouldn't worry a damn about having one. Well, I would for Caleb in case anything ever happens to him, and I need to call for help.

I can't remember anyone's number from the club, so I can't let anyone know I don't have the other phone. Everything was programmed into the phone, and all I had to do was click on their name, and that's it. I feel so lost without the damn thing because, in a twisted way, I *need* to hear about what's going on with Playboy.

Playboy is still on my mind every second of every day. I can't stop thinking about him sitting in a jail cell. Or maybe he's in prison now if the Prosecution got their way and locked him up for good. My heart breaks when I think of everything he could be going through right now. Still, I feel as if it's my fault, and I should be the one sitting inside while he's with his family.

"Mama, I'm hungry," Caleb tells me as he stops by the couch where I'm lying.

"Okay, buddy. I'm getting up," I say. "What do you want?"

"Peanut butter and jelly," he answers.

Nodding my head, I get off the couch. It's not a pretty sight because I basically have to roll off and get to my feet with the use of the side of the couch. Caleb doesn't once leave my side to ensure he's there if I need help. With only Edna and Carson's numbers in the phone, he knows to call one of them if something happens to me.

Yes, I've finally told Caleb about the babies. There's no way I can hide it from him now. Or anyone else. So, I explained to him how I'm going to be a mommy again to two new babies. He seems to be excited, but he also worries over me. If I cry out, Caleb is right by my side. He's even taken to sleeping in my room.

Caleb makes a bed on the floor with blankets and the cushions from the couch. When I asked him why he was sleeping in my room, he told me so he could hear me if I needed help at night. That's all Playboy right there. I cried for hours after that because it made me miss him so much more than I already do.

Walking into the kitchen, I make Caleb his lunch and then sit down on the couch. If I lay back down again, I'm going to fall asleep and miss work. Carson would definitely understand, but I'm not going to leave him in a bind because I didn't go to work.

Besides, I'm going to have to start getting ready soon. Taking a shower takes a lot longer these days, and I feel as if I'm constantly running behind. It's a horrible feeling to have. But, this is my life, and I have to live each day as it comes to me.

I'm not feeling all that great today either. The worry over bills, work, Caleb, and Playboy bombard me constantly. I know I have money for our bills and food. There's still a constant worry that something is going to change in the blink of an eye. For some reason, I can't make the feeling go away.

"Buddy, I'm going to get my clothes around for a shower. Edna will be here soon, and I have to be ready when she gets here," I tell him.

"Okay, Mama. I'll sit outside the door," he tells me.

Yes, Caleb even sits outside the bathroom door when I'm in there. He takes the role of my protector very seriously. I've never seen a child the way he is before. Though, I've heard stories of the way the kids in the Wild Kings were growing up. Especially Jameson and Anthony.

Once I have my clothes around, I waddle into the bathroom so I can get in the shower. The first thing I do is turn the water on so I can wait for it to get warm while I'm undressing and finding a towel for me to dry off with. As soon as the water's up to temperature, I carefully step in the tub, so I don't slip and fall. I've come close a time or two, and I don't want to ever do anything to hurt the babies I carry.

I quickly shower. Well, as quickly as I can with the size I am currently. Everything takes two or three times the length of time it normally does for me. I'd say I hate being pregnant, but I don't. I love having my children, and I love carrying them even now. The only thing I don't like is how I feel.

"You okay, mama?" Caleb asks me as I shut the water off.

"I'm okay, honey. Getting out now," I answer him.

"I'll be here until you open the door," he informs me.

A smile forms on my face. Caleb is so cute most days and lately, it's even more so because he's ultra-protective. I'd like to think Playboy and the rest of the men at the Phantom Bastards would be proud of him. Hell, of all the clubs they associate with. It's one of the things they try to instill in their children. Especially all the boys.

As soon as I'm dressed, I open the door so Caleb can go in his room or do whatever it is he's going to do until Edna gets here. She's worried about me too and I know it's just a matter of time before the mother hen in her comes out in full force. I see it more and more on a daily basis.

I'm brushing out my hair when there's a knock on the door. Edna has a key so I'm not worried about her coming in while I finish up. The only thing I have left to do is put on some make-up to hide the bruising under my eyes. Yeah, I'm tired, but when it's time to go to bed, I have a hard time falling asleep. I tend to toss and turn most of the night. Then I can't get comfortable because one of the babies is either on my bladder or they're pressing on something inside that shoots pain through my body. It's a no-win situation.

"Sam, I'm here," Edna calls out as Caleb runs down the hall to get to her.

"I'm almost ready. How was work?" I ask her as I put my make-up away.

"Busy as hell," she answers honestly.

"That's always a good thing. Means the day will go by fast," I respond, taking my dirty clothes to the laundry room and tossing them in the washer.

"Yes, it does. But, I'm ready to be off my feet. Think I may order in dinner for Caleb and I tonight. That okay with you, Sam?" she asks, looking at me as I walk back into the living room. "Are you okay, Sam? You don't look so good."

"I'm okay. Just a little rundown today I guess," I respond.

"You be careful tonight. If you need to come home, I'll go in and finish your shift for you," she tells me.

Edna pulls me into a hug before releasing me. She gives me one more thorough look over as I turn to kiss Caleb goodbye. He wraps his arms around me and I let him hug me for as long as he needs to. Once he pulls back, I bend over and kiss him on the top of his head.

"Be a good boy for Edna. I'll see you in the morning," I tell him as I grab my purse and head out the door.

"Did you ever find your phone?" Edna asks me.

"No, I haven't. I can't even remember the last time I had it," I respond before closing the door behind me.

Walking out to the car, I get in and head to work. I don't even worry about music because the trip is so short there's no point in playing anything from my playlist. As soon as I pull up to the truck stop, I park close to the building and get out. Once my car is locked, I make my way in the back door for Torrino's. Carson is in his office as I walk through.

"How you feeling today?" he asks me as I tie my apron around my waist.

"Not the best," I answer honestly. "But, I'm here and I'm ready to do my job."

"You take it easy. Have you found your other phone yet?" he asks, standing from his desk and following me to the floor.

"No. Still can't remember the last place I had it. I've looked everywhere," I say, grabbing a coffee pot while looking to see what section I'm in today.

"Alright. Well, you be careful and holler out if you need anything," he says before filling a cup with water and heading back to his office.

I walk around my section and see very few people sitting there. In fact, the entire place is the slowest I've ever seen it since starting here. So, I make my rounds and refill any coffees for customers who want it. Once that's done, I go through and clean up any empty tables. I always do this to ensure the tables in my section are clean to my standards.

It's not long before I'm restocking the salt and pepper packets at the tables and making sure the ketchup and other condiments are clean and full too. Then it's on to napkins, checking customers, and anything else to keep me busy while I wait for new customers coming in.

"Sam, it's time for your break," Sandy says, walking up to me.

Sandy is a new girl we hired and she's working out great so far. She's on time for every shift and helps me out whenever I seem to fall behind. I share my tips with her when she helps me and they seem to always find their way back into my tip jar. The girl is sweet and I want to know what makes her want to work here. There's a story there and she'll tell it when she's ready to share.

"Okay. Thank you," I say, walking from the floor and to the bathroom.

When I get in the stall, a horrible pain rips through my stomach. I cry out and hold on until the pain subsides. As soon as I can move about without pain making me cry out, I pull down my pants and go to the bathroom. What I see has me crying out once more. I'm bleeding. Not spotting or anything; full-on bleeding.

I finish in the bathroom and make my way back to the restaurant. Carson sees me as I breach the opening and rushes to my side.

"What's going on?" he asks me. "You're awfully pale."

"I'm bleeding. Really bad," I respond.

"Okay. You sit right here and we'll get you taken care of. I'll be right back," Carson says as he rushes from my side.

Panic is beginning to set in and I want Playboy. If I lose these babies and he has no clue about them, I'll feel horrible. It's not fair for him not to know about them. Maybe it's time to figure out a way to get in touch with someone at the clubhouse. I'm not sure how I'd even go about that because I don't have internet at the house and there's no data on the phone I have now. I highly doubt the number for the clubhouse is in the phone book.

"Ambulance is on the way," Carson says as he rushes back to my side. "I don't want you getting up or moving until the EMTs are here. Is there anyone I can call for you?"

"No. The only person I want by my side can't be reached. At least by me right now," I answer, fear continuing to take over.

"I'll figure it out. For now, let's just focus on you," he tells me.

It's not long before I hear the sirens of the ambulance pulling into the parking lot of the truck stop. The EMTs rush in and Carson quickly speaks for me as I'm loaded up on the stretcher. He lets them know I'm bleeding and how far along I am. The paramedics begin to take my vitals as I'm strapped down before they wheel me from the restaurant.

"Sam, I'll be right behind you. And I'll let Edna know what's going on. But, I won't let her bring Caleb there. He doesn't need to see you like this," Carson says.

"Sir, I'm sorry. We have to head out. She's in good hands," one of the EMTs says when they're ready to take me from the restaurant.

Carson steps back and I know he's worried as hell about me. He's more of a dad to us than we truly realize. Honestly, Carson reminds me a lot of Slim. They both take their roles seriously and treat everyone under them as family. They're the father figures to so many of us and they don't seem to notice they're doing it.

I've been at the hospital for a little while now. Doctors and nurses have been in and out to see me. They're monitoring the amount of blood I'm losing and it seems to be slowing down. I'm still panicking, though, because you never know what's going to happen and life is too precious to take any chances with. Especially a new life that hasn't had a chance even to take their first breath of air yet.

"Miss Hart, how are you feeling?" the doctor asks, walking back in my room.

"Not better. Well, a little better," I answer. "Do you know what's going on? Are the babies okay?"

"We're going to have the ultrasound technician come in soon. They'll take pictures and make sure nothing is going on to hurt you or the babies," he tells me. "Other than working more than you should be, what's been going on?"

"Well, just the normal. Bills needing to be paid, and I just moved here from Benton Falls," I say.

"So, a lot of stress then," he says more to himself than to me.

"I guess you could say that. I've been extremely tired and things lately. I just figured it was due to carrying twins," I answer.

"It can happen. I just don't think it's the case this time," the doctor tells me.

"Then what is it?" I ask him, concern feeling me.

"I think you're under way too much stress and you need to dial everything back," the doctor tells me. "Once we make sure the babies are okay and there's nothing else going on, I think you're simply going to need to be on bed rest for a few weeks. It may be longer than that actually."

"What about working just a few hours a week?" I ask him.

"Can you take it easy and not be run ragged?" the doctor asks me.

"No, she can't. She's a waitress," Carson answers, coming inside my room.

"I see. I know you don't want to take any unnecessary risks so it's bed rest for now. You'll need to reevaluate with your doctor when you go back," the doctor tells me.

Carson nods his head and assures the doctor I'll be resting. I'm not sure how he's going to make that happen, but knowing Carson, he'll find a way. I wouldn't be surprised to see him sending the different women from the truck stop in to make sure I'm resting and taking care of myself. And to make sure Caleb is taken care of so I can rest.

I'm left alone while Carson goes to make phone calls and I stare at the ceiling while I wait for the ultrasound tech to come in and see me. It's not long before a young woman is coming into my room so I can see and hear the babies.

As I look at the screen in front of me, I'm in awe of two babies resting inside my body. They're twisting and turning and I laugh as they seem to be playing inside me. Yeah, I saw Caleb moving around when I had ultrasounds done, but nothing like this. Now, there's two of them and they seem to be playing instead of just moving around.

"Everything looks good here," the technician assures me. "Would you like to know the sex of the babies?"

"Yes, please," I say, excitement filling me.

"Baby A looks to be a boy," she says before moving the wand around. "Baby B is also a boy."

"Oh, lord! Help me now," I say, still in awe of adding two more sons to our family.

Then, the reminder of knowing Playboy isn't here with me hits and I'm filled with regret and pain. A deep sadness fills me and I let my tears slide down my cheeks.

"Are you sure everything is okay?" I ask her.

"Yes. There's no tears in anything and nothing else looks to be off," she once again assures me. "Let me get you some pictures printed out and make sure you contact your doctor to make an appointment."

"Yes, ma'am. I'll call her tomorrow and make arrangements to get in to see her," I respond.

It's a while later the doctor comes in to let me know everything looks good and this is probably nothing more than a case of extreme stress. So, until my doctor clears me, I'll be on bed rest and won't be able to do much more than get up to go to the bathroom and make sure I have something to eat and drink. When I don't have someone at the house with me, that is.

Things could definitely be a lot worse than they are now. I still have our children resting comfortably in my stomach and as long as I take care of myself and stop obsessing over things I have no control over. So, I thank him for making sure my babies are okay and Carson comes in to take me home. It looks like I have no choice but to make sure I'm resting because Edna is staying the night with me.

Chapter Fifteen

Playboy

I'VE BEEN ON a run for the last three days. It's the last thing I wanted to do, but with my dad filling in while I was inside, I had no choice but to head out with my brothers. Unfortunately, we should've been back in Benton Falls by now and we're not. We're still with Butcher and his club. The shipment we're waiting on has been delayed because of something that happened with the other club.

I don't have any idea what's going on with the other club, and everyone is being very silent about what's happening. A few of us have a horrible feeling about this and we don't want anything to do with it. But, we have orders to fulfill and can't stop because of a gut feeling we have.

"Playboy, you okay?" Killer asks, walking up to the bar where I'm watching the activities in the common room take place.

"Yep. Well, no, not really," I answer.

"What's goin' on?" he asks, tapping his knuckles on the bar top for a beer.

"I just don't have a good feelin' about this run. It's not like this usually. And, for us to not know what's goin' on with Knight's Rebellion isn't right. We should be the first fuckin' men to know why they're not ready to deliver to us," I tell him.

"Yeah, I'm glad I'm not the only one who thought it was weird. Butcher doesn't know anythin' either. I talked to him and he assures me he has no clue what's goin' on," Killer tells me.

"I didn't even want to be here. I'd rather be out lookin' for Sam and findin' out what's goin' on with her," I say honestly. "Gwen still hasn't heard from her?"

"Not a word. It's like she's gone radio silent to everyone and no one can figure it out," he tells me. "I think the women are talkin' about makin' a trip to her house and figure out why she won't answer anyone. Even the other ol' ladies are havin' a hard time with her not respondin' to anyone. Especially the women from Dander Falls. They met her first."

"I know. This isn't like Sam at all," I say, not knowing what else to say. "I'm off to get a tattoo done. See ya later."

"What you gettin'?" he asks me, downing his beer.

"Aphrodite with 'Playboy's Goddess written around it," I answer.

Killer tries not to laugh his ass off at me. It doesn't work as he busts a gut while I stand up and flip him off. He doesn't get it; no one does because every man who wants an ol' lady has theirs with them at home. I'm the only one who fucked up enough to lose my woman before I got to make her mine officially. Sam is my Goddess of love, she's true beauty, and she has so much passion in her to give without realizing it.

However, in my tattoo, her face will be Sam's. I have a picture of her on my phone and I've already given it to Garth. He's the club's tattoo artist and he does amazing work. It's not the first time I've been to him and it won't be the last time. Garth is a solid man and Butcher has been trying to get him to patch into the club for as long as I've been a member.

"I'm ridin' with ya," Killer tells me.

We get on our bikes and head to the shop in town. I try to enjoy the freedom and peace of the road and it doesn't work. I haven't found a single second of peace since Sam took off. Nothing will be right until I find her and bring her home. At least that's what I'm hoping for.

It's taken us less than a half-hour to get to the shop. I back my bike into the spot in front of the shop. Once Killer and I are parked, I take off my helmet and slide my sunglasses up to the top of my head. I've got a blue bandana on and I keep it in place, so my hair stays off my face. I don't want to be messing with it while Garth is trying to ink me.

We head inside and Killer starts chatting up the woman at the front desk. I don't know why he doesn't get his head out of his ass, but it's not my business. Hopefully, he doesn't lose Gwen because he wants to give her time. She won't be around forever and he has to realize that. She's going to see something she doesn't like one of these days and that's going to be the end of things for the two of them.

"Playboy, it's good to see you again," Garth says, walking out from the back.

"Good to see you too, man," I reply.

"Let's get this shit started," he says and turns to walk back to his room.

Killer doesn't follow me; he chooses to stay and talk to the bitch at the front. She'll be in his bed before we leave here. He's usually up for a piece of strange but I thought he'd tone that shit down with Gwen here permanently now. I guess he's going with 'what happens on the road, stays on the road' philosophy. I'll never do that. I have everything I need in Sam.

"Where's this goin'?" Garth asks me.

"On my chest," I tell him, taking my cut off and hanging it on his door before removing my shirt.

I sit back in the chair and get relaxed while Garth finishes setting up. He sets the ink out and then places the stencil on my chest where I want it. I love the design and can't wait until Sam sees it. Hopefully, it's soon.

Killer and I are back at Butcher's clubhouse. As I suspected, the bitch from Garth's shop followed us back here and is sitting on his lap while he plays cards with Butcher and a few of his men. I'm at the bar nursing a beer and playing with my phone.

I've tried calling her several more times and it just continues to go straight to voicemail. My level of worry goes through the roof. I won't rest until I talk to her; no, I won't rest until I see her in the flesh. Sam is my other half and I'm not the man I should be without her.

"What's up?" my dad asks, answering his phone.

"Anyone heard from Sam yet?" I ask, getting straight to the point.

"Not yet, son," he answers.

"What the fuck? Somethin' is wrong, dad," I say, letting my concern shine through.

"We'll figure it out, Playboy," he assures me. "Now, what's goin' on with the run?"

"I have no clue. We still don't know dick all and no one from Knight's Rebellion is talkin'. All we know is there's a delay but we don't know when it's goin' to come. I'm not stayin' here for long, dad," I tell him. "I know we've got orders to fill and we need this shipment, but there are other ways. We're wastin' our fuckin' time here."

"I'm callin' them as soon as I get off the phone with you. I'll get an answer from Lash or we'll take our business elsewhere," my dad says.

"Thanks. And let me know if someone hears from her," I say.

"Will do. If the women don't hear from her in the next few days, Shy and Gwen are talkin' about goin' down there," he assures me. "We'll get her home where she belongs. I miss my little buddy."

"I miss them both so much I can't stand it," I tell him.

"We'll get them home," he tells me before hanging up the phone.

I finish my beer and set the bottle on the top of the bar. Looking around the room, I have no interest in being out here. The men are partaking in smoking joints and having the house bunnies climb all over them. This is definitely not my scene these days. I'd rather head to the room I've been using here and be talking to Sam on the phone. Instead, I'll be using my hand to images of her.

"You headin' to bed?" Valor asks me.

"I'm headin' to my room. I won't be goin' to bed just yet," I say.

"See ya in the mornin'," he returns.

"Oh, Butcher, dad is callin' Lash to find out what's goin' on. He may call you," I say, giving the President a warning to stay somewhat clearheaded.

"Gotcha. I'll make sure my phone is on and ready," he says, placing his bet against Killer.

Heading to my room, I strip off my cut so I can hang it on the back of the door when I get inside. As soon as I'm stripped down, I head to the attached bathroom and start the shower. I look in the mirror as the water heats up. I'm exhausted and the worry I feel over Sam and Caleb is plain to see on my face. I can't hide it and I don't want to.

Stepping in the shower, I imagine Sam in here with me. She's got water cascading down her body and I want to lick every single drop of it from her smooth, silky skin. In my mind, she turns around and I glimpse her full tits pointing straight up at me, her nipples begging for my mouth.

Sam drops to her knees in front of me and takes my hard cock in her mouth. She sucks, licks, and teases before swallowing as much of my length as she can. At the same time, she reaches up and rolls my balls in her hand. I'm sliding my hand up and down my cock as quick as I can. I can feel myself already close to cumming all over the shower.

One more image of Sam sucking my cock while her other hand disappears between her legs. She's playing with her pussy while sucking my cock. I can't stop my orgasm from exploding from my body as Sam's name falls from my lips. Fuck! I want her so much I literally ache for her.

It's been over five months now since the one and only time I got a taste of her. That's way too long for us not to be tasting and touching one another. I want to have her in my life more than I want to keep breathing. Sam is my life, my partner, and my best friend. She's the only one who will ever own my heart and no one will ever come close to having a piece of me if we can't bring her home.

Getting out of the shower, I hear my phone ringing. I wrap the towel around my hips and don't bother wiping off the water dripping from my hair and down my body. Reaching out for my pants, I grab my phone and see it's my dad calling once again.

"Yeah?" I ask answering it.

"Talked to Lash. He's meetin' you with our shipment. Same location as before. Tomorrow mornin' at nine. He's pissed at the time, but I don't give a fuck," he tells me. "This is his last shot and I've made that clear. Still have no clue what's goin' on with the club and shipment on his end. Watch your six and make sure you're not followed."

"Thanks. We'll see you tomorrow night then. We're headin' straight through. I'll make sure our only stops are for gas and we'll fill up before headin' out. We should only have to stop once on the way back," I say.

"See you tomorrow," he says before hanging up once again.

I put my jeans on so I can let the rest of my guys know what's going on. They'll need to be up early so we can head out. Walking into the common room of Butcher's clubhouse. I see Killer getting a blowjob by the table he was playing poker at. Valor is sitting at the bar, Boy Scout is sitting at a different table, and our Prospect Connor is the last one I see. Fox must be in his room already. I'll message him, later on, to let him know. Hopefully, he's just on the phone with Kim and not sleeping.

After letting the men know we're heading out at a little after eight in the morning, I head back to my room. Everyone other than Killer follows me to their rooms. Killer will finish his blowjob before kicking the bitch out and heading to bed. I shoot a quick message to Fox and get in my bed to grab some sleep. Thoughts of Sam and Caleb fill my head as sleep claims me.

Chapter Sixteen

Sam

TODAY IS A very important day for Caleb. It's his sixth birthday and I'm having a small party for him. It's just going to be Edna, Carson, Sandy, and myself. Since I still haven't found my phone, I can't get a hold of anyone from the club to celebrate with him. I know it's breaking his heart and I wish I could change it for him.

I'm still taking it easy, very easy. Carson is only letting me work one day a week for now and I hate it. I'm thankful to get out of the house and have job. But, I want to feel as if I'm pulling my weight and be able to pay my bills. I want Caleb to have a good life and be able to provide for him. I've got a few more months and then I'll be back to normal. Well, busy as hell with three kids, but I'll manage.

"Mama, it's my birthday!" Caleb says, running into my room.

"I know, buddy. Are you ready to see Edna, Carson, and Sandy today?" I ask him.

"Yeah," he answers, putting his little head down.

"What's the matter?" I ask him.

"I want Papi here. And everyone else. Where's Playboy?" he asks me.

"I wish I could get them here for you, buddy. If I had my phone, I'd call them and see if they could be here. But, I don't know where it is still. And I also have to work later today so we don't have much time bud," I say, pulling his body to mine.

Caleb places one hand on my ever-growing belly and rests his head on my shoulder. This is how we usually lay down together. I give us some time because I'm still supposed to be resting more than I am up and about. Doctor Manning didn't want to let me go back to work, but I talked her into one day a week for now. And I'm truly trying not to stress about anything.

After several minutes pass, I tap Caleb on the shoulder to get up. He sits up in my bed and I try to sit up myself. It takes a few minutes before I manage to sit with my stomach sticking out like several beach balls are attached to my stomach. The first thing I have to do is run to the bathroom. Well, I can't run, but I can waddle my ass there.

While I'm in taking care of business, there's a knock on the door. Caleb stops in front of the bathroom and we wait to see who's here. I'm thinking it's Edna because she was picking up the cake and wanted to decorate for Caleb.

"It's just me," Edna finally calls out. "Are you okay, Sam?"

"In the bathroom," I answer her as Caleb runs to see her.

It takes a little while, but I'm finally able to make my way out of the bathroom. I walk from the bathroom to the couch and park my ass there. At least for now because I have to get us breakfast.

"How are you feeling this morning?" Edna asks me.

"I feel like a beached whale. It takes forever to get up from anything. And I still have to make breakfast for us," I tell her with a laugh at the end of my words.

"Don't you worry about that. Carson will be here in fifteen minutes and he's bringing breakfast with him," Edna tells me.

"Oh, thank you," I say, grateful I don't have to get up right this second.

Edna goes in the kitchen and places the cake on the counter. This year, I'm not trying to surprise him with anything because I know his heart is broken and there's nothing I can do to fix it. The only thing would be Playboy, his Papi, and the rest of the club and women coming here to see him.

The only thing I'm hiding is his gifts. Edna managed to pick me up a few things for him when she went shopping for her own gift to him. Carson and Sandy also got him gifts, but no one will let me know what they got him. Apparently, I'm going to be surprised right along with him.

It's not long before Edna is opening the door to Carson and Sandy. They rode over together for some reason. Maybe because we both have to work tonight, and she figures I can ride in with them, so I have a ride home. Yeah, I'm not supposed to be driving a lot right now, either.

"How are you feeling?" Carson asks me, leaning down to place a kiss on my head.

"Been better. But, this will be over with one day and then I'll have two more babies in my life to love and care for," I answer him.

"That you will. We'll see if you're still here when that happens. Either way, you better let us know when you have them," he tells me, looking at Edna as he walks away from me.

"Why wouldn't I be here when I have them?" I ask him.

"You never know what's going to happen," he tells me cryptically.

"What have you done?" I ask him.

"I don't know what you're talking about," he says.

"Uh-huh," I murmur.

Carson brings me over a plate and I thank him while giving him the stink eye. He's done something and he won't tell me until he's good and ready to let me in on the secret. However, I'm betting Sandy and Edna both know what's going on because they're avoiding me. Sandy is eating with Caleb and Edna is making herself busy by cleaning my house. She's been taking good care of me since I got put on bed rest and then moved to extremely light duty.

Tears fill my eyes as I realize I've made a new family for Caleb and myself. We have Carson, Edna, and Sandy, who have all been by my side since I got taken to the hospital. At least one of them has been here since I got released and they've done everything to help me out around the house. Edna is even talking about painting the walls for me. Or making Carson have someone come in and do it for her. We laughed over that one because of her facial expression.

Both families Caleb and I have are as good as one another. One is just smaller than the other one. And less rowdy for sure. But, I love them all dearly and know they care for my son and I. Just like they'll care about my other sons when they get here. Although, no one here knows what I'm having. Edna and Sandy have tried to get it out of me, but they won't. I'm keeping that secret as long as I possibly can.

"You need anything else?" Sandy asks, walking up to me on the couch.

"No, thank you. I'd rather be up moving around, but I'll be working later so I have to rest now," I respond.

"Yeah, I know. If you need anything, let me know," she says, going back to Caleb's side.

Caleb's party was amazing. He got a Nerf gun from Carson with a ton of extra bullets. I glared at him while Caleb went over to give him a massive hug. Edna got him some summer clothes, a new pair of sandals, and some bubbles. Sandy got him a new movie and things so he can have a movie night with her. Edna also picked him out some clothes, movies, and a few books from me. Caleb has started reading and I wanted to make sure he has some books so he can read to the babies when they're here.

"Caleb, I gotta head to work now. You be good for Edna and I'll see you soon," I tell him.

My son runs up to me and stops just before colliding against my legs. He's very careful around me these days. After wrapping his arms around my legs, I hug him back and kiss the top of his head. I won't be able to do that much longer because it's getting harder to bend down to him.

"I love you, mama," he tells me.

"I love you too," I say.

Carson and Sandy help me out to his truck. Once I'm sitting in the front seat, Sandy and Carson get in the truck. We head out to the truck stop and Carson lets me off at the front door with Sandy helping me inside. I walk to the backroom without looking around the restaurant and put my purse in my locker before grabbing my apron. I'm glad the thing has long strings, so I can still use it.

"If you need me, let me know," Sandy says as we walk back to the floor to relieve the other waitresses.

"I will. Thanks, Sandy. For everything," I say before heading to my section.

As I take the coffee pot around to refresh the customer's coffee, I see two people sitting in the last table. They're huddled together and seem familiar to me. But, I can't quite place them because they have menus in front of their faces.

"Can I get you, gentlemen, some more coffee?" I ask when I get to their table.

"Sam?" I hear Playboy ask.

Looking at him, I almost drop the coffee pot to the floor.

"What are you doing here?" I ask, shock filling me.

"What are you doin'?" he asks, looking at my stomach.

Slim looks at me at the same time and there's nothing I can say. Tears fill my eyes and Playboy stands to take me in his arms. I wrap my own around him and cry for the time we've lost and the fact he's going to be leaving me again. His life is in Benton Falls with the Phantom Bastards.

"Is this why you left, sweetheart?" Slim finally asks me.

I nod my head, not letting go of Playboy in case this isn't real. My fear is I'm dreaming and I'll wake up soon. That Playboy is still in jail and we're still separated.

"Why?" Playboy asks me.

"Because you wouldn't see me or accept my letters. If I couldn't tell you, I didn't want anyone else to know before you. The best way I could figure to make that happen was to leave," I tell him.

"Baby, I'm so sorry," he says, lifting my head to kiss me.

"Well, you know the surprise now. What you don't know is we're having twins," I say, exhaustion taking over as I suddenly feel weak.

"Sam, are you okay?" Carson asks, walking up to us.

"You did this?" I ask my boss.

"Yeah, I did. I got a hold of Slim. Turns out, I've known these guys a long time. They stop in whenever they're in the area. I had his number.

And, look at this," Carson says, holding out my phone.

"Where was it?" I ask him, taking my phone from his hand.

"Behind the counter in the kitchen. I believe it fell back there when Vanessa got fired," he tells me.

"This is why you haven't gotten any of our calls or messages?" Playboy asks, looking down at my hand.

"Yeah."

"Why don't you guys take her home. Playboy, she's supposed to be on bed rest. She can fill you in," Carson says. "You'll get paid for today. Go make your boy happy."

Playboy and Slim lead me from Torrino's. Slim has his truck today and Playboy helps me into the backseat before climbing in after me. He rests his hand on my stomach and looks at me with wonder and excitement filling his eyes.

"You've made me the happiest man on Earth," he tells me, leaning down to place a kiss against my lips.

"Are you sure. I don't want to push this on you. Caleb and I are fine staying here and you can see the babies as much as you want. Or not at all," I say, rushing out the words.

"You're comin' home with me, baby. Told you I love you and I meant it. When we get home, I'm makin' you my ol' lady. Everyone misses you and Caleb so much. I'm so fuckin' sorry, Sam. For not seein' you, for not callin' you, and for not readin' your letter. I just knew it would be hard as fuck because I couldn't comfort you and our son," Playboy tells me.

"Next time, you come to us," Slim says. "We would've made sure this ass saw you if we knew the news you had. Though, I get why you wanted to hide it. We all gossip like a group of damn hens."

Playboy and I laugh as Slim pulls into my driveway. He helps me down from the truck and then to the door.

"Now, why are you on bed rest and light duty?" he asks me as we walk to the door.

"I started bleeding a few weeks ago. The doctor said it was stress-related. So, now I'm on light duty because they don't want to chance anything with the babies. I have pictures inside," I tell him as we get to the porch.

"Are you okay? Are the babies okay?" he asks me, concern lacing his face and voice.

"We're okay. I just need more rest than normal," I answer.

Opening the door, I hear Caleb's laughter. It warms my heart as I hear him so happy when he's been heartbroken. The three of us stop and listen to him for a minute before Playboy can't stand it anymore.

"Caleb, where are you, buddy?" he calls out.

"Playboy? You're really here?" Caleb yells out, running to him with his arms spread open and a smile on his face larger than I've ever seen. "And Papi!"

Everyone laughs as tears run down my little boy's face. Playboy whispers something in his ear and Caleb furiously nods his head in response. As soon as Playboy sets him down on his feet, Caleb is up in Slim's arms. Slim whispers something to him as well.

"Mama, I got my birthday wish," Caleb tells me.

"Today your birthday?" Slim asks him.

My son nods his head and gets down so he can show his two favorite men the gifts he got today. Playboy and Slim have a conversation with their eyes before following Caleb into the living room.

"Edna, this is Playboy and Slim. Slim and Playboy, this is my friend Edna," I say, making the introductions.

"It's nice to meet you," she says, eyeing Playboy.

"You too, ma'am," he responds.

Playboy and Slim sit down on the couch and I watch as they take in our small home. Neither one of them are happy about it, I can tell by the look in their eyes. That's not my problem, though. For now, my only problem is sitting down and getting off my feet.

"Sam, get off your damn feet," Edna tells me, getting up from the couch so I can sit down. "I'll get you some juice and something to eat."

"I'm fine," I tell her.

"Nonsense. I know you need to eat something. You visit with your friends here and let me worry about things before I leave. I'm gonna leave and go cover your shift," she lets me know.

"Thank you. I'm sorry you have to cover for me," I say.

"Don't worry, child," she says. "You guys have a lot to catch up on."

The rest of the day, we talk and laugh. Slim and Playboy spend the entire afternoon focusing on Caleb. The only time they leave is to get dinner. And to get him some birthday gifts. I'm exhausted and Playboy makes me go to bed. He puts Caleb to bed and then walks his dad to the door. Just before I fall asleep, I feel him climb into bed with me and pull me against his body.

"I've missed you so much. And I've missed out on so much," he says, placing a kiss on the top of my head. "I love you, Sam."

"I love you too, Playboy. I missed you every single day," I say, my words ending as sleep pulls me under.

Instead of dreaming about Playboy, I sleep wrapped up in the safety of his arms. This is where I'm meant to be and I can't even believe I ever thought he wouldn't want the babies or me. Playboy is mine and I'm his. Caleb is our son and we're about to add two more boys to our family. Life can't get much better than this.

Chapter Seventeen

Playboy

JUST AFTER I got home from the run, my dad pulled me into his office. I sit down in the chair across from his desk and wait for him to talk. This isn't about the run we were just on; otherwise, the rest of the guys would be here with me. Whatever he has to say is personal and I'll have to wait for him to fill me in on the details.

"Son, I had a phone call from an old friend of the club. His name is Carson and we need to head to Torrino's. Now," my dad says, not holding back at all.

"Why? What's goin' on there that means we have to show up to lend our support?" I ask him, confusion filling me.

"Nothin' we have to lend support for. Sam's there and she needs help. She's okay for the most part, but we need to get there," he says.

"When are we leavin' because I'm ready to go now?" I ask him.

"Now."

Dad and I head out of his office. He stops at the bar where Shy is sitting and whispers something to her. I watch on as she looks at me with tears in her eyes. My dad obviously knows more than what he's letting on. I'm not sure what to do or think about things right this moment. All I know is I'm about to see my woman and something is going on with her.

Shy walks over to me and pulls me into her arms.

"You bring our girl home," she whispers, a tear falling and landing on my shirt.

"I will. I love that woman with all my heart," I respond.

Shy backs off and my dad and I go to our bikes. She'll let everyone know where we're going. But, I'm not sure our bikes are the way to go right now.

"Dad, should we take the bikes?" I ask just before he starts his up.

"What do you mean?"

"Well, if somethin' is goin' on with her, shouldn't we take one of the SUVs?" I question.

"Fuck! You're right. We'll take my truck," he says.

We get off our bikes and run to his truck parked along the side of the clubhouse. As soon as we're both in, he's got the engine on and we're taking off. It should take us about four hours to get there, but with the way he's driving, I don't think it will take that long.

"So, what's the plan?" I ask.

"We're gonna show up to Torrino's before Sam does. Then, we can find out what the hell is goin' on with her. If I had even thought she'd be workin' for Carson, I'd have called him before now. I just thought she was workin' somewhere else in town," he tells me. "I dropped the fuckin' ball on this one."

"No, you didn't. I did when I wouldn't let her come see me or have any contact with her," I reply.

The rest of the ride goes by in silence. I'm thinking about how this is going to go and hoping I can talk her into coming home with me. If I have to stay here a few days, then that's what I'll do to ensure she comes back where she belongs. Sam and Caleb belong in Benton Falls and that's where they're going to live. With me.

The second Sam walked into the truck stop; my eyes were on her. She kept her back to us because of where we were sitting, but I knew there was something different about her. I could feel it down to my bones. Now, the trick will be to get her to talk to me long enough to find out what her secret is.

When she walked hesitantly up to our table, my eyes never once strayed from her face. I couldn't tell you what she was wearing or how she looked. The only thing I saw was pain in her eyes and exhaustion marring her beautiful features. Until I let my eyes fall lower to land on her huge stomach. She isn't fat; far from it. No, Sam is pregnant and no one could be the father except for me.

Her boss telling us to take her home was the best thing I've ever heard apart from her telling me she loves me. I don't waste any time getting her out of there. Especially knowing she was in the hospital for bleeding and is mainly on bed rest and light duty until the babies are born.

Sam can't be on her own anymore. With Edna being here when we got to the house, I'm sure she's been one of the main people here with Sam and Caleb. Carson seems like the type of man who would be here for my family too. Just from the few minutes he was near us at the table in the truck stop, Carson reminds me a lot like dad. I'm grateful Sam had him and the rest of her friends here. But, she has a family and friends back home too.

Lying in bed with Sam in my arms and Caleb across the hallway asleep in his bed is the calmest and most peaceful I've been since the day I got arrested. I relish the feeling of her laying against me, her hair fanned out over my chest, and her stomach pressing against my arm. This is where I'm meant to be every day for the rest of my life.

I have a lot to make up for with Sam and Caleb and that starts tomorrow. As soon as we're awake, I'm going to explain everything to my woman and hope she forgives me. There's no other option for me. I refuse to let Sam get away and leave me again. Not with Caleb or our two new children she's carrying in her belly.

Waking up, I hear Sam crying softly next to me. Instantly I'm awake and hovering over her.

"What's the matter, baby?" I ask her, concern etched in my every muscle.

"I can't get up and I have to go to the bathroom," she says as I catch a tear sliding down her face.

"Why didn't you wake me up?" I ask her.

"Because if I woke you up, I thought I was dreaming and you'd disappear again," she says as her tears fall faster.

"I'm not goin' anywhere and you're not dreamin'," I tell her. "Now, let's get you out of bed."

Stepping on the floor, I hold out my hands and let Sam put her hands in mine. I slowly pull her from the bed, so I don't hurt the babies or her. Following her, I make sure she gets in the bathroom okay and then wait in the hall for her to be done. Just in case she needs help up from the toilet.

When she opens the door, I lead her to the living room and help her sit down on the couch. As soon as she's comfortable, I make my way to the kitchen and start making breakfast. Sam doesn't have much, but it's enough for us and that's fine by me. For now.

"Why are you still here?" Sam asks me.

"Because we need to talk. And I'm not leavin' you again if I can help it," I tell her.

"But why now after all this time?" she questions.

"Because I've been tryin' to get a hold of you since the second I got out. All the ol' ladies have been. We had no clue you didn't have your phone," I tell her. "Sam, it's not that I didn't want to see you. I couldn't see you. If I saw you, I'd want to be with you to comfort you and be with you at home. If I heard your voice, I'd want to be with you. And, if I saw your letters with the tears stains on the paper, I'd feel horrible because I couldn't be there with you. That's why I wanted no contact."

"But you saw Shy," she says.

"She forced her way in and I know better than to try to tell her no," I say on a laugh.

"True, but you could have sent a letter explaining this all to me," she tells me logically.

"I know. But, I didn't want you to be even sadder because I was tellin' you in a letter I didn't want you to see me as a caged fuckin' animal," I say, walking over and bending down in front of her. "I felt like a caged animal in there and I didn't want you to see me that way. I'm so sorry, Sam."

"You have no idea how much you hurt me," she says, a fresh tear sliding down her cheek. "Especially once I found out I was pregnant."

"I know, baby. And if I could take it all back, I would. But, I still wouldn't have you see me in there. I can't do that," I tell her, begging her with my eyes to believe me.

"I don't know what to do," she tells me. "This all feels so surreal."

"I know. It does for me to. But, we'll get through this. Now, what I want to know is everythin' that's been goin' on with you and the pregnancy. I've missed so much of it already," I tell her.

"Well, I didn't find out until I was almost four months pregnant. My cycle has never been normal, so it's always a hit or miss if I'm going to get pregnant or not. All it took was one time for us to be together to result in a positive test. I went to the doctor and they did an ultrasound because I had no clue how far along I was. That's when I found out we're having twins.

"I will still basically not showing when the women showed up to see me. It was like the day I hit five months, I'm where you see me now. And I'm only going to get bigger from here as they grow," she tells me.

"So, what about you goin' to the hospital?" I ask her.

"I was at work one day and I started bleeding really bad. They said it was stress-related and I had to be on bed rest. When I went back to my doctor, she said I could work one day a week and I have to do as little as possible for now. I go back in a few days and we'll see what she says then," Sam tells me.

"But you and the babies are okay other than that?" I ask, still worried as hell about her.

"We're fine."

Finishing up cooking, I make our plates and set them out before going to wake Caleb up. When he sees me in his room, Caleb jumps out of bed and rushes to my arms.

"Hey, buddy. Did you sleep okay?" I ask him, pulling him up for a hug.

"Yeah. I thought I was dreaming," he says.

"You're not. I'm really here. Go to the bathroom and come out for breakfast," I say, setting him down on his feet so he can do his morning routine.

I walk back out and grab the juice out of the refrigerator and pour us each a glass. As soon as everything is set up, I help Sam off the couch and hold her hand as we walk into the kitchen where the small table is.

"So, there's no reason why you can't come home with me. Is there?" I ask her.

"I don't know, Playboy. There's a lot I need to think about," she says evasively.

"Well, then it looks as if I'm here until you make up your mind," I say, waiting for Caleb to get up in his seat.

The rest of the morning, we spend together. I sit on the couch with Sam while we watch one of Caleb's new movies. Shy calls and wants to know what's going on, but I don't tell her about the babies. I know dad hasn't either because she would've said something about it. He's letting us tell everyone in our own time.

Chapter Eighteen

Sam

PART OF ME is happy as hell Playboy is out of jail and here with us. The other part of me is trying to figure out what this all means. What it means for him as an individual, us as a couple not that we ever labeled what we were, and us with Caleb and the new babies on the way.

I feel as if the only reason he's still in Torrino is that he saw me, found out I'm pregnant, and now wants to be in the babies' lives. I'd never keep our children from him, but it doesn't mean he has to pretend he wants to be with me either. Playboy simply could want to be here because I'm pregnant and he wants to make sure I don't disappear with the babies.

While I understand his concern, I would never take his children from him. The only reason I left Benton Falls to begin with is so no one would tell him I was pregnant before he and I talked. Now, it seems to have backfired on me and I don't know what to do about it.

"Playboy, I think we need to talk," I tell him after lunch.

"About what?" he asks, sitting down on the couch next to me.

"Well, I think you need to go back to Benton Falls. I have a lot to think about and you have things to do for the club, I'm sure," I tell him.

"I'll think about moving back there, but for now, we don't need to be on top of one another."

"Where's this comin' from?" he asks, turning his full attention to me.

"Playboy, you didn't want to have anything to do with me while you were inside. And I get why you chose to do that. However, if something happens again and you're locked away, I won't be able to do this again. It hurt so much when you didn't want to have anything to do with me. I've been going through all this alone except for my friends here. Yes, it was my choice because I wanted to be the one to tell you about the baby," I tell him. "But, I can't have you here now just because I'm pregnant. It's not fair to Caleb or myself. It's not fair to you either when the one for you could be out there waiting for you to find them."

"Sam, I know I fucked up when I didn't have anythin' to do with you. But, I've told you I meant it when I said I love you. You're the only one I want in my life. It has nothin' to do with the babies you're carryin' or anythin' else. The only thing I want is you and Caleb by my side. The new babies are just a bonus and I can't ask for anything more than us spendin' our days together," he tells me, holding my hand while looking into my eyes. "I have a house waitin' for us to move into. I refuse to live there without my family with me. Caleb has his own room waitin' for him and there's plenty of room for the new babies as well."

"I just need some time," I try to tell him.

"Well, take all the time you need. I'm not goin' anywhere. I'll be here every single day until you decide to go back with me. And if you choose not to go back, I'll talk to my dad and leave the club. For you," he says, his eyes locked on mine and I know he's speaking the truth.

"Playboy, you can't do that. The club is not only your family, it's your life," I respond.

"Well, until you're ready to go home, right here's where we'll be," he informs me. "They can come visit for now and once the babies are born, we'll go there to visit."

"You can't do that," I try again.

"I can do anything I want to do. This is my life and I don't have one without you and Caleb in it. The babies are just a bonus," he says. "By the way, do you know what we're havin' yet?"

"I do. We're having boys," I tell him. "If you grab my purse, I have something to show you."

Playboy doesn't say or do anything for a few minutes. Then, his face breaks out in the biggest smile I've ever seen. He's happy we're having sons. The next generation of the Phantom Bastards MC are resting in my stomach, growing until we can meet them and hold them in our arms.

"Look, we may not have anything here, Playboy. But, Caleb and I have a few friends, I have a job since I couldn't find one in Benton Falls, and I won't ever stop you from seeing your kids," I tell him.

"This isn't about the babies, Sam. This is about me bein' head over heels in love with you and wantin' to have you in my life. I want to make you my ol' lady, marry you, adopt Caleb, and grow old with you. Why can't you understand that?" he asks, kneeling in front of me.

"I've never had anyone want to be with me and only me before. It's always been about what I could do for them on my back," I answer honestly. "Now it just feels as if you're doing this because I'm pregnant with your kids and you want to make sure you stay in their lives. I love you, Playboy. I just can't go through the heartache again."

"And you won't. I'll be by your side every single step of the way and we'll get through anythin' together. This will only work if. you're by my side, though," he says. "Please say you'll come home with me. That we'll work on earnin' the trust I blew out of the water."

"I have a lot to do if I'm even going to consider moving back there," I tell him. "I have to give my notice, make this place better so Carson can rent it out easier, and I have to pack everything up. It's not an overnight process, Playboy," I tell him.

"Well, I'll be here to help you do it all. I'm dead serious. I'm not leavin' without you," he says.

I nod my head because I won't ever be able to deny this man anything. He owns me, heart and soul. Caleb runs from his room; he's been listening to us talk and I know he's wanted to go home since we left. No matter how I've felt, Benton Falls is my home.

"What about a job?" I ask him. "I'm not gonna live on your money or the help of the club. I can't do that anymore."

"We'll find you somethin'. But, when these babies are born, I want you to finish school. Get your degree in nursin' and get a job doin' what you've always wanted to do. It's not gonna be easy, but everyone in the club will be there to help," he replies.

"It's been so long since I've been in school, Playboy," I begin to say.

"Mama, we're going home?" Caleb asks to make sure we're really going back.

"Yeah, I think we are," I tell him.

Caleb runs around the small living room like a mad man. He's talking a mile a minute about seeing his Papi, Rayven, and everyone else. Playboy and I are laughing at him until he launches himself at the man who is making his dreams come true. As I said, Playboy can do no wrong in the eyes of my young son.

"Mama, you need to drink," Caleb suddenly announces.

As he goes to the kitchen to get me a bottle of water, Playboy just looks at me.

"He's been like this since finding out I was pregnant and went to the hospital," I answer his unspoken question.

Playboy nods his head and I see the smile he's trying to hide. Yeah, he's proud as hell of Caleb stepping up to 'fill his shoes'. My son is missing out on his family back home and I need to think of him too. I can't just stay here because I'm scared to let Playboy back in and something happen.

Caleb hands my water to me and then runs off to his room. I'm not sure what he's doing, but I can hear all sorts of racket and noise coming from in there.

"I'll check," Playboy says, getting up and making his way down to Caleb's room.

After a few minutes, neither one of them is back. So, I push myself up off the couch and go in search of them. It takes me long enough to get off the damn couch. But, as I get close to his room, I hear Caleb and Playboy talking softly to one another. I can't make out what they're saying, and I don't want to interrupt the moment.

Looking around the open door of my son's room, I see Playboy sitting on the floor holding the bear he got for Caleb. My son is busy packing his things as if we're moving today instead of in a few weeks. A smile covers my face as I realize he's excited to be going back to Benton Falls.

Turning around to head back to the living room, I question every decision I've made since Playboy got arrested. Was I right to leave Benton Falls? Should I have let the ol' ladies know I was pregnant? So many questions run through my head as I sit carefully back down on the couch and wait for them to come back out of Caleb's room.

We've had dinner, Caleb's room is completely packed and ready to move back, and now Playboy is helping me get to bed after helping me in the shower. He's not happy I've been showering alone with only Caleb sitting outside the door. Now, he's helping me in bed after putting one of my oversized tee-shirts on and a pair of panties.

Well, the panties make it as far as landing on the bed. They never make it on my body. Instead, Playboy fits his body between my legs and stares up at me for a minute. We simply look at one another and don't say a word.

"Tonight is all about you, baby. I've been dreamin' of tastin' you since the one and only night we were together," he tells me.

Before I can respond, Playboy lowers his head and swipes his tongue through my slick folds. I hear and feel him groan at his first taste of me. Closing my eyes, I let the sensations Playboy is causing flood my body take over.

"Look at me, baby," he says, his voice husky and low as he pauses his ministrations for a minute.

Opening my eyes, I glance down toward Playboy. He's concentrating on sucking my clit in his mouth while locking eyes with me. He doesn't miss a beat as he slides a finger in my pussy while continuing to suck on my clit.

It's not long before my body begins to tighten and I know my release is going to slam into me.

"That's it, give it to me, babygirl," Playboy says.

I reach down and thread my fingers into Playboy's long hair. It's so soft and feels like silk in my fingers as I keep my eyes locked on his. I can tell by his eyes that he's smiling as my grip tightens in his hair the closer I get to the edge of the cliff he's leading me to.

Finally, when I can stand no more, my orgasm crashes over me. Wave after wave flows from my body as Playboy doesn't let up.

"Griffin!" I yell out, my head thrown back and my eyes closed.

Still, Playboy doesn't let up as he brings me back down from one of the few orgasms I've ever had in my life. Actually, from the second one I've ever had in my life. Both have come from him and I don't know what to make of it.

As Playboy sits back from me, he wipes his mouth with the back of his hand. Leaning over me, he places a kiss on my lips. It's soft, sweet, and gentle. I'm the one that deepens the kiss, opening my mouth and sliding my tongue against his closed mouth. Playboy immediately opens his mouth and lets me deepen the kiss. I can taste myself on him as I wrap my arms around his neck and hold him close to my body.

When he finally breaks away, Playboy stares at me for a few minutes.

"I truly love you, Sam Hart, and I want to make you mine in every sense of the word. I'll spend the rest of my life makin' this up to you; of earnin' your trust and respect," Playboy vows to me.

"I love you, Playboy," I answer him, running my hand down the side of his face.

"Get some sleep and we'll get more things taken care of tomorrow," he says, rolling from holding himself above me to lying next to me.

He wraps his arms around me and pulls me close to his body. One hand slides under my neck while the other one rests on my belly as it sticks out from my burgeoning belly. I burrow down into him and place my head on his chest. If I could lay like this in his arms for the rest of my life, I'd be content.

My only hope is that Playboy is telling the truth and he really wants to make this work between us. And that it's not just because of the twins. It would gut me to think this is just because of them. But, he's going to have to work to prove he wants me for me and nothing else.

That's my last thought as sleep claims me. I dream of the life I've always wanted with the man in my bed. He's always in my thoughts, dreams, and now he's in my life. Time will tell what our story is going to be and how things are going to play out.

Chapter Nineteen

Playboy

I'VE BEEN IN Torrino for the last two days. While I've loved it being just Sam, Caleb, and me I know I have to get back to the club. Not saying things are going on, but I don't have a reason to stay away. Not in the eyes of the club, at least.

I'll stay no matter what for Sam and Caleb. But, the club needs me and I've already been on a run and was in jail for weeks. It's time for me to start pulling my weight and I can't do that from four hours away. My problem is I don't want to leave Sam and Caleb here alone either.

Caleb has been up my butt when we're not busy. He's been talking more than ever before and I love that he wants to help and wants to talk to us. Now, we can't get him to stop talking and we laugh because it's like he's finally learned he doesn't have to be quiet or express his opinions because he's afraid we're going to be mad or yell at him. None of us ever will.

I'm up early this morning. Caleb and Sam are still sleeping and I want to take a shower and have breakfast ready before they get up. So, I jump in the shower after checking on them and quickly wash. I don't linger in the shower at all. Just as I go to get dressed, I hear my phone ringing in the pocket of my jeans. Grabbing it out quick, I head to the living room so I don't wake either one.

"Yeah?" I ask, not bothering to look at the caller ID.

"Son, need you home," my dad says, not bothering with any small talk.

"What's goin' on?" I ask him.

"Got another shipment and somethin' is goin' on with Lash's club. I think we're gonna have to head there to help out. Not makin' any plans without you here," he tells me.

"Okay. I'll talk to Sam as soon as she wakes up," I answer.

"How's she doin'?" he asks me.

"As good as can be expected, I guess. I don't know much about this kind of thing," I respond.

"Well, I've kept a lid on it, but you know things are goin' to change once you get back here," he tells me.

"I know. We need to get her a doctor there because she's still on light duty and I want to see for myself that everythin' is okay and the way it should be. I've missed out on so much already, Dad," I tell him.

"You have. But, there will be more than just this baby and you'll see everythin' for that pregnancy," he says, laughter in his voice.

"We'll see," I say. "I'm gonna make breakfast and then talk to her about comin' back sooner than planned."

"Let me know what's goin' on. I'll have some guys meet you at the halfway point," he says.

"Do I need to be worried?" I ask him.

"Not at all. Just don't want to take any chances," he responds. "Call me before you head out."

My dad hangs up before anything else can be said. We don't need to say anything else. I've got my marching orders and now I need to get Sam on board with heading home now instead of doing everything we talked about doing, giving notice to Carson, calling her doctor to make arrangements to get everything switched, and taking our time packing the house up.

Heading to the kitchen, I grab the eggs, bacon, and pancake mix. There's orange juice that we'll finish this morning and I grab out an apple to split between the three of us. Sam is going to bitch about the amount of food, but she needs to eat a good, healthy, balanced diet and that's what I'm giving her.

It doesn't take me long to get the food made. I'd kill for a cup of coffee, but Sam doesn't have it in the house because she can't drink it. She told me it was too much of a temptation and she doesn't want to do anything to put the babies at risk. She gave up coffee when she was pregnant with Caleb too.

Once I have the plates filled and set out, I fill our glasses with orange juice and make my way in to get Caleb and Sam. I wake Caleb up first so he can use the bathroom while I get Sam up and help her out of bed. She's in a pair of shorts and a long tee-shirt, so I don't have to worry about helping her dress. Or wanting to get another taste of her before letting her get out of bed. One is never going to be enough.

"Sam, baby, I need you to get up now," I say gently, sitting on the edge of the bed closest to her.

"No. Need sleep," she murmurs in her sleep.

"Breakfast is already on the table and Caleb is up. Need to talk to you too," I tell her.

This gets her attention. Sam wakes up and glares at me. No, she didn't get a lot of sleep last night because the babies were apparently sitting on her bladder and she had to keep getting up to go to the bathroom.

"What's for breakfast?" she asks, her voice sleep laden as she struggles to sit up in bed.

"Pancakes, bacon, eggs, and apple slice. We have orange juice to drink with it," I answer her question.

"Fine," she grumbles.

I help Sam out of bed and she waddles to the bathroom. My gaze is locked on her ass as she walks away from me. When she turns to go into the bathroom, she looks back at me and catches me looking at her. I shrug my shoulders at her and give her a mock innocent look because I'm not going to be ashamed or feel guilty for looking at my woman's body. Sam is sexy as hell to me and I'll look as much as I can.

As soon as she's done in the bathroom, I grab her hand and we walk to the table together. Caleb is already in his seat as I pull Sam's chair out and wait until she's comfortable before moving to my own. She looks at the table and I can practically hear the lecture she wants to give me. Instead, she surprises me by digging into her food instead of uttering a word.

"So, what did you have to talk to me about?" she asks once she's eaten some of her food.

"Got a call from Dad this mornin' while you were still sleepin'. He needs me to come home. Today," I tell her. "And you already know I'm not leavin' you here alone. Even with Edna, Sandy, and Carson here, I want you and Caleb with me."

"I haven't talked to Carson or anything yet," she tells me. "I'm not just going to walk out on him and leave him with nothing."

"Sam, I'll talk to him. I'll explain Dad needs me back. You only work one day a week," I tell her.

Which is obviously the wrong thing to say based on the look she's giving me. Well, glare, not so much as a look. Will I ever not fuck up when it comes to Sam?

"Playboy, I can take care of my own affairs," she begins telling me. "I don't need you to take care of me. I've been doing it on my own for a long ass time now."

"I didn't mean it like that and you know it, Sam," I say, keeping my voice light and calm. "I'm just askin' you and Caleb to come home with me today instead of a few days from now. I can finish packin' everythin' up while you talk to Carson and Edna. Then we can be on the road in a few hours and be in our own home tonight."

She sits and looks at me for the longest time. Sam doesn't say a single word. The only thing she does is continue eating her breakfast in silence. At this point, I'm not sure if I'm in the doghouse with her right now or if we're going to be okay. Only time will tell when it comes to Sam and what's running through her mind.

"Fine. I'll come home with you today as long as Carson is okay with it. Playboy, you need to understand that you can't make all my decisions for me. And you can't do everything for me. I have to do things on my own," she tells me.

"Thank you, baby. I'll try to remember that. But, you're goin' to have to help me out every now and then. Cause I'll be the first to tell you I'm gonna fuck this up between us more times than we'll be able to count," I tell her.

After breakfast, I wash up the dishes and let them air dry. When I'm done with those, I start packing up the rest of the house. The only thing I leave out is a change of clothes for Sam. Caleb's already dressed and ready to go. He's got a bag packed with toys and books to keep him occupied on the ride home and he told me he's going to grab something for a snack. I'm sure we'll be stopping for something to eat on the way because of Sam anyway, but he doesn't need to know that.

It doesn't take me long to pack up the house for Sam. She's resting on the couch with a book in her hands. Though she did tell me she talked to Carson and he had a feeling about her leaving with me. He's happy we're finding our way together. I can't thank the man enough for looking after my family while they were here. He's in my debt for the rest of my life and there's nothing I won't do for the man. I'll be sure to let him know how much

I appreciate him and that he's got a marker from me. Markers aren't something I give out lightly.

"Baby, you ready to get changed?" I ask Sam walking back out to the living room after grabbing the last of the clean clothes from the dryer.

"Yeah," she answers, setting her book down and holding out her hands for me to help her up.

She may only be five months pregnant, but if I didn't know any better, I'd think she was due to give birth any day now. It's very awkward for her to get up and down, much like Shy was when she got farther along in her pregnancy with Rayven. Sam's only going to get bigger as the months go by and I can't wait to see her fully round with our children nestled safely in her belly.

While Sam is getting dressed, I finish loading everything up in her car. It's going to be a tight fit, but it's only for a few hours and then we'll be home. We'll have the guys in the club help us once we get back. Caleb is bouncing around the house and trying to help me load things up, but he doesn't have the attention right now to focus on the task at hand. So, I just let him follow me to and from the house with bags.

By the time I've finished loading the last of the things in the car, Sam is making her way back into the living room. Instead of sitting down, she grabs her purse, cell phone, and her book. We walk out of the house and Edna is waiting for us outside. Tears are already filling her eyes as she looks at us.

"I'm gonna miss you two," Edna says as we get close to her. "You be sure to stay in touch. I wanna see pictures of those babies."

"We will," Sam says, tears falling down her face. "I'll call you all the time."

"You better," Edna replies.

Sam hands over the keys to the house so Edna can get them back to Carson. Edna hands her over an envelope and I see money in it when Sam opens it up. She looks up at Edna with questions in her eyes.

"It's your deposit back from Carson," Edna says.

"That's way more than my deposit," Sam tells her.

"I just know what he said. Call him and take it up with him," she tells Sam with a small smile on her face.

The women hug and then Edna hugs Caleb before he climbs in his booster seat in the back of the car. I fasten him in while the two women finish saying their goodbyes. Then, I help Sam in the car and close the door before heading to the driver's side. As soon as I get in, I start the car and we head for home. I breathe a sigh of relief that my family is coming home with me. Today is the first day of the rest of our lives and I'm going to take every second I can get with Sam, Caleb, and the new additions to our family. This is my life now; my destiny.

Chapter Twenty

Sam

THERE WAS NO way I could say no to Playboy when he told me Slim called and needed him to come home. Honestly, I want to be with him and I can't fight the feelings I have for him. No matter what anyone thinks, Playboy does make me happy. I was just hurt when he pushed me away because he didn't want me to see him in jail.

I appreciate that he wanted to take care of things for me, but I wasn't lying when I said I need to do things on my own. I'm independent because I've had to take care of everything my entire life. It's only been the last little bit when Playboy's been around to help with Caleb or anything else I need to do. So, I tend to push him away when it comes to needing to do anything.

Now, we're almost to the halfway point of our trip and it's taken a lot longer because I have to stop so much to go to the bathroom. I've apologized repeatedly to Playboy and he just brushes it off. I know he's not upset or anything about constantly having to stop, but I still feel horrible about it.

Just as I start dozing off in the front seat, I hear the loud rumble of several bikes. Looking out the window, I don't see anything. So, I look in the side mirror and see a group of bikes coming up to us. Playboy places his hand on my thigh and a smile graces his face.

"It's our welcome home, baby," he assures me without me having to say a single word.

"Oh. Everything okay with the club?" I ask my concern level rising.

"Yeah. Dad just wanted them to escort us home," he answers.

"They for us?" Caleb asks as two bikes ride in front of us.

"Yeah, they are, buddy," he answers.

I turn to watch Caleb looking out the window as bikes pull up on either side of the car. When he turns to the front after waving to Killer based on the long black hair flying behind him, he sees Slim is in front of us.

"It's Papi! He's here!" Caleb yells excitedly.

I can't help the laughter erupting from me. He's so excited the guys are here and he has no clue they can't hear him. Caleb is trying to wave to all the guys surrounding us. We have Slim and another guy in front, Killer on one side, another bike on the opposite side, and one more bike behind us.

The rest of the ride back to Benton Falls seems to fly by in the blink of an eye. Caleb is chattering endlessly as he watches the bikes and tries to concentrate all of them at one time. When he finally realizes he can't do that, he focuses on his Papi in front of us. He keeps asking who's up there, but I have no clue and Playboy isn't saying a word about who it is.

When we got to Playboy's house, our house, the guys helped bring everything in from the car. Slim made sure to hold the women off so I can relax. But, the guys were shocked as hell to see me as big as I am. I swear, Killer's eyes were about to pop out of his head when Slim pulled me out of the car and then into an enormous hug. I love his hugs and I've missed them.

Shortly after everything was brought inside, Playboy had to leave for church. All I got told was its club business. I'm more than fine with not knowing what's going on unless it concerns Caleb or myself. I'll do anything to protect us and that includes wanting to know exactly what's going on if there's a threat to either one of us. Or Playboy.

Yes, I care about the rest of the club members and the ol' ladies of the club. Not so much the house bunnies because they don't care if one of the guys has an ol' lady or is seeing someone outside of the club; they only care about getting laid and trying to become an ol' lady themselves. But, everyone has their own problems and if it doesn't concern all of us here, I don't need to know about it.

I have to admit being back here I want to see the women I call my friends. I'm just so damn tired right now and want to go to bed even though it's way too early to do so. Caleb needs to eat and I have to figure out where we're all sleeping. Hell, I don't even know who's room is who's here. Playboy didn't have time to show me around before he headed out with the rest of the guys.

For a little while, Caleb and I explore the house. The outside looks like a log cabin. I remember telling Playboy once I always wanted to live in one. When you walk in the door, the entire downstairs is an open floorplan with the exception of a hallway on the left side of the house. There's a laundry room, a bathroom, and a door that's locked in the hallway.

Walking back out to the main room, I take in the kitchen. It's huge with a ton of cupboard space and stainless-steel appliances that are brand new. A sink faces the front of the house and overlooks the porch and front yard. There's an island with four barstools separating the kitchen from the living. Just before the hallway is a kitchen table large enough to sit eight people. Then you see the living room.

The living room is spacious and bright, with the entire back wall of the room nothing but windows. An enormous TV is mounted to the wall with shelves built-in on either side of it. There's already movies stacked on one side with the opposite side blank. A large leather couch takes up the middle of the room with a recliner in front of one of the windows. The only other piece of furniture in the room is a coffee table.

There's a staircase directly opposite the door and I don't dare go up it without Playboy here with me. I'm too tired and I don't want to fall or have anything else happen. So, I sit down on the couch and turn the TV on to see if he has cable or not. Finding out he does, I put on a show for Caleb as I get comfortable and try not to fall asleep.

I'm woken up when Playboy leans down and kisses me softly. I immediately wake up to see Caleb sitting on the end of the couch, still watching the show I put on for him. My heart is racing with the thought something could've happened to him while I was asleep. Damn, I've never done that before. Maybe I should've called Gwen over to visit.

"What do you need to do before we head out?" Playboy asks as he sits down next to me and Slim stands at the end of the island.

"Nothing. I just need to get my purse and we can head out," I answer him.

"Shy and Dad will have Caleb while we're gone. We'll pick him up there when we get back. And I'll warn you now all the ol' ladies will be there. They're waitin' to see you both," he says.

"Okay. Caleb, you be good for Papi and Shy. I'll see you in a little bit," I tell him, stopping to hug him to me.

Playboy ushers me out to the car and helps me inside the passenger seat before closing my door and walking around to the driver's side. He gets in and starts the car as I fasten my seat belt. We're leaving the clubhouse entrance before I can blink. I already know he's going to ask about us having sex because we both want to go there. But, he doesn't want to hurt the babies.

We're at the doctor's office before too long and I hope I can start doing more. Not just around the house, but just in general. The only thing I am these days is tired as hell. I get so tired easily and have to rest. The same happened when I was pregnant with Caleb, and it's just worse this time around. I'm guessing it has to do with the fact I'm growing two humans inside me instead of just one.

"Penny for your thoughts?" Playboy asks as he pulls into the parking lot.

"Just thinking about how different this pregnancy is compared to when I was pregnant with Caleb," I respond.

"How so?" he questions me.

"I'm just tired more easily and I have to rest more," I reply. "I want to get a job and do things with Caleb, but I seem to always be resting."

"We'll talk to the doctor about it then," he tells me.

I nod my head as we exit the car and make our way inside. After giving my name to the receptionist and grabbing the paperwork from her to fill out, I let her know there should've been paperwork faxed over from my previous doctor and the hospital.

"You won't need to fill out those papers," she says, looking at my chart. "We got them from the previous doctor."

"Do you mind if I do fill these out? This way, the father's information can be added in," I ask her.

"Not at all. Just bring them up when you're done," she answers with a smile.

Sitting down next to Playboy, I see the other women in the waiting room eyeballing him. He's not paying them any attention as he answers a text on his phone. When I sit down, he looks up at me with a smile on his face.

"Everythin' okay?" he asks me.

"Yeah. We just need to fill these out. If you want to start with your section, they can add it to my chart," I tell him, handing over the clipboard.

"Okay," he tells me, putting his phone back in his pocket and getting started on filling out the papers.

By the time he's done with it, my name is being called by one of the nurses. He helps me up and we head back after he stops briefly to turn in the papers to the receptionist. Playboy focuses on everything the nurse does as she takes my weight, blood pressure, and everything else that's normally done at these appointments. I'm waiting for him to bark out instructions, but he just stands back and watches her like a hawk.

We're then ushered into one of the exam rooms and told the doctor would be in with us shortly. This visit I don't have to have an exam done because it's just a check-up since I'm now living here. And they'll be doing an ultrasound so we can see the babies. I'm excited Playboy gets to experience this with me today. And a little nervous because this will make the situation a reality and I don't know how he's going to react once he sees our children on the screen.

"Are you sure you're ready for this?" I ask him as he pulls a chair next to my bed and holds my hand.

"I'm ready, babe," he assures me.

"You know it's different seeing my bulging stomach to actually seeing two little babies on the screen, right?" I ask him.

"I know, Sam. We've got this. I'll be fine seein' the babies on the screen and whatever else happens today. I'm not gonna run scared or take off like some little bitch," he tells me, laughing at the end of his words.

I nod my head and relax back against the bed I'm sitting on. It's not long before Doctor Sanchez knocks on the door and enters the room with my file in hand.

"Sam, I'm Doctor Sanchez. It's nice to meet you," she says, holding out her hand to shake.

"It's nice to meet you too," I answer.

"Playboy, it's good to see you again," she says before diving in. "Now, it looks as though you were placed on bed rest and then mandatory light duty with mainly resting for the last month or so. Can you tell me what was going on?"

"Yeah. Um, I left here and moved a few hours away. I got a job in a restaurant at the truck stop. One day I went to work and started bleeding shortly after starting my shift. They rushed me to the hospital and said it was from stress and placed me on bed rest until I could get in to see my doctor there," I tell her honestly.

"Okay. Any bleeding since you've been up and moving around?" she asks me.

"No. The only thing I have right now is that I get extremely tired and want to rest more than anything else," I reply.

"You'll probably feel that way carrying multiples. Anything else going on with you?" Doctor Sanchez asks.

"No. My morning sickness went away fairly quickly and other than being tired, I feel good. Too good to be laying around the house most of the time," I tell her.

"And, I'd like to know when we can have sex again," Playboy pipes up as the doctor and I both look at him.

My face is turning several shades of red; I can feel it. Doctor Sanchez has a look on her face as if she would expect nothing less from the man sitting next to me. I guess she's used to the way the men in the club talk and worry about having sex because every single one of the ol' ladies from Phantom Bastards and the Wild Kings come to Doctor Sanchez. She has two different offices now because of the clubs.

"Playboy, as long as Sam is feeling okay and there's no bleeding, you can have sex. No rough, monkey sex, though," she says with a straight face.

"Got it," he tells her with a smile on his face. "I'll leave the rough, monkey sex for when we're havin' our next kid."

I groan low at the thought of having sex with him to get pregnant once again after the twins are born. He'll see exactly how much it takes to push a kid out of a body when I go into labor. Maybe then he'll rethink his decision to have more kids. Or maybe he won't. Who knows when it comes to Playboy?

"Okay, I'm going to keep you on light duty for now. I don't want to take any chances and have you start bleeding again. You can have sex as long as you're not in pain and are comfortable. My suggestion is to play with different positions that keeps you both off your stomach. Now, let's get the ultrasound tech in here so we can get a visual of the babies," she says before opening the door of the exam room we're in. "You can go to the store if it's a quick trip. No browsing through the aisles or taking your time."

I pull my shirt up over my stomach and lower my pants a little bit. Playboy is looking at me as if I've lost my damn mind. If I weren't nervous about what we'd see today, I'd be laughing my ass off right now.

"The fuck you doin'?" he asks.

"They need to get to my stomach in order to see the babies. So, I'm lifting my shirt up and lowering my pants a little bit so they can see the babies no matter what position they're in," I answer him.

There's another knock on the door and Doctor Sanchez comes back in the room with another woman pushing the ultrasound machine in front of her. Looks like time is here and we get to see and hear our babies.

I get comfortable on the table as Playboy scoots even closer to me. The technician drops some gel on my stomach and I flinch as the coldness hits me. Playboy looks at her with anger in his eyes.

"It's okay, Playboy. It's always a little cold," I tell him, grabbing his hand and holding it with mine.

Once the wand is placed on my stomach, we hear the whooshing of the babies' heartbeats filling the room. Playboy looks up at me with awe and shock on his face as tears fill his eyes.

"Heartbeats sound good," the technician says, clicking a few buttons on the keyboard of the machine.

I nod my head as I keep my eyes on Playboy since this is all new for him and I want to look at his expressions while he witnesses our babies first-hand. I'm sure he mirrored my expressions when I experienced this all while I was pregnant with Caleb. He looks at me and leans down to place a soft, gentle kiss on my lips. The doctor and technician disappear from the room as I relish the way his lips feel against my own and the way the sensations flowing through me at the simple contact.

"Alright, Mom and Dad, let's take a look," the technician says.

Playboy pulls his lips from mine as we turn our attention to the screen in front of us. He stands up so he can get a closer look at the monitor. Never once does he let go of my hand. It takes seconds before the screen is filled with the images of our children safely nestled in my belly.

"Everything looks good," the tech says. "Do you want to know what you're having?"

"I was already told, but I'd like to be sure," I answer.

The tech and Doctor Sanchez laugh as she moves the wand around on my stomach.

"Baby A is a boy," she tells us, moving the wand around to get a look at the second baby. "Baby B is also a boy."

Nodding my head, I turn my eyes to Playboy. He's got his attention firmly on the screen as he watches are sons turn and move in my stomach. The look on his face shows me he can't believe what he's witnessing at this moment; a moment just for us.

"Thank you, baby," he suddenly tells me.

"For what?" I ask him, taking my attention off his face to look directly in his eyes.

"For givin' me the gift you're givin' me. Two sons are bein' added to the family and I can't wait to see them and hold them," he answers.

"You had a hand in making this happen," I tell him with a slight laugh.

"But you could've gone a different route with this and the way I was actin'," he tells me. "You're stronger than you know. So much stronger."

"I love you, Playboy. There was no way I'd deprive you of this. Of growing our family," I tell him honestly. "We just need to work on some things to make it even better and ensure we last."

He nods his head as the tech hands us photos of our children. Playboy takes them and places them in the pocket of his cut. He grabs my hand and uses the towel I'm handed to wipe the excess gel off my stomach. Once that's done, he tosses the towel in the bin for it and leads me from the room so I can make my next appointment.

"Let's go get our son," he says once I'm done and we're heading from the office.

Playboy helps me in the car once again and we pull from the parking lot of the doctor's office. He points the car in the direction of the clubhouse and I watch the scenery pass by. We're holding hands and they're resting on his thigh as he drives carefully back.

I zone out, thinking of the babies as he drives. By the time we're at the clubhouse, I have no clue where the time went because I was in my own head.

"You ready to face the ol' ladies?" he asks me.

"I guess so," I answer nervously, not knowing what to expect from them when we walk in Slim and Shy's home.

Playboy leads me inside and I see Shy holding Rayven, who's gotten so much bigger in the little time I've been gone. Kim, Gwen, and Jennifer are here too. When Playboy clears his throat, the women look up and in our direction. They all have shocked looks on their faces and stare at my burgeoning stomach.

"Holy shit!" Kim says. "This is why you left."

It's a statement and not a question, so I don't say a word to her in response.

"Are you okay?" Gwen asks me.

"I'm okay. I just have to take it easy; light duty for me only right now. I'm sorry I didn't tell any of you sooner. I just wanted Playboy to be the first to know and that couldn't happen when I found out," I tell them, letting the truth of my words shine from my eyes.

"We get it. I know I'd have done the same thing as you if it had been me," Shy tells me. "But you're back now and not going anywhere again.

We'll all help you guys out whenever Playboy has to be gone."

"Thank you. For everything," I tell her, looking at them all in turn. "Where's Caleb?"

"He's with his Papi at the clubhouse," Shy answers. "Playboy, take her home and I'll bring him over in a little bit. Get some rest while you can. And I'm making dinner tonight.

"Got it," Playboy says.

We leave her house and Playboy puts me back in the car to head to our home. Once inside, he leads me to the couch and we spend the next while watching movies on TV while I doze on and off. It's the perfect day and I couldn't think of a better way to spend our time together.

Chapter Twenty-One

Playboy

AFTER SEEING OUR sons at Sam's appointment two days ago, I've been in awe of what she's been going through. Yeah, I've seen the ol' ladies of our club and the Wild Kings go through pregnancies, but I never paid much attention to them. It's different when it's the woman who owns your heart though, and when it's your children growing inside her.

So, I called my sister yesterday and Tank and Maddie will be here today. I didn't tell Sam because I know she'll fret and worry about every little detail if she knows they're coming here. I know how she is and worrying is the last thing she needs to do right now because she'll start bleeding again and have to go back on bed rest.

Sam is already going crazy being on light duty. She wants to be able to clean the house and cook meals, help the ol' ladies out at the clubhouse, and find a job. Or start going to school again. Right now, she can't hardly do any of it. The most she does is start the washer and switch the clothes over to the dryer. I won't let her carry the laundry baskets or anything else.

We've fought more than I ever wanted to because I'm being an 'overbearing asshole' according to her. I'm just being cautious and making sure nothing happens to her or our sons. While she understands where I'm coming from, she doesn't like how I go about it. I've had more silent treatments in the last two days than my entire life. I'll live with it if Sam is okay.

"Baby, we're gonna have a cookout at the clubhouse today. The ol' ladies want to celebrate you comin' home and want to know the sex of the babies. You up for it?" I ask her, walking in our bedroom to see her sitting up in bed with her Kindle in her hands.

"Yeah. It will be nice to get out of the house for a while," she tells me, a soft smile on her face.

"Okay. I'm goin' to let Dad know we'll be there and then help you in the shower," I tell her.

Sam nods her head at me and goes back to reading her book while I pull my phone from my pocket and head into the hallway. After letting him know we'll be there in a little while, I head back in the room and help Sam out of bed and to the bathroom.

Today, I'm going to join her in the shower. Since I saw her in the truck stop and went home with her, I help her in and then sit on the toilet or something out of her way. She's refused to let me in with her but wants me close by in case something happens. Thankfully, nothing ever has and I've just been in the room with her. I don't know what I'd do if something happened to her or the babies.

Once I have helped her undress, I turn on the water and let it get to temperature while she pulls the hair tie from her hair and sets it on the counter by the sink. When she goes to get in the shower, I help her and then quickly strip out of my clothes. I step in behind her, and Sam gasps as I wrap my arms around her body.

"What are you doing, Playboy?" she asks me.

"I'm showerin' with you," I answer. "Not wastin' any more time now that we've been given the green light by your doctor."

She doesn't say a word as I grab the shampoo and she carefully turns around to get her hair wet. As soon as she's ready, I wash her hair. Making sure to massage the suds into her scalp. Helping her turn once I'm done, she rinses it while I grab the conditioner. Her hair is still short, so it doesn't take long to complete the tasks.

Once her hair is done, I grab her loofah and body wash. It smells of lilacs and I can't get enough of the scent on her. I make sure the suds from her body wash are enough to wash her body before placing the loofah against the smooth skin of her shoulder. I slide it along her skin and let my fingers graze her skin. It's not helping the raging hard-on I have right now, but I don't care. Tonight is when I'll be with Sam; after I make her my ol' lady in the eyes of the club.

I run the loofah over her ample tits, which have only gotten larger since she got pregnant. A shiver runs through her body and I relish the fact I'm doing this to her. I'm the one making her horny and want me; no one else will ever get this response from her. I'll gut any man who thinks he can touch what's mine.

When I get to her rounded belly, I bend down and place a kiss where our sons rest. Once I wash her entire body, I stand back up and let her rinse off. I'm wet enough now I can easily wash my hair while she's rinsing the suds from her gorgeous body.

When she's done, Sam takes a seat on the small bench in the shower and I condition my hair and wash my body. She's watching every move I make; I can feel her eyes on me. Instead of stroking my hard, aching cock like I want to, I simply wash my body and rinse before getting out of the shower with her.

I help Sam dry off and grab a towel for myself so I can dry my body before we head into the room to get dressed.

"What do you want to wear today?" I ask her.

"One of the dresses you just bought me," she answers, sitting on the bed.

I walk in the closet and pull out a long summer dress in a pale purple color. At the same time, I grab my jeans and a tee-shirt before making my way back to the bed where Sam's waiting for me. She managed to get her underwear on while I was getting our clothes. I look at her wearing a white lace matching bra and panty set. Sam looks beautiful and I want to strip the material from her body and have my way with her.

Instead, I hold out the dress and drop to the floor as the towel begins to loosen around my waist. Sam puts her feet in the center of the garment and I slowly slide it up her legs. My fingers graze her skin and again, a shiver runs through her entire body. This time I place a kiss on her belly and stand up, pulling her with me so our bodies are flush.

Well, as flush as they can be with her belly between us.

"Tonight, babe, I'm goin' to have my way with you," I warn her. "You have until we get home to get right with it."

"Nothing to get right with, Playboy. I want you now," she says, looking me in the eyes.

"Have to head out. Caleb is waitin' for us to get to the clubhouse," I tell her.

Caleb went with my dad earlier to the clubhouse. They were going to play on the playground that was added to the backyard when kids started being born into the club. Now, Caleb is enjoying it with my dad chasing after him. I'm sure there's a Prospect or two helping him because I'm sure Caleb isn't the only kid out there already.

I help Sam downstairs once her hair is brushed and put up in a ponytail. Half of her hair is already escaping the hair tie and I know she'll be putting it up a million more times before the end of the day. I love it when she gets frustrated with her hair. Her nose scrunches up and her lips thin instead of being full and kissable. Then, she pulls the hair tie from her hair and flings it letting it hang all around her face.

We stop in the kitchen so she can grab the salad she directed me to make. I followed all of her instructions, but I still don't know if it's going to be the same as she usually makes. For now, I don't give a shit about the salad. I just want to get her to the clubhouse and sitting down in the shade with a cold drink in her hand.

As we step out of the front door, I can already hear the music blaring from the clubhouse.

The cookout is already in full swing and we're probably going to be the last ones there. I don't even care about that, though. I'm surprised my phone isn't blowing up with Maddie calling and messaging me about where we are.

"You ready for this?" I ask Sam as I point the car toward the clubhouse.

"Yeah. Today is going to be a good day," she answers, smiling at me.

Her smile is radiant and lights up her entire face. It's one of the things I used to picture while I was in jail. And honestly, it kept me going when I didn't think I was going to make it through the day without getting in a fight or killing some dumb fuck who wanted to press their luck with me.

I pull up behind the clubhouse and close to the chairs, so Sam doesn't have to walk far before sitting down. Yes, I'm being the overbearing asshole once again, but I don't give a flying fuck about it. Sam is not going to get too tired and not enjoy the day while we're here. I have too much planned for her. I'll just move the timing of things up. Maybe once everyone is sitting down to eat.

When I park the car, I race around the front to help Sam out as I see Maddie and Tank talking with my dad. Chance, Shawn, and Brax are playing with Caleb while Zoey is pushing Rayven in the baby swing. Other kids are playing in various parts of the playground while their parents stand close by to keep an eye on them. Soon, I'll be over there watching our sons play and run around, causing trouble because I have no doubt our sons will always be right in the thick of things just as I was.

"Playboy! Sam!" Maddie calls out when she finally spots us.

Sam looks up at me and I know if Maddie weren't making her way over to us, she'd be giving me an earful for not letting her know sooner about their arrival. I smile down at her glare and place a kiss against her cheek.

"I love you," I tell her, moving out of the way so my sister can look at her.

"I love you too," she says grudgingly.

Yeah, she's mad at me. But she'll get over it.

"Oh, my God! Is this why you called and wanted Tank and I to come visit?" Maddie asks, hugging me in greeting.

"It is. I didn't want you to hear it from anyone other than me," I answer her.

"Congratulations!" she says, carefully pulling Sam into a hug as well. "I'm so happy for you."

"Well, so you know, we're havin' twins," I tell her as she turns her shocked gaze toward me.

"Holy shit! I don't believe it," she says, covering her mouth as Tank approaches us.

"Playboy, it's good to see you," he says as we greet in a man hug. "Sam, well, it's good to see you too. Why don't you sit down before you fall down?"

I look at her and I know it's time for her to sit. She's been on her feet too long and I don't want her to overdo things before I have the chance to present her rag to her. Tank and I help her sit in a lounge chair before he hands me over a case holding something special for today. We're going to reveal the genders today and I have something special planned. Even though Tank brought it for me, he doesn't even know what we're having.

Once Sam is situated and Maddie is keeping her company, I make my way over to my dad for a drink and to find out how long it will be before the food is ready.

"How's she doin'?" my dad asks when I get over to him.

"She's okay. Gettin' restless because she wants to be able to do things and not be restin' so much," I answer as Caleb and my nephews run over to me.

"Uncle Playboy!" Brax yells out as he hugs my legs.

"Boys, how are you doin'" I ask the triplets. "Been a long time since I've seen you. You're gettin' big and strong, just like your dad."

They all smile at me and I rumple their hair. Before I can ask about the food, I see the ol' ladies making their way through the back door of the clubhouse. While they're all coming out, I excuse myself from the boys and head into my room. I have Sam's rag in there and I want to give it to her while we're all here as a family. We can't do the gender reveal until later on tonight and this will hopefully excite her.

When I'm back outside, I place the box on the ground behind the chair Sam's sitting in. Caleb is waiting for me to walk through the food line with him. I pile my plate, a plate for Sam, and help Caleb put food on his plate. He wants to eat with my nephews and niece since they're sitting with us; it's not a big deal. Maddie has been glued to Sam's side since we got here and it excites me to know my sister likes my woman so much.

After the plates are filled, I walk back over to where Sam, Maddie, Tank, and the kids are sitting. I hand off her plate to her filled with chicken, salt potatoes, pasta salad, a biscuit, and corn on the cob. Pulling a water from my back pocket, I hand it over to her as well. I remain standing and nibble on my food as I wait for the remaining members and ol' ladies to make their way through the food line.

I'm nervous as hell and I can't remember the last time I was nervous about anything. Part of me worries Sam is going to turn me down about being my ol' lady in front of the club. While I have to do this in front of the club, there's no guarantee of what she's gonna say. Sam is hormonal because of the pregnancy and part of her still thinks I'm with her because of our boys. It's not the case at all and I'm hoping by claiming her she'll realize I'm serious about her.

Once Boy Scout, the last person is walking away from the tables under the canopy, I whistle. Loud. Everyone stops and looks at me while I step behind the chair Sam's sitting. She's got her head at an angle and is looking at me. There's questions staring at me from her eyes and they're about to be answered.

"As some of you know, I've been stayin' with Sam for a while now. What only a few of you know is that before I went to jail, I was plannin' on askin' her to be my ol' lady. There's no better time than with you all here today and my sister and Tank joinin' us," I say, opening the lid of the box. "Sam, I love you more than I could ever put into words. Will you be my ol' lady?"

Sam has tears in her eyes as she pulls the leather rag from the box. On the back is our club colors with 'Property of' above the colors and 'Playboy' underneath them. My girl leans forward as she tries to slide the rag on her shoulders.

"I'll help you, baby," I tell her.

As I slide the rag on her, everyone erupts into whistles and catcalls. She's got a smile from ear-to-ear on her face as she looks up at me with love shining from her eyes.

"I love you, Playboy," she says, pulling me down to kiss her.

"I love you too," I answer as I break the chaste kiss.

The ol' ladies come over to congratulate her as Sam eats her food. She's starving and no one is going to keep her from her food. I sit down next to her as everyone files away and we eat the rest of our meal in relative silence. Well, without everyone being up in our faces. The kids are talking a mile a minute and we're laughing at them as they try to outdo one another with their stories. Unfortunately, the stories from my nephews are more than likely true.

When I see Sam put her plate down on her lap, I know she's done eating for now. It will be a different story in a little bit, though because I plan on giving her a workout now. I can't wait until we get home. Especially when I have a perfectly good room in the clubhouse we can use.

"Come with me, baby?" I ask her, holding out my hand to help her up.

"Where are we going?" she questions.

"Inside for a little bit. Caleb's okay out here with the kids and my sister. No one here will let him get into trouble or hurt," I tell her.

Sam nods her head and accepts my help up from the chair. I lead her inside and take her up to my room. Once we're inside, I shut the door and make sure it's locked. I step up behind her, wrap my arms around her and place a kiss on the side of her neck. Sam relaxes back into me as I run my hands up from her rounded stomach to the amazing tits she has.

A low groan escapes her as I rub circles around her nipples through the thin fabric of her dress and bra. I can't wait. I need her now.

I slide the rag off her shoulders and fold it before carefully place it on the dresser to my left. Next, I remove my cut and place it on top of her rag. Turning her around, I kneel down and begin to slide the dress up her body. My hands skim her legs as I raise them higher and higher on her body.

When my hand reaches the junction between her thighs, I rub a finger under her soaked panties before continuing up her body. The second her stomach is uncovered, I place a kiss on her and don't linger there. I want her naked and under me right now, not minutes from now.

Finally, her dress if completely off her body and I step back to look at her body only covered by the bra and panties she's wearing. Before I can ask her to take them off, she reaches around her back and undoes the clasp on the bra and lets it slide from her shoulders until it falls to the floor. My jaw drops open as I stare at her bared tits.

"Don't," I growl out when she goes to push her panties down.

Sam immediately stops and I take a step forward until her body is up against mine. I raise my hands just enough to pull the shirt from my body so I can feel her skin against mine. My movements halt when Sam gasps in shock.

"What's the matter, baby?" I ask her.

"When did you do this?" she asks, looking at the spot over my heart.

Looking down, I see the tattoo I got her for her when I was out on a run.

"I got it just before I found you in Torrino," I tell her. "You don't like it?"

"I love it," she tells me as a lone tear slips down her cheek.

Sam reaches up on her tiptoes and presses her stomach against me. She pulls my head down and places a kiss against my lips. For a second, she just lingers there. Knowing she won't deepen the kiss, I lick across her full, bottom lip and she doesn't hesitate to open her mouth to me. As I kiss her, her hands reach between us and I hear her undoing my belt so she can unbutton and zip my pants. As soon as she's done, she reaches her hand inside and wraps it around my hard cock.

"On the bed, baby," I tell her, knowing this will be over with too soon if I don't get her ready for me first.

She walks over to the bed and I watch as she climbs up and lays directly in the middle of the mattress. Sam looks just like a goddess lying in the center of my bed with her hair surrounding her head. I take a minute just to take her in. The way her body has changed with the pregnancy, the golden hue of her flawless skin, and emotions flooding her eyes.

Before joining her on the bed, I kick off my boots and let my jeans fall to the floor. I kick them off and pull my socks off before walking to the bed. Climbing on the bed, I don't slide in next to Sam, I go between her legs. She opens them up to accommodate my body as I lower my head to slide my tongue between her slick folds.

I lick from her opening to her clit several times and feel her body tremble under me. Sam reaches down and slides her fingers into my hair. This tells me she's already close and I know what I have to do. I suck her clit into my mouth and flick my tongue over it while pushing a finger inside her pussy.

"Yes!" she moans out. "Don't stop. Please!"

I have no intention of stopping anything I'm doing. My only goal is to get her to fall apart under me and I won't stop until she's completely sated.

Sliding my finger in and out of her body, I add another finger as I suck harder on her clit before gently biting down. That's all Sam needs to fly over the edge and her release rush over her.

"Griffin!" she screams out as her body clamps down on my fingers and I lap up her release.

I slowly slide my fingers in and out of her as I bring her back down. When she's lying spent in the bed, I slowly climb up her body and rub my cock through her folds, getting it wet with her juices. I kiss her lips as I slide in. I continually slide in and out of her body until I'm fully seated in her. I don't want to hurt her or anything as I wait a minute for her to adjust to my size.

"Move, please, Griffin," she pleads with me. "I'm fine, I promise."

I listen to her and begin to slide out of her body. She feels so good, I know I'm not going to last long. I truly don't care as long as she's taken care of. I'll never leave her unsatisfied and I'll always make sure she gets hers before I even think about letting go.

"Harder," she says, urging me on as she wraps one slim leg around my hip subtly changing the angle a little bit.

There's no way I'm going to deny her what she wants, so I slide in and out of her faster and harder. I bend my head down and take a taut nipple into my mouth, gently biting down on it. Licking it, I take the sting out of it and I'm rewarded with a moan from Sam as she throws her head back and slightly arches her back.

I sit up my haunches and never once lose my rhythm of sliding in and out of her. My only reason is I don't want to put any pressure on her stomach and have something happen. So, I slowly pull out of her and shift her to her side. Once she's in the position I want her in, I climb behind her and slide back inside her warm, wet pussy. I feel like

I'm in heaven and coming home all at the same time. It's a feeling I never want to lose.

"You feel so good," I tell her, kissing her on her neck.

"Playboy, please. I'm so close," she grinds out.

"I got you, baby," I tell her.

Reaching around her body, I find her clit as I begin to thrust a little harder and faster in her. Her body begins to tighten up and I know she's ready to explode. I stretch up and bite down on the skin between her neck and shoulder. Sam explodes.

"Griffin!" she yells out.

As her body tightens around me, I feel the telltale tingling in my spine and know I'm not going to last much longer. I thrust a few more times into her and still once I'm completely in her.

"Sam!" I yell out as I fill her with my cum.

For a few minutes, we lay still with my cock softening still in her. I rub my hand over her stomach as we try to catch our breath and we lay in complete silence. The only sound filling the room is our labored breathing.

"I love you, Playboy," she suddenly says, her voice groggy.

"I love you too," I respond.

Before I can pull from her, Sam is already asleep. I make my way to the bathroom and clean up before wetting a washcloth with warm water. After cleaning her up, I place a kiss on her forehead, pull the blankets up over her and make my way out of the room, locking the door behind me so no one can sneak in on her.

Sam slept for about two hours while I was out with everyone at the cookout. I want to keep an eye on Caleb, so no one else is watching over him. Not that anyone out here would mind one damn bit. We're a family and he's been spending all his time with the triplets, so it's been easy to keep track of him.

Just as it's getting dark out, I take out the case Tank brought me and walk over to Sam, who's back in her lounge chair. She's talking and laughing with Maddie, Shy, Gwen, Kim, and Jennifer. They're having a good time and I don't want to interrupt, but I know she's going to want to go home soon. It's time to do the gender reveal.

As I crouch down next to her, I open the box and inside are two sparklers. Grabbing a lighter from Stryker, I hand one to Sam and light hers just before lighting mine. Everyone is gathered around us as blue flames begin to fill the air while we wave the sparklers around.

The men and women of our family begin to cheer and applaud. I'm handed a shot and a beer as Sam accepts the bottled water being held out to her by Valor. My dad, Shy, Maddie, and Tank are surrounding us and hugging the hell out of us.

"I getting brothers?" Caleb asks, running up to us.

"Yes, you are," I answer him as he wraps around my legs.

"Yes! Girls are gross," he yells out before letting go and running off toward Brax, Chance, and Shawn.

We all burst out laughing at him and his antics. Maddie and Sam talk about planning out the nursery. I don't care what she wants done to it, I'll make sure Sam gets everything she wants for it. From the color of the walls to the carpeting on the floor, she can redo the entire room.

Within an hour, Sam is yawning and ready to head home for the night. Tank and helps me wrangle up the kids since they're staying at our house until they head home. the women are still sitting in the same spot when I go to help Sam out of the chair and get her in the car.

Once we're home, the boys all head to Caleb's room. They take turns in the bathroom and get dressed in their pajamas so they can get to bed. I grab the movie they want to watch and put it on the TV while the other adults kiss them goodnight. Next, we get Zoey situated in one of the other rooms close to Maddie and Tank. She's easy to get into bed. Now, Sam and I can get to bed.

I walk her in our room and help her change into a large tee-shirt before I strip down to nothing. Walking into the closet, I grab a pair of pajama pants and a pair of shorts for Sam. I would normally sleep naked, but not with my sister, Tank, and the extra kids in the house. You never know who's going to come bursting in a room.

Laying down next to Sam, I pull her into my arms and let her rest her head on my chest as I wrap an arm around her. Her eyes are already closing and I know it's not going to be long before sleep claims her. So, I tip her face up and place a gentle kiss on her lips.

"I love you," she murmurs, already falling asleep.

"I love you, too," I tell her, placing one more kiss on the top of her head.

With all the activities of the day, sleep doesn't take long to claim me either. I dream of Sam having our sons and finally being able to hold them. Because we're both asleep, we miss the kids kicking in Sam's stomach for the first time.

Chapter Twenty-Two

Sam

YESTERDAY WAS ONE of the best days of my life. Playboy claimed me in the eyes of the club and I could see the love he feels for me as he gazed down at me. This isn't about the babies I carry or any other reason but love. There was no way I could turn him down because I know the guys don't usually ask their woman to be their ol' lady; it's more of a demand. Something they all do when they want something.

Then, Playboy gave me what I've been wanting since seeing him in the truck stop in Torrino; him. I know he was holding back and I hate it for him. Part of me wants to tell him to find someone he can do what he truly wants to while the other part of me knows I'll never be able to stay with him if he were with someone else. This is just temporary and he won't have to hold back forever. Not that he complained a single bit about holding back.

After I took a small nap, we did the gender reveal, which was greeted by cheers, applause, congratulations, and the men drinking to help Playboy celebrate bringing two new sons into the family and club. It was a good day, but a tiring one. I'm still worn out today and want to spend the entire day in bed. Not that I will because I can't do that.

Maddie and Tank are staying with us because the boys all want to spend time together so I need to get up to head to the store for a few more things while they're here. We have more than enough food, but the kids want a picnic and then they want to roast marshmallows later on tonight. I've called the other ol' ladies and no one has anything for that.

Playboy wanted to send a Prospect to the store, but I want to get out of the house. I need to get out of the house. I'm going stir crazy here. Sitting around isn't something I'm used to doing. I usually am up and about doing whatever needs to be done or helping the ol' ladies. Now, I can't do any of that because I'm stuck on light duty. While I understand it, I'm just not used to it.

After getting ready for the day, Playboy leads me out to my car and I get in.

"Be careful. If you need anythin', call me. I'll have my phone on me," he tells me, leaning down to give me a kiss.

"I will. I'll be back before you know it," I assure him.

Turning on the car, I take a minute to connect my phone to the radio and put on *Pass Slowly* by Seether. I turn up the volume and leave the driveway to our home so I can leave the compound. Once I'm outside the gate, I put the window down, so dirt doesn't get into the car, causing me to choke.

I don't pay attention to my surroundings as I make my way through town and to the small grocery store in Benton Falls. We always go to this store instead of the big box store on the outskirts of town. Even knowing I should always pay attention in case someone is following me or something else like that. Today, I'm just happy to be out of the house and away from the clubhouse.

When I get to the store, I park as close as I can, which is easy because the parking lot is virtually empty at this time of day. Getting out of the car, I waddle into the store and grab a cart on my way in. Women nod at me until they notice I'm wearing a rag proclaiming me the 'Property' of Playboy. The few men in the store don't come anywhere near me because they don't want to get on the wrong side of anyone in the club.

I walk in search of the items I need and don't linger in the store as per the doctor's orders. Once I have them all, I head to the checkout line. I've got a sudden feeling as if I'm being watched and it's not in a good way. There have been times the Prospects have followed us when we've left the compound. I feel safe and protected when they're following us. This time, I feel as if I'm in danger. But I don't want to call Playboy or anyone else if it's all in my imagination.

"How are you today?" the young girl asks as she begins to ring my purchase up.

"I'm good, thank you. How are you?" I ask her with a smile on my face.

"I'm okay, thank you," she responds.

I look over my shoulder to find out why I feel as though I'm being watched and don't spot anyone, or anything, out of the ordinary. Just a few people from town in here shopping and nothing else. They're going about their own business and not looking at anyone in particular. Shrugging my shoulders, I tell myself it's all in my mind.

The cashier tells me the total and puts the bags in the cart for me. I pull out the money and hand it over to her. While she's getting my change, I can't help but continue to look around to find out who is looking at me and where they are. The feeling is only getting worse and not any better. Maybe this isn't only in my mind.

"Here's your change," the cashier tells me as I zone out again.

"Oh, I'm sorry. Thank you," I respond, tossing my change in my purse and pushing the cart out of the store.

I'm about halfway to my car when I feel the presence of someone behind me. I try to walk faster, but it's not easy considering I'm as big as a house and more likely to trip and fall on my face than to get to my car before anyone captures me. Though, I don't think I'm going to be successful in this instance.

As I reach the side of my car to put the groceries in, I'm turned and slammed against the door. My head whips back and slams against the edge of my car and I see stars in my vision. An instant headache builds and makes my vision blurry.

A hand is wrapped around my throat and before I can blink, I'm punched in my face. What the fuck is happening right now?

"Do I have your attention now?" the man asks, his sour breath filling my senses.

"Y-y-yes," I stutter out.

My eyes rake down the man. He's wearing a cut, but I can't tell what club it is. The patch on the front tells me his road name is Rancor and he's the Sargent at Arms of the club. His hair is greasy and longer than even Killer's hair is and his eyes are a dull and lifeless brown. The other thing I notice is he's not fit at all for a man who's in charge of protecting the club and anyone associated with it, he's fat with a huge stomach that hangs down below the top of his jeans. I can't even see his belt in the front.

The other thing I notice is his clothes are dirty, they're stained, and his cut isn't taken care of the way I usually see them. Instead of being aged from everyday wear, it's stained and covered in the same grease which coats his hair. Plus, he smells as if he hasn't showered in months. I almost get sick from the body odor emitting from the man as he chokes me out.

"You're gonna go back to those bunch of pussies you fuck and let them know a new club is in town and we're gonna take everything from them. Starting with the sluts who warm their beds. I can't wait to get a taste of you. Though we may have to do something about that baby in your belly," the man gnarls out. "You make sure you tell them, or I'll pay you another visit. And I'd hate for an accident to happen when you least expect it."

Just when I believe the man is going to leave me alone, he leans in close, pressing a knife against my stomach and I gasp at the thought of something happening to my babies. Next, he licks up the side of my face and I throw up on him. I can't do anything to stop it from happening.

"You fucking bitch!" he yells at me, pressing the knife in a little deeper to the point I feel a burning sensation before punching me once again in the face. "I'm gonna take my time killing you. Too bad you need to deliver a message or you'd be mine now."

Before I can utter a single word, the man rushes off from me. The back of his cut has a symbol I've never seen before. There's a devil holding a scythe. Devil's Rule is on the top rocker of the cut and there is no bottom rocker. I've never seen a cut with no bottom rocker but there was once one because I can see the cut looks newer in that spot. They must be waiting on the new ones claiming Benton Falls as their territory.

I want to sink to the ground and catch my breath, but I know I can't. The thing I have to focus on doing right now is getting ahold of someone at the club. I'm not sure how much damage has been done. Plus, there's no way I can drive back there now.

Instead of calling Playboy, I pull out my phone and squint my eyes until I can focus on Slim's number. Hopefully, he'll answer and I won't have to try to call anyone else. I click on his name and hold the phone to my ear as it begins to ring.

"Yeah?" he asks, answering the phone.

"Slim, are you alone?" I ask him.

"Yeah. What's wrong, Sam?" he asks, instantly alert.

"I've just been attacked in the parking lot of the store. Can you come get me? I don't know what's been done to me and I don't want Playboy to see me yet," I ask him.

"Do you need to go to the hospital?" he asks, as I hear a shuffling noise in the background.

"I don't think so. He punched me a few times and choked me. I have a cut in the side of my stomach, but I don't know how deep it is," I inform him.

"Fuck! Killer, you're with me," I hear him yell out before a door slams shut closely followed by another one.

"Slim, I think I need to go now," I tell him, my head feeling like it's going to explode.

"Not happenin', Sam," he tells me. "We'll be there in just a few minutes. Killer, get Doc here. Now!"

"I don't know, Slim. I'm tired," I tell him.

"Don't go to sleep, darlin'. Why are you in town alone?" he asks, trying to keep me talking to him.

"I just had a few things to pick up with Maddie, Tank, and the kids staying with us," I answer him.

I can hear Killer talking in the background and I'm guessing he's on the phone with Doc. I've seen him before and I'm honestly not sure if it's better to see him or go to the hospital. Slim and he can make the decision when they see me, though. Right now, I don't know anything I should be doing.

Pain and fear are starting to settle in my bones and I know it's a delayed reaction to what the monster did to me. Now, my adrenaline is crashing and everything is starting to hurt more. Especially my head.

"Darlin', you there?" Slim asks me. "Where are you at the store?"

"I'm sitting on the ground next to my car. There's a shopping cart right next to me too. I didn't even get a chance to put the groceries in the car," I tell him.

"I see you, darlin'," he tells me as I slowly turn my head to see his big truck pulling up to behind my car.

Slim and Killer quickly get out of the truck and help me off the ground. They put me in the back of Slim's truck, so I can lay across the backseat. With the door still open, I watch as Killer puts the groceries in the back of my car and shoves the cart in the corral next to where I parked.

"We'll have you back at the clubhouse in no time at all," Slim tells me as he shuts the door.

I know he's going to have to call Playboy and fill him in on what happened to me. It's the last thing I want to happen because he'll never let me out of his sight if he finds out. It's going to be impossible to hide the damage done to me from the maniac, though. Just like I know I'm going to have to fill Slim and the rest of the club in on what I was told and what I saw about the man.

Right now, I close my eyes and let the rumble of the truck's engine and Slim's voice lull me to sleep. It's not a deep sleep, but it's enough to let me relax some so I can try to get rid of this headache that's behind my eyes and throbbing where my head met the side of the car.

"Sam, you have to get up now," Slim suddenly says to me.

Killer and him once again help me up and I look around to see we're at the clubhouse already. I guess I dozed off a little harder than I thought I did. That's not what I meant to do, but it happened. Slim has a worried look on his face and I know the damage is worse than I thought it was in the beginning.

They walk me into the clubhouse and I hear a shocked gasp from the side, but I don't have the energy to see who it is.

"Not now," Slim says, continuing to move me toward the back of the clubhouse.

There's a room here for medical purposes and I've never had to be in it; until now. I let them lead me in there and see Doc waiting on us. They get me settled onto the bed and I know what Slim's about to do without him even telling me.

"Darlin', I need to go get Playboy and let him know what's goin' on. He'll want to see you with his own eyes," Slim tells me as Doc begins poking and prodding at my face.

"I know. I'll be right here," I say, trying to ease some of the tension in the room.

"Killer ain't leavin' until Playboy gets here to be with you," Slim says before turning and walking from the room.

"Nothin' is broken in your face. It will be tender and bruised for a while, though. Don't try to force your eyes open if the swelling gets worse," Doc tells me. "Where else are you injured. Besides the obvious cut on your side."

"The back of my head," I answer him. "It was slammed into the edge of my car."

Doc steps behind me and begins to exam the back of my head.

"There's a big goose egg there. No bleedin', though," he tells me.

Before he can move to the cut on my side, I hear a ton of commotion from outside this room. Playboy has arrived. Killer looks at me and a grin appears on his face. He's going to enjoy watching Playboy go out of his mind when he sees me. I flip him off, which makes him start laughing his ass off just before the door to the room slams open.

"What the fuck?" Playboy yells out. "What happened, baby? Why didn't you call me?"

"Because I knew this is how you'd react. I didn't want you to be this way at the store when I was already feeling like shit," I respond to him.

"Can I finish examin' her?" Doc asks before Playboy can rant anymore.

"Yeah," he answers him.

Doc asks me to relax back against the bed and he lifts my shirt up so he can clean and then exam the cut. Playboy brings a chair over to me from somewhere in the room and sits down next to my head. He holds my hand and looks at what Doc is doing. He's like an animal staring down its prey with the way he's watching the man work on me.

"It doesn't need any stitches. I'm goin' to finish cleanin' it out and put a few butterflies on it. I'll give you an antibiotic just to be on the safe side. You should call your doctor and get an appointment to make sure no damage was done inside. If you have anythin' else happen like bleedin' or anythin' get to the hospital immediately," Doc tells me.

"I will. Thank you," I respond.

Once Doc leaves the room, Slim, Stryker, Fox, and Tank make their way into the room with us. I know now is the time for me to let them know what happened so they can have church about it. Playboy is not going to be happy.

I look at Slim as he stands in the room by the door. He nods his head and makes his way over to his son's side. Slim knows Playboy is going to need him to keep him calm and not trash the medical room. Just like every man in this room knows the same. Tank walks to Playboy's other side and silently stands in case he's needed.

"What happened today, darlin'?" Slim finally asks me.

"I went to the store to get a few groceries. As I was standing in the checkout line, I felt like someone was watching me. I looked around and couldn't see anyone standing out. There were just a few customers in the store shopping while I was there," I begin. "Nothing happened until I walked out to the car. Suddenly there was someone following me. It's not like I could run to get away.

"Anyway, I went to open the back door of the car and that's when I was turned around and the guy slammed my head against the edge of the car. The guy punched me and then put his hand around my throat. He told me to deliver a message to you that a new club was in town and they want everything you have. Starting with the women."

I can feel the anger radiating from the men in the room. They're pissed for several reasons, I'm sure. Slim is looking at me with questions in his eyes.

"Did you see anythin' about the man?" Slim asks me.

"Yeah. His name is Rancor and the club name I saw when he turned around was Devils Rule on the top of the cut. There wasn't a bottom rocker, but there had been. He's the Sargent at Arms for the club," I answer him.

"If you saw him again, you'd know him?" Killer asks me.

"Yeah. I'll never forget the man who did this to me," I reply.

"He was the only one there?" Playboy asks me, gritting his teeth and tightening his hand on mine.

"As far as I know, he was the only man there. If there were more, I didn't see them," I tell him, wanting to comfort my man.

Playboy gives me a kiss on the top of my head and stands up so fast the chair he was sitting in goes flying backward. It barely misses both Slim and Tank. He storms from the room and slams the door shut behind him. Tank and Stryker silently follow him out of the room.

"Is there anythin' else you remember?" Slim asks me.

"I threw up on him, which made him tell me he would enjoy taking his time with me before taking his time to kill me," I tell him, glad Playboy isn't in the room to hear this part.

"Alright, darlin'. I'm gonna send Shy to the house with you. I want you in bed and restin'. Let Shy and Maddie take care of Caleb and anythin' else that needs to be done," Slim tells me. "Killer, you and Valor get her to the house and I want Valor to stay there until Playboy and Tank get there."

"On it, Prez," Killer answers as the rest of the men start to leave the room.

"Proud of you, darlin'," Slim tells me. "Killer, we'll just go over what Sam told us until you get to church. Tell Valor to keep his phone on him in case we need his vote."

Killer nods his head and waits for Valor to enter the room so we can head to the house. I lay back and close my eyes, not as tired this time, as we wait for him to come into the room. This is definitely not how I expected today to go when I got up this morning.

Chapter Twenty-Three

Playboy

WHEN MY DAD showed up at the house, I knew something was wrong. Not only is Sam not back yet, she's not answering her phone. I've called more than a dozen times panic is beginning to set in. I'm trying not to show it as the kids are all in the house with us.

"Playboy, need to come to the clubhouse," he says.

"What's goin' on?" I ask him.

"Not answerin' in here," he tells me, his tone leaving no room for arguments.

Nodding my head, I follow him out of the house with Tank walking out behind us. If something is going on, he's going to be here for us as a part of the family if nothing else. Tank may be a member of the Wild Kings MC, but he's also the son-in-law to the President of the Phantom Bastards MC and brother-in-law to the Vice President. Tank can sit in on whatever is going on right now since my dad isn't saying a word about it.

We get in my dad's truck, which is also weird. I sit in front while Tank slides in the backseat to ride to the clubhouse.

"Son, you need to prepare yourself. Sam was attacked at the grocery store. Doc is in with her now," he tells me.

"What the fuck? How did you know?" I ask him, my level of rage boiling in my body.

"She didn't want you to freak out at the store and lose your cool. She needs you to be calm right now," he tells me. "Don't go in there and lose your shit in the room with her. She's exhausted and I know she's tryin' to hold her shit together right now."

"I'll be fine. I just want to see her. I *need* to see her, dad," I tell him, almost pleading with him.

As soon as he pulls up to the clubhouse, I jump out of the truck and rush to get to Sam's side. Stryker tries to slow me down, not sure what's going on right now. I start yelling at him.

"Get. The. Fuck. Out. Of. My. Way," I yell at him.

"Playboy, what's goin' on?" he asks me, not moving.

"I need to get to my woman. You're stoppin' me," I answer, picking up the nearest chair to throw if Stryker doesn't move out of my way.

"Playboy, calm down," my dad barks out, coming in the clubhouse.

"Tell him to get the fuck outta my way then," I tell him, not turning around or moving at all.

"Stryker, let him go," my dad finally says after what seems like hours but is only seconds.

I push past Stryker and make my way down the hallway to get to the medical room. Nothing is going to stop me from laying eyes on my woman. I'm not angry she didn't call me, I'm upset she called my dad instead, but I get the reason why. I would've taken off and gone in search of the fuckers responsible for this if I'd been the one to show up.

Pushing the door to the makeshift exam room open harder than necessary, it slams against the wall. I see Killer standing in the room with a smirk on his face. Yeah, he's waiting for me to lose my shit.

Sam is lying in the bed we have in here and she looks like shit. Her eye and cheek is already bruised a darker purple. There's a small cut under her eye and her hair looks as if it's a tangled mess. Looking further down her body, I see blood soaking into her shirt. It takes me seconds to catalog what my woman looks like.

"What the fuck?" I yell out. "What happened, baby? Why didn't you call me?"

"Because I knew this is how you'd react. I didn't want you to be this way at the store when I was already feeling like shit," she responds to me.

"Can I finish examin' her?" Doc asks before I can rant anymore.

"Yeah," I answer him.

Grabbing a chair from the side of the room, I pull it close to the bed and hold her hand. My eyes never once leave what Doc's doing to my girl. He cleans out the cut on the side of her stomach and then exams it to decide if she needs stitches or not. After he puts a few butterflies on it, he gives her instructions and I let my mind wander.

Whoever did this to Sam is going to pay with their motherfucking life. I don't care who the hell it is or how many men I have to take out. They'll die for harming my woman and unborn babies.

My dad and a bunch of other guys come in the room and I know it's time for Sam to tell us what happened to her. I'm surprised my dad waited to hear the news, but it makes sense that he's not the only one to hear it and have to relay the news to us. More than one of us will hear the tale and be able to tell the rest of the guys who aren't in here.

While I listen to all the details of Sam's story, I can feel my rage simmering just below boiling point. I'm about to explode and I know it. I give her a kiss on the top of her head and stand up so fast the chair I was sitting in goes flying backward. It barely misses both my dad and Tank. I storm from the room and slam the door shut behind me. Tank and Stryker silently follow me out of the room.

I head to the bar and tap the counter with my fist. The Prospect slides me a shot and a beer. It's the last thing I need right now because there's no doubt in my mind we're going to have church. But, I need something to take the edge off and have the red haze I'm seeing disappear. I need to be able to focus on what's being said in church and make a rational decision.

Heading into the room we hold church in, I slam the door open and set my bottle down on the table. Tank is the only one to follow me in. He just stands back and lets me get my anger out.

Picking up the first chair I come to, I throw it against the wall to my left. It shatters into multiple pieces and collapses at my feet. After the first chair, I make my way around the table and destroy every single one of the chairs. The pictures hanging on the walls are smashed to the floor and there's now a brand-new hole in the wall close to the door.

As I pick up an ashtray off the table, my dad and the guys file in the room. Killer is the last to enter and I know it's because he took Sam home to rest.

"What the fuck happened in here?" my dad bellows out.

"Playboy lost his shit and rightfully so. He didn't do it in front of the women or anyone else. Everythin' in here can be replaced and no one got scared," Tank responds as I bend over and try to catch my breath.

"Okay. Well, I'd tell everyone to sit, but that's about impossible right now. So, get to your spot around the table and stand there. I'll have a Prospect clean this shit up when we're done," my dad says.

As soon as he's in his spot at the table, my dad picks up the gavel and bangs it against the table.

"Now, if you haven't heard by now, Sam was attacked when she went to the store a little while ago. She's okay, but banged up. Apparently, a new club is in town and they want our territory. If we don't comply, they're goin' to take it by force and start with the women," he tells the room.

You can feel the rage and tension from every man in the room. We don't tolerate anyone going after women. Especially not our women. They'll die slow, painful deaths for even insinuating they're going to take our land and go after our women.

"Playboy, because of your outburst, you're sittin' this one out," my dad says as I turn to look at him.

"What? I deserve to go out and find these fuckers!" I explode.

"No, you don't. Not this time, son," he responds. "You're goin' to stay at home with your woman and make sure nothin' happens to those babies. Take her to the doctor like Doc told you and make sure your woman stays right. Hold her, comfort her, and make sure she knows this could've happened to anyone."

"I deserve to be out there, makin' sure justice is dealt to these fuckers," I tell him, forcing myself to be calm.

"What club is this?" Fox asks, opening his laptop.

"Devils Rule," Killer answers. "No bottom rockers."

"The fuck?" Valor says.

"They're already to put Benton Falls as their bottom rocker it seems. We're not gonna let them have it. Now, I want you all out in shifts to find these fuckers. If you find one of them, call it in and follow them so we can figure out where they're goin'," my dad tells the room. "Playboy, see if Sam saw anythin' else on the cut that will help us out."

I nod my head, ready to get home and be with Sam and the rest of my family. If I can't be out helping the rest of the guys, I'm going to be home where I'm needed. And I need to make sure she made a doctor's appointment to double-check the babies.

"Killer and Stryker, hand out shifts. I'll take one now with Boy Scout and Valor," the men nod and remain in their seats.

My dad slams the gavel down on the table, dismissing us. We all leave the room and I make my way out of the clubhouse without talking to anyone. The only goal I have is getting home to see how Sam's doing. But, I need to take the long way around the clubhouse and to our house because I have to calm down a little before I face her.

Sam doesn't need to see me pissed off and wanting to kill someone with everything she's been through in the last little while. She needs me to be calm and help her get through this.

I walk in the house and Caleb comes running up to me. He wraps his arms around my legs and begins to cry. I pull him up into my arms and he buries his head in my neck. His tears hit my neck and slide down to my shirt collar and cut. I don't give a shit, though.

"Mama hurt," he tells me, sobs still choking him up.

"I know, buddy. She's gonna be okay, though. We just have to help her out for a few days until she can feel better," I tell him, rubbing my hand up and down his back.

"I help," he informs me, trying to stop crying.

"She'd like that, buddy. Why don't we go check on her," I say, heading to the stairs.

I get to our door and hear her talking to someone. I'm not sure if she's on the phone or if Maddie or Shy are in with her. Not that it matters to me. Caleb and I both need to see her.

Opening the door, I see Maddie and Sam sitting in the bed. They're talking and I know Maddie is trying to keep her mind off things. Hopefully, it's working.

"Hey," Sam says gently as she looks up at us. "You okay?"

"He's okay," I assure her. "Just worried about you. So, I think we're gonna have lunch in here with you and watch some movies."

"That sounds perfect," Sam responds with a smile on her face.

Maddie gets up and leaves the room. She hugs me and presses a kiss to Caleb's head as she passes us by. I place Caleb on the bed and head down to make us something to eat. Shy's already ahead of me, though, as she hands me three plates loaded down with food. I thank her and then head back up with my family.

Caleb is snuggled up next to Sam with his hand resting on her belly. I pull out my phone and take a picture of the two of them because I can't help myself. Getting close to the bed, I hand Sam her plate and wait for Caleb to sit up so he can eat. I don't care if we have to change the bed because of any messes.

Shy comes in to bring us drinks and then leaves the rest of us alone. We pick out a movie and eat our lunch. I keep my eyes on Sam instead of the movie because I need to reassure myself she's truly okay and here with us. This is where I'm going to be until the physical evidence of her attack is gone. My main concern is her mental health at this point. We'll cross that bridge when we get to it, though.

Chapter Twenty-Four

Sam

IT'S BEEN TWO days since I was attacked in the grocery store parking lot. I haven't left the house other than to go to the doctor's office the day after it happened. Playboy called and wanted to get me in as soon as possible to ensure nothing was wrong with the babies.

Doctor Sanchez told me there's nothing wrong with the babies. The cut did absolutely nothing to harm them or anything else internally. She went over the antibiotics Doc put me on and assured us they wouldn't do anything to harm the kids either. So, now it's just a matter of healing and going on with life until the babies are born.

Playboy, Tank, Maddie, and the kids have been outside and down to the clubhouse to hang out with everyone. I've remained home because I don't want to leave the safety of the house. While I know rationally no one can get in the compound, I still don't trust it that this club will do something to breach the boundaries and find me again.

Rancor threatened to kill me slowly and I know he means it. I don't want to die and leave my children without a mom. Especially Caleb. While he has gotten to know and love the men and women of the club, he's not close to them like he is with me. I worry about what will happen to him. So, the only way to make sure nothing happens to me is to stay inside and not go anywhere.

Kim came over to see me yesterday. We got talking about her designing book covers and how Kiera was one of her clients. She pulled out her laptop and showed me some of the work she's done and I fell in love with it. Then, she showed me how easy they are to make and let me try making one with her guidance. So, I'm going to be working with her to make book covers and other graphics for the authors she's been working with for some time.

The next thing I have to do is start a social media platform under her business page and try to add new clients. I'll be posting some pre-made covers I've done myself and things like that. It's definitely going to keep me busy and help me keep my mind off things instead of worrying about Rancor and the rest of his club being out there still.

Sitting on the couch, I open the laptop Kim brought me. She has an extra one I can use until I can get my own. So even though I can't work outside the house, I can work from home until the twins are born and then look for work. Or finish school and find a nursing job. Book cover designing can still happen when I'm not working or doing something with my family. At least that's my hope.

I open the first email Kim sent me. It contains everything I'll need to work on this cover for Keira. She's entrusting me to do this and I'm going to do the best job I can. I worry I'm going to mess it up, but I'm still learning, so I don't expect to be perfect the first time I do a cover alone.

Before I start working, I turn on the TV and put *Uneasy* by One Less Reason on. Now that I have background noise on, I pull up the program I need to design the cover and put in the picture of the model Kim sent in the files.

I read through it again and find pictures from Kim's account on a royalty-free website and find the perfect image to put in the background. Once I've inserted all the images and made sure they blend together, I save the file in a folder for Keira. Time to get started on the next one.

Before I can get to work, there's a brief knock on the door before I hear it open. My entire body tightens up and a cold sweat breaks out on my body. I freeze as my heart beats so fast and hard in my chest, I feel as if it's going to break free and fall to the floor in front of me. Even as Maddie comes into view, I can't stop my body's reaction.

"Sam, are you okay?" she asks, her voice laced with worry and fear. "Is it the babies?"

"I-I-I'm okay," I finally manage to stutter out. "I got scared when you came in the door is all."

"Why?" she asks.

"Because I thought you were the man who attacked me coming back for another round," I answer her.

"Oh, honey. He's not going to come back. The guys will find him before he can come here and get you. That's why you're not leaving the house, isn't it?" she asks me.

"I don't feel safe when I leave the house," I tell her truthfully. "I can be surrounded by everyone here, but I see glimpses of the man who attacked me out of the corner of my eye and in every shadow."

"Have you told Playboy this?" she questions me. "Or anyone else?"

I shake my head in response. Looking down at my hands wringing in my lap, I realize things could've changed in the blink of an eye and I may not be sitting here right now. I could be in the hospital or worse all because some man, some club, wants what the Phantom Bastards have worked their asses off for. They don't sit around and come in to take things from other people; they realize they want something and they work hard to obtain it.

The anger at this man's audacity has my rage building. How dare he come at a woman who's pregnant because he doesn't have balls enough to take a meeting with the club itself. If Rancor is the Sargent at Arms, that speaks about every man in the Devils Rule; they're cowards who would rather take their chance going after a woman instead of standing toe-to-toe with a man of equal size and strength.

"There you go," Maddie says, never once taking her eyes off me. "I can see the anger and fire in your eyes again. That's what you need to get through this and come out the other side."

"I'm still scared, Maddie. I don't think I ever want to leave the compound alone until I know every single man is taken care of and not left alive," I say honestly.

"It's completely natural and understandable. You know almost every single one of us have been through some shit and our men have had to rescue us and take care of the problem. What you need to think about is taking some self-defense classes once you have my nephews," she says.

"I think I might. I'll talk to Playboy about it," I respond.

"Now, what are you doing here?" she asks, coming over to look at the computer.

"I'm helping Kim out. She designs book covers and things so I'm taking some of the load from her since I can't work right now," I say.

"You're doing Keira's next book?" she asks, excitement filling her voice and closing her eyes. "We all get sneak peeks of the covers back home when she gets them back from Kim. I don't want to see it before she shows us."

"You can look. I've closed out of it," I say with a laugh. "I'm getting ready to do a premade cover if you want to watch me do that."

"Yes, please," she answers. "I've never watched one be made, so this is exciting."

For the next hour or so, I find images and put them together to design a book cover fit for a motorcycle club book. That's not all we're going to cater to, though, so I do one more with a shifter theme to it. Maddie silently watches me work and gives me praise as I show her the finished product.

"You're really good. Are you going to do this full time?" she asks when I save the file to send off to Kim later on.

"No. When I deliver the babies, I'm going back to school to finish my degree in nursing. I'm almost done if they'll take the credits I already earned. If I remember correctly, I have one semester left and I'll be done," I answer.

"Wow! That's amazing. I know Playboy will support your decision to go back and finish it."

"He already does. When he was locked up, he wanted me to go back and finish. I've been talking about it more and more recently. So, he wanted me to use the money he gave me and go back. Before I could do that, I gave his card back to Shy and moved from Benton Falls," I say.

"I heard you left from Dad, but he didn't say why," she says.

"Well, I found out I was pregnant and your brother refused to see or talk to me. He wouldn't even read any letters I sent him; just sent the first one back unopened. So, if I couldn't tell him I was pregnant, I didn't want one of the men or ol' ladies to inform him. Playboy had the right to hear the news first and hear it from me," I inform her genuinely.

"I love my brother but he can be a fucking idiot sometimes. Did he at least talk to you about it after he got out and found you?" Maddie asks.

"Yeah. And I get why he did what he did, just like I told him there was no way in hell I'd go through it again. If he goes inside again, I'll be right there to see him and talk to him whether he likes it or not," I answer.

"Good. You give him hell, Sam. Playboy has to get used to being part of a couple and not just making decisions for himself whenever he wants to. It's something they all have to learn," she says, giving me advice I need to remember.

I work on putting one more cover together for a premade before sending everything to Kim to look over and send me back notes on. As soon as

I'm done, I close out of everything and put the laptop away. Maddie is in the kitchen preparing dinner for a small impromptu cookout at our house today.

Tank and Maddie are heading back to Clifton Falls soon and we want to spend as much time with them as we can. It's not often we get to see them and with having kids, I want to get together with them more often. It's important to have family surrounding you and I want to watch our kids grow up. Together.

Caleb has been glued to the sides of Brax, Shawn, and Chance since they got here. I don't want to deprive him of their presence in his life so I have to figure out a way to get together with them on a more regular basis.

I walk out to the kitchen and sit on one of the stools so I can help Maddie prepare the salads and everything else for dinner. As long as I'm sitting down, Playboy can't bitch at me for doing too much. I get busy chopping up tomatoes and cheese for the pasta salad while Maddie prepares a potato salad. We're also going to have cheeseburgers, salt potatoes, and a few desserts Maddie has been hiding from Skylar.

Skylar sent up some fudge, brownies, and a few pies. We had the pies at the cookout with the club the other day, but Maddie knows how to be stingy and has hid the rest for just us. I can't wait to dive into those desserts because Skylar is amazing when it comes to baking and cooking. I'm surprised she hasn't opened her own shop up yet. She would make a killing there and sell out on a daily basis.

As we're preparing the meal, Playboy, Tank, Slim, Shy, Killer, Gwen, Fox, Kim, and the kids all show up. The music is turned on before Playboy and the guys make their way outside with a tub full of ice and beer so they can cook the burgers on the grill out back.

Today is what the club is all about. Family, friends, and being there for one another. We have one another's back and I know we don't have to worry about the outside threat as much as I made it out in my mind. Yes, I was the one attacked, but that doesn't mean that any single one of the men in this club won't have my back. So, I need to worry more about days like today than days where something bad happens.

Chapter Twenty-Five

Playboy

TODAY I HAVE to get back to work. I'm making my rounds through the club's businesses to see if they need anything or if the club who attacked my ol' lady have been causing any problems for them. The last thing we need is for these assholes to start costing us money because they want to take our shit from us.

Thankfully, Tank and Maddie are still in town and they're staying with Sam and Caleb while I'm out making my rounds this afternoon. I don't want to leave her alone, especially after we talked last night about her being scared to leave the house. Even while staying inside the gates of the clubhouse. I don't want her to be afraid of them because we will take care of it and end the fuckers once and for all.

So, she's going to be working while the kids are playing outside and then they're going to just relax and hang out. Maddie's going to try to get Sam to go outside to get some sun and just be out in the fresh air. I don't know if she'll go or if it will work, but I'm hoping it does. With Tank and Maddie there and her being outside right next to the house, I'm hoping she'll hang out with them all for a bit.

I've just left Bottoms up, the club's bar, and I'm making my way to Allure. If I were the guys in Devils Rule, I'd hit up our bar and strip club before any of the other business. So, those are the first two places on my list to go today. I need to check in with the girls anyway. Make sure they have what they need and no one's bothering them outside of the club.

As I'm riding through town, I notice a bike in front of me. The rider is wearing a cut and it looks as though it fits the description Sam gave of what she saw the day of her attack. It's hard to believe it's been a few days already since we learned of their existence and my woman was beaten.

When it looks as the biker is about to pull into the strip club, I gun the throttle and speed up to stop him before he gets inside. There's no way any of these fuckers are going to touch anyone who works for us or any of our businesses if we can help it.

As I speed up, the lone biker speeds up and doesn't turn into the club's parking lot. At least that's something I suppose. I push the Bluetooth button on my helmet and call my dad. He needs to know I'm following this fucker so we can find out where the hell they're staying and how many of them. Plus, I want this man to come back to the clubhouse with us for a little visit. I'm not playing games with these fuckers any longer.

"Yeah?" my dad asks, answering the phone.

"Dad, I'm followin' one of the fuckers as I speak to you," I tell him. "We're headin' out of town. I want a van to bring him back with me. I'm just goin' to let him think he's beatin' me for now and see where he heads."

"We're on it. I'll send Killer, Wood, and Valor out to find you. Your GPS still on so Fox can track you and let them know where you are?" he asks me.

"Yeah."

"They just left and will be with you as soon as they can. I'm gonna get Fox to trace you now so he can send them in your direction," my dad says. "Be careful, Playboy."

With that, he hangs up the phone and I continue in my pursuit of the bastard from Devils Rule. We're definitely heading out of town and I can only hope he's not on the phone with the rest of his club. If he is, I'm about to ride right into an ambush. That's the last thing I want, but it's a risk I'm willing to take if it means we can stop these wannabe men. As far as we're concerned, they're not men going after women. Especially pregnant women.

It looks as if we're going to the part of Benton Falls with the abandoned farms. There's several farms that have been left abandoned by the farmers who used to work the land for whatever reason they had. These homes and land have been sitting empty for so many years now, it's just a part of our town.

The club has looked into buying several of the properties, but we don't know what we'd do with the land just yet. I'm sure if we can come up with a sound plan, we'll follow through on it. Until then, these homes sit empty because no one wants to put in the time or effort to repair them or bring them up to code and date.

I hear the faint rumble of bikes following me and I glance in my side mirror to see Killer and the guys coming up on my tail. There's a van coming up behind them. I just hope they hold back just enough not to spook this damn guy. So, I hold one hand down when I'm sure Killer can see me and motion for him to back off. He flashes his light once to let me know he gets it.

They back off and I continue to follow the man as we turn down a dirt road toward one of the homes that have been left standing. Yeah, that's what I thought. I speed ahead and cut the fucker off. He has no choice but to slam on his breaks or take both of us out. Thankfully, he stops just before hitting me and I pull my gun from my cut and point it at him as Killer and the rest of the guys surround him.

Turning off my bike, the rest of the guys follow suit and there's sudden silence filling the air. I can hear the birds chirping and the faint sounds of traffic as cars head out of town for one reason or another. The highway isn't far from here so it's easy to hear without so many bikes rumbling at the same time.

"You're done fucker!" I tell him, not moving my gun from him.

"That's where you're wrong," he says, looking around at the four of us surrounding him with the van pulled up behind us.

"How do you figure?" I ask him.

"You think my club hasn't heard you follow me in here?" he questions. "You'll be surrounded by all of them in a matter of minutes."

"Really, cause I don't hear anyone comin' to your rescue," Killer says. "Based on your looks, I'd say everyone is too fucked up to even realize we're out here. Sucks ass for you though."

"You don't know shit about my club," the man tells us.

"I know you're not a man, not a single one of you. You go after women because they're weaker and smaller than you are. I also see the track marks on your arms tellin' me all I need to know about drug use. And, if I keep goin', your cut is an insult to every single club in the world. You don't respect the club enough to keep it clean," I tell the man in front of me. "So, you're gonna go for a ride with us and we're gonna have a little chat."

The man looks at me and his eyes are lifeless. There's no fear, anger, or anything else in them. Sam actually described Rancor's eyes much the same, so I look down at his name patch and see this man is Hades. He's the clubs Vice President. Good luck for us.

I put the kick stand down on my bike and Killer does the same thing. We walk on either side of Hades and pull him off the bike. He doesn't struggle because he knows he's not only outnumbered, but he's also out muscled. Hades won't put up a fight because we're not women he's going after. Fucking pussy.

We get him in the van and I watch as Valor pushes the man's bike to the thick brush on the side of the property. No one will be able to see it if they come or go from the property. Works out perfectly for us. Devils Rule won't know where their second in command is until we're ready for them to know we have him. Even then, they'll probably get him back in bits and pieces. It just depends on how cooperative Hades decides to be.

Craig, a new Prospect handcuffs Hades to the bar we have running down the side of the van. Then he uses zip ties to hold his ankles together. The final piece is slamming the duct tape over Hades' mouth. He won't have to hear him or worry about him finding something to escape with him handcuffed and zip tied.

"No stoppin'. Head straight back to the clubhouse. Killer and I will be in front while Valor and Wood stay behind you. Don't fuck up," I threaten Craig.

Before getting out of the van, I make sure the asshole doesn't have any weapons on him. He has nothing, that's why he didn't pull a damn gun. Apparently these jackasses feel as though we're going to cower down to them just because they told us they want our territory. Fuck that!

Killer and I get back on our bikes and turn around. Craig pulls out right behind us after turning the van around. I already know I don't have to worry about Wood or Valor because they know how this shit works. Even if Valor is one of the newest patched members. He's been around the club since birth and I'm proud to call him brother.

We're not stopped on the way back to the clubhouse. It takes us a half hour to make our way there and I release the breath I'd been holding as soon as we're through the gates. Killer leads Craig around to the side of the clubhouse where there's a door hidden in the wall that leads down to the basement. We don't know who's inside and there's no way in hell we'll bring Hades through there to get the lay of the land or anything else.

Parking my bike in my designated spot in the line of bikes, I shut off the engine and make my way inside. What I see shocks the hell out of me. There's not a single kid, ol' lady, or house bunny anywhere in the common room. None of the house bunnies are cleaning and another Prospect is behind the bar. This is an unusual occurrence for sure. Especially the house bunnies who are usually at least cleaning this early in the day.

Walking over to my dad, I accept the beer the Prospect hands me and take a seat next to him.

"You do okay?" he asks me.

"Yep. The package is delivered and goin' to be waitin' downstairs for us," I answer him.

"You want time to head home before we take care of business?" he asks me, knowing I hate leaving Sam alone right now.

"Nope. I want to know what their end game is and what we have to do to stop them," I reply.

My dad nods his head and waits for me to finish my beer. At this point, I'm just giving Craig and Killer time to string Hades up so we can go down and begin our interrogation. If we take our time and let him hang there for a little bit, maybe it will give Hades a chance to decide if he's going to talk or not. Either way, I'm going to get my hands bloody because I know it's his club that's out for us and his Sargent at Arms who put his hands on my woman. Hades will know it today too.

"We know who it is?" my dad asks once the Prospect isn't near our table.

"The Vice President, Hades," I tell him. "He should know about the attack on Sam and anythin' else we want to know unless the President is keepin' him outta the loop. But, I think there's a bunch of users in the club. Hades has track marks up both arms."

"So we really don't want these fuckwads in our town any longer than necessary?" my dad questions.

"Nope," I tell him as Killer and Craig make their way in the clubhouse. "Killer take a seat and have a drink. He give you any problems?"

"Not a single one. Hasn't uttered a damn word either. I'm wonderin' if we should strip him down and make sure he doesn't have a tracker on him somewhere," he returns.

"We'll do that when we get down there. I'm not worried about that band of pussies showin' up here," my dad says. "Let them. All the women and kids are up at Playboy's house and that's far enough away, they won't have a chance to get there."

I nod my head as the three of us sit there. We finish our drinks and talk nonsense while we're in the clubhouse. Since Devils Rule has come into town, we've been cautious. You never know if they've planted someone on the inside or gotten to one of the house bunnies when they've been in town. So, we don't talk about anything unless we're in church because Fox has the room set up with whatever gadgets he needs to disrupt any signals or interrupt any bugs so nothing can get through.

Chapter Twenty-Six

Sam

I KNOW PLAYBOY and the rest of the guys in the club have been working on something at the clubhouse. Yesterday when he got home, Playboy was in a better mood than he has been since I got attacked. I couldn't help but overhear him talking to Tank about catching one of the men in the club. Of course, I didn't say a single word because no one needs to know what's going on. And, I have no clue what they're doing with the man or if he's someone who is giving them information to take down the bad members of the club. It's not actually my business as long as they don't get near me again.

Today, I'm working on more covers while Tank and Maddie spend some time with Shy and Rayven before they head home tomorrow or the day after. Well, Maddie, at least, is spending time with her. I'm not sure if Tank is or if he's in the clubhouse with the rest of the guys. Gwen is keeping me company because she's bored as hell at Kim and Fox's house. They don't let her out of their sight unless she's at the clubhouse and it better not be a party night because she's not allowed anywhere near there.

I honestly feel horrible for Gwen. She came with Kim and Fox so she could finally have some freedom and experience things she's never been allowed to do before. Instead, I feel as if she's traded one prison for another one. Especially if

Killer is around. He really doesn't let her do a damn thing for his own reasons.

If I had been thinking, I would've brought her with me when I left Benton Falls because she needs to get out and go to school, date, and several other things she's never had a chance to do before. Gwen is an amazing young woman and she'll do amazing things if she's ever given a chance to spread her wings and fly. I have no doubt about that.

"Sam, can I talk to you for a minute?" she asks hesitantly, her eyes not meeting mine.

"Absolutely. What's going on?" I ask her as I save my work and close the laptop so she has my undivided attention.

"It's about Killer," she tells me, which isn't surprising in the least.

"Okay. What about him? Has he done something to hurt you?" I ask, leaning forward a little bit.

"No, he'd never intentionally hurt me," she says, hinting at the fact she is hurt.

"Okay, then what's going on?"

"Well, ever since I saw him when I came home with my sister, I've wanted him. He thinks I'm just some young, dumb girl with no experience for anything," she tells me. "I'm so tired of everyone seeing me as some young kid."

I don't say anything for a minute as I process what Gwen has told me. It's honestly not a secret about her wanting Killer; we all see it. I've also seen the looks he gives her when he doesn't think anyone is watching. Killer wants her bad and won't say a word to her or make any moves against her. He refuses to fight for what he wants and that's only going to end up with them both being miserable in the end.

"So, what are you going to do about it?"

"I don't know what to do. I've never experienced feelings like I have for him. I'm not dumb and I know he's having sex with the house bunnies, if not other women. My problem is, why does he treat me like no other woman in the club. He's nice, caring, loving even," Gwen tells me. "I have no experience with men other than the asshole my father let me be with. He used force and violence to get what he wanted, including my virginity. No one other than you knows that, though. Please don't say anything."

"I won't, Gwen. Whatever you share with me stays between you and me," I assure her. "I've been with a ton of guys, not by choice. Gwen, do you see the way Killer looks at you?"

"No. As far as I know, he sees me as a little sister because of Kim and Fox and nothing more," she tells me and I can see by the look on her face she's being completely honest.

"Honey, I wish there was some good advice I could give you. I just don't know Killer well enough to say why he's doing what he's doing. Maybe he wants you to get some experience under your belt before he makes you his. Honestly, the only one who can give you answers is the man himself," I tell her.

"I can't do that. Every time I get close to the man, he disappears without a trace," she says, forcing herself to laugh a little. "Sam, how can I make him see me as more than Kim's little sister?"

"Hmm. Another good question," I say, trying to come up with an answer for the young woman. "Well, you have to talk to him and figure out what he's looking for. Then show him you're that person if you are that person. Don't pretend to be something you're not, Gwen. If Killer doesn't want you for you, then he's not the man for you. Only time will tell and you'll have to talk to him, spend time with him, and figure out if he's truly the man you want and why."

Gwen takes a few minutes to think over what I've told her. She needs to do this on her own, none of the other ol' ladies or men in the club can give her information on how to get Killer to notice her; that's not the problem. The problem is something within Killer and how he feels toward Gwen. Or something he's waiting for.

"I get what you're saying and I want to talk to him, but I can't. I'll either talk to him or get over wanting him. Killer is Killer and he's going to do what he wants no matter what anyone thinks or how they feel about it," Gwen finally says. "I'll figure out what to do one way or another. Thank you, Sam."

"You're welcome, honey. You know I'm here to talk no matter what's going on, right?" I ask her.

"Yeah, I know. I appreciate it. So, I'll think over what you said and try to come up with something. Or I'll walk away from Killer. And the club," Gwen states.

"Woah! Why would you walk away from the club?" I ask her.

"Because it already hurts to see him go off with those bitches. If I have to keep doing it, it's going to drive me insane," she responds, wiping a tear from her eye.

"Please, don't walk away from us," I beg her. "I don't want to lose you as a friend or not have you in my life."

"You'll be in my life no matter what. I just won't come around the clubhouse anymore. We can meet up away from here or whatever you want to do. I'll even come up here to the house as long as Killer isn't here," Gwen assures me.

"I love you," I tell her.

"I love you too, Sam. You're my best friend," Gwen tells me.

This brings tears to my eyes as I realize I've never had a best friend before. I consider all the ol' ladies of the club my friend and I do hang out with Gwen the most, but I never thought to call her my best friend. I'm thinking it's because I've never had one so I don't know how to choose one. But, if I had to choose one right now, I'd have to say Gwen is my best friend.

For the next few hours, Gwen and I sit and talk. We laugh, she cries, and I listen to everything she has to say. I don't get any more work done, but that's okay. Our minds both turn to the men and what they're doing at the clubhouse; we all know they're there with someone else. I don't let us go down that path, though, because if they wanted us to know what they were doing, they'd have told us.

We prepare dinner together, and I call Maddie to bring Caleb home so he can eat with Gwen and me. She brings him home and we eat dinner before Gwen puts on a movie for us to watch. When Playboy eventually comes home, freshly showered and clothed, he sits with us as we enjoy our night.

Gwen eventually goes home when Fox comes to get her. She hugs me tight and promises me she'll think about what we talked about today. I sit on the couch until Playboy takes me upstairs for bed. He proceeds to show me the rest of the night, exactly how he feels about me. He shows me just how much love he feels for me as he worships my body. The perfect end to the perfect day.

Chapter Twenty-Seven

Playboy

TODAY IS THE day the club made a hard as hell decision. One we never dreamed we'd have to make. We need to keep our women and children safe. So, we decided in church to send them home with Tank and Maddie. It's the only way to keep them out of harm's way and ensure they're here with us after the dust has settled and we can go on about our business without the threat of Devils Rule taking them from us.

Grim and the Wild Kings are fully on board with them going there and making sure they're safe until we're done with these asshats. He even told us he'd send in some help if we need it. So, we're keeping them on standby for now. We won't know what direction to turn in until we know what this pathetic excuse for a club wants. It's more than just our territory and businesses; that we're sure of.

Now, I have to tell Sam she's going to be heading out with my sister and brother-in-law when they head home in an hour or so. It's not much time, but enough for everyone to pack some bags and say their goodbyes. Even the house bunnies are going with them because they're under our protection as much as the ol' ladies and children are. We don't want anything happening to them either.

Walking into the house, I hear music coming from the living room, but I don't see Sam or Caleb anywhere. I know Tank and Maddie are at the clubhouse because their things are already packed and loaded in their SUV. They're going to hang out there until everyone else is ready to go. So, now my dad, Fox, Wood and Boy Scout, and I are preparing our families to head to Clifton Falls.

"Sam, where you at, baby?" I holler out.

There's no answer and now I'm starting to worry. Caleb isn't coming out from anywhere, either. And I know for a fact he's not at the clubhouse since I just left there. Where the fuck are they?

My heart is racing in my chest as panic and fear grip me. I frantically search downstairs for my family and they aren't there. The laptop Sam's been using is out on the couch and the screen saver is flashing across the screen. So, she was doing work not too long ago.

I run through the house and the last room I come to, our bedroom, the door is shut. As I open the door, my heart stops in my chest. Sam and Caleb are in bed, completely passed out. They're snuggled up together and I don't want to disturb them. Unfortunately, we're on a time crunch and they need to get on the road soon if they're going to get to Clifton Falls before dark. And if we're going to go down and question the asshole in the basement.

We've been leaving him alone. I've gone down a few times and busted him up a little bit. Just giving him a taste of what's about to happen to him. The only reason we haven't gone full board yet is that we've been trying to figure out how to keep the women and kids safe and take out the rest of the club. Now that we have it figured out and they'll be leaving soon, we can get the answers we need.

"Sam. Sam, wake up," I whisper so I don't disturb Caleb just yet.

"Huh? Playboy?" she asks, her eyes barely open and her voice laced with sleep.

"Yeah, baby. Need you to get up so we can talk," I tell her.

"What's going on? Are you okay?" she asks her first thought never on herself.

"I'm okay, baby. I need you to get up and pack some bags for Caleb and you," I tell her.

"Why? We're not going anywhere," she tells me.

"Yeah, you are. All the women and kids are goin' to Clifton Falls with Tank and Maddie. You're gonna stay with the club until we can get this mess taken care of," I tell her as she fully wakes up.

"Why? I don't want to leave you. We have doctor's appointments and other things to do for the babies," she tries to argue.

"We'll still do all that, sweetheart. Right now, we need to eliminate the threat against us and have you guys out of the way, so we're not worried about you," I assure her.

"Fine. How long are we leaving for?" she asks, holding out her hands so I can help her up.

"I don't know yet. But, you'll have Shy, Kim, Gwen, Jennifer, and the kids there with you. Not to mention the ol' ladies and kids from Clifton

Falls," I say. "The time will fly by quicker than you think."

"You trying to convince me of that, or yourself?" she asks, heading into the closet.

I follow her in and pull down two suitcases for her to use. She grabs her dresses, some leggings and extra-large shirts she's been wearing. Next, she gets in the drawers and grabs some bras and panties to take with her. Sam won't worry about footwear because they only thing she's been wearing lately are her sandals. She can just slip them on and off and says they let her feet breathe. I don't give a shit what she wears on her feet as long as she's comfortable and not in any added pain.

Once she's done shoving her clothes in the suitcase, we head to Caleb's room so she can pack for him. She grabs him several short outfits, tee-shirts, jeans, his underwear and socks with his sandals and sneakers. Then she grabs some of his toys to take with them and packs a bag of things to do while they're in the SUV so he's occupied and the ride there.

"Are you sure we have to go?" she asks me once more as I grab the suitcase from her.

"Yeah, baby. If there were any other way, we'd have thought of it in church. We can't see another way out," I tell her.

"Okay. I'm going to miss you so much," she tells me, tears filling her eyes as she wraps her arms around my waist and leaning her head on my chest.

"I'm gonna miss you too, baby. I don't want you to go, but I can't be worryin' if somethin' else is gonna happen to you, Caleb, our babies, or any other woman and child here. These men don't know the meanin' of fightin' a real man," I say to her, holding her close for just a little while.

"I know. I trust you and the club will do what's best and handle the situation the best way possible," she answers, putting her full trust in me and the brothers in my club.

"It'll be over with before you know it. I'm gonna go wake Caleb up so we can head down to the clubhouse. Tank and my sister are waitin' for you all there," I tell her, not wanting to let go of her.

Walking into our room, I pick Caleb up from the bed. If we can keep him awake until we're at the clubhouse, I'd rather do it. The only reason we really have to wake him up is to go to the bathroom so they're not stopping every few minutes for all the kids to use the bathroom. There's going to be five kids going from our club plus my three nephews and niece. Plus, there's all the kids left at the clubhouse in Clifton Falls. I don't envy the Wild Kings men for the time being.

"Daddy?" Caleb questions once I pick him up.

For a minute, I'm stunned speechless. Caleb has never called me daddy before. Not that I don't feel as if I am his father, because as far as anyone is concerned I am. I'll always be his father.

"Yeah, buddy," I answer him finally.

"Where we going?" his sleepy little voice asks.

"You, mommy, and the rest of the kids and women are goin' on a trip. You'll be with Chance, Shawn, and Brax for longer," I respond.

"Really?" he asks, waking all the way up.

"Yeah, buddy."

"You coming, too?" he asks.

"Not this time," I say.

Caleb struggles to get out of my arms and I set him on the floor. Once I know he's steady on his feet, I let him go and step over to Sam. He's looking up at us with wonder and excitement in his eyes.

"Mama, we going on a trip!" he says excitedly.

"Yes, we are," she says.

"Let's head to the clubhouse," I tell them, picking the suitcases up and heading downstairs in front of Sam and Caleb.

"He called you Daddy, didn't he?" Sam asks once we get downstairs.

"Yeah. Why do you ask?"

"The smile hasn't left your face since you came out of the room with him," she answers as I feel the smile on my face get bigger. "Caleb, get your other sandals on so we can go."

Caleb sits down and puts his sandals on because he doesn't want to be delayed in getting to his cousins and friends. The sooner he's ready to go, the sooner he can be with them. Sam grabs the laptop, cord, her phone, phone cord, purse, and sunglasses while Caleb's putting them on. I hand her over the laptop case and she puts it inside to protect it on the ride there.

"You got everythin'?" I ask her before we head outside.

"Yeah, I think so," she answers with sadness in her voice.

The three of us head outside and load up the car to make the short trip to the clubhouse. Once I have the suitcases and bags in, Caleb's fastened in, and Sam's in the car, we head down and I park close to the front door right next to Shy's SUV. That's where Sam and Caleb will be riding anyway.

As soon as Caleb is unfastened, he gets out of the car and runs to the door of the clubhouse. It's already sitting open and he rushes right inside. I help Sam from the car as one of the Prospects comes out the door to load their bags in one of the SUVs. After telling him to put in Shy's SUV, I lead her inside and sit her down at a table.

"I'll be right back, baby," I tell her, heading over to my dad for a minute.

Talking to dad about when they're leaving, I find out we have a little bit of time still. Gwen isn't happy and doesn't want to leave Benton Falls. So, Fox and Kim have to talk her into leaving with the ol' ladies. This means I get to take Sam up to my room.

"We got Caleb," Maddie tells me, a knowing smile on her face.

Once we're in my room, I kick the door shut behind us and lock it. Sam is already stripping out of her clothes as I shrug out of my cut and hang it on the back of the door. It takes me seconds to strip out of my own clothes and join my woman on our bed.

"This is gonna be fast, baby. I'm sorry I can't take my time with you before you leave," I tell her honestly.

"I know. I just want you," she says, looking up at me with love shining from her eyes.

I lean down and kiss her. Sam opens her mouth for me and our tongues tangle. I reach up to find her nipple and pinch and pull it between my fingers. She moans into my mouth and arches slightly up into me, her belly getting in between us. I roll us to the side so she's more comfortable.

Breaking the kiss, I kiss a path from the corner of her mouth to her chest. Stopping only to suck gently on her neck. Taking a nipple in my mouth, I suck and bite down on it just enough to cause her a little pain with her pleasure. Sam likes it that way and I try to accommodate her as much as possible given her pregnancy.

"Griffin, we don't have time for this," she tells me, reminding me we have to make this quick.

"I know, baby."

I pick her leg up and bring it over my hip. Reaching between us, I check to make sure she's ready for me and my girl definitely is. Gripping my cock in hand, I line myself up with her opening and slide inside. This is definitely where I want to be buried every second of every day.

Without hesitation, I slide in and out of her tight, wet pussy. I have to hold myself back from slamming into her the way I want to because there's no way I'm doing anything to hurt her or the babies. No rough sex, I keep telling myself.

I also know Sam won't be able to get off if there's not a little bit of rough in there. So, I increase my speed just a little and run a hand down Sam's body. Once I get to her clit, I rub it before pinching in with just enough force to give her the bite of pain she needs. Even if she's not ready to fly over the edge yet.

Curving my body around Sam's belly where our sons lay nestled safe and sound, I kiss her. Sam deepens the kiss this time as I open my mouth to her and let her control our kiss. When she finally breaks free, her hands are tangled in my hair and I pinch her clit once again.

"Griffin!" she yells out, her orgasm sneaks up on her.

Sam's body goes taut and she continues to moan out as wave after wave crashes over her. Three more thrusts into her body and I'm following her over the edge.

"Sam!" I roar out and continue sliding in and out of her body to prolong our mutual releases.

When I finally stop sliding in and out of her body, I remain firmly in place, surrounded by her wet heat still.

"I love you so much, Griffin," she tells me when our breathing slows down, a tear sliding down her face. "I'm going to miss you more than you know."

"I love you too, baby. I'm goin' to miss you too. It's not that I want you to leave, I need you to leave so I can make sure you're safe and protected until we get this taken care of," I tell her, placing a soft kiss against her lips.

I finally slide out of her and walk to the bathroom. Once I'm cleaned up, I wet a washcloth with warm water and make my way back out to clean Sam up. It's not long before I'm helping her out of bed so she can get dressed again for us to make our way back out to the common room where I see everyone waiting for us. Catcalls and whistles erupt as Sam turns multiple shades of red and buries her head in my chest.

"Knock it off," I tell them. "Everythin' ready to go?"

"Yep. Just waitin' on you two," my dad answers.

"I'm ready to go now," Sam responds, her voice small and just above a whisper.

Everyone leaving, gets up, and walks out to the SUVs waiting in the parking lot for them.

"Mama, can I ride with Tank?" Caleb asks as I go to lift him up in the SUV.

"I don't know, honey. I think you should ride with me," Sam answers.

"Sam, it's really no problem. We were thinkin' Caleb could ride with us and Zoey can ride with you guys and help keep an eye on Rayven while you're drivin'," Tank answers.

"Well, I guess if it's okay with you guys, he can. Here, take this bag so he things to do. Caleb tends not to like long car rides," Sam answers, handing Tank the bag she packed earlier.

"Alright. Let us know if you have to pull over and stop for a bit," he returns, heading off to his SUV.

"Okay, baby. I'll see you soon. Call me when you get there and we'll talk as often as possible," I tell Sam, leaning in to get a kiss.

"I love you," she tells me.

"Love you, too," I respond, closing her safely in the SUV.

We all stand outside and watch as the SUVs pull away from the clubhouse. This isn't the norm for our club and it feels as if my heart is leaving, making my world go black. Now, it's time for business.

With the women and kids away from the clubhouse, the officers of the club and I make our way down to the basement where our friend is staying. I'm the first one in the room and the smells assault me to the point, I pull my bandana from my back pocket to cover my nose and mouth. As I said, he's been down here for a day or two.

"You ready to talk?" I growl out toward the asshole strung up from the rafters in the ceiling.

"Fuck. You," he grits out, spitting at my feet.

"You're not my fuckin' type. So, I'm gonna ask you one more time; are you ready to talk?" I ask again, stepping up and landing a punch to his ribs, digging my knuckles in just a little bit deeper.

"I ain't telling you shit," he grits out as his eyes water.

"Killer, why don't you bring me a knife. You know the one I like to use," I say, never once taking my eyes off the man in front of me.

I watch as Hades watches Killer's every move. He saunters over to the stand loaded down with our 'tools' of the trade. Killer picks up the largest knife on the table and runs the blade against his own skin. Hades can see how sharp the damn thing is and his eyes bug out slightly.

I place the blade against his chest and dig the tip of the blade in slightly. Once I know I have his attention, I look into his eyes and see his fear for the first time. When I start sliding the blade down his chest, directly in the middle, he screams out.

"No one's gonna hear you down here," I tell him, acting as if people are still upstairs.

He won't ever know the ol' ladies and kids were sent away. Not that he'll be leaving here alive. Hades will meet his maker sooner rather than later.

"I'll. Talk," he finally says as I get to his belly button.

"What are you guys doin' here?" I ask him, pulling the blade from his skin but letting it hover over him.

"We want your territory," he answers me after a minute, regret and hatred filling his eyes.

"Why?" Slim asks, not my dad right now.

"Because you've got everything settled and set up already," Hades answers.

"So, your club doesn't have a single real man in it to put in the time and effort it takes to start your own club in a new territory? You're a bunch of fuckin' pussies?" I ask him.

"We're not fucking pussies!" he yells out, trying to kick out at me even though he's chained to the floor.

"Then why take over our territory because it's already established?" Slim asks him.

"Because you have the cartel in your pocket and Terror wants that hook-up," he finally answers, hating he's ratting his club out.

"Why does he want the cartel in his pocket?" I ask him.

"Because he wants to have help in running the girls from the states south of the border," Hades answers me. "Among other things."

"And you guys think the cartel is just going to start workin' with you?" Slim asks. "That's not how it works."

Hades doesn't say a word.

"Anyone check him for a phone?" Killer asks.

"Got it, it's locked but I just need a thumbprint," Fox answers me.

"Get it," I respond, holding out the fuckers thumb for Fox.

Fox walks close and I know Hades wants to pull his thumb back from me.

"Either you cooperate or you're goin' to lose your fuckin' thumb," I growl out.

Hades doesn't move a muscle as Fox gets his print to open the phone. Once it's open, he goes in to change it up, so there's no lock on the phone in case we need to get back into it. Fox always thinks of that shit; it never occurred to me to make sure the password was off once we got into the phone. That's why he's our tech guy.

"Don't need him anymore," Fox lets my dad know as he sets the phone down on the counter behind the guys.

"What are you gonna do now?" Hades asks.

"Well, do you have anythin' else to tell us?" I ask him.

"What do you wanna know?" he questions back.

"Who gave the order to put their hands on my ol' lady? Who's pregnant with my babies," I question the man.

"Terror told us if we saw one of the women from the club out, to give them a message. Rancor took it too far," Hades says, trying to make it seem as if it was all Rancor's doing.

I see his eyes shifting for the first time since I started asking questions. Now, I know he's lying and the order came from Terror. Or himself.

"Fellas, I don't want to talk to him anymore," I say, turning my back on the fuck.

Without using words, I let my dad know he's lying about the situation with my woman. He nods his head in response. Turning back around, I lay into Hades with the blade. I cut his entire body with slices that aren't deep enough to kill him. The rest of the guys are going to get their licks in on him too.

Once I'm done, Killer steps up and takes his turn. He lands punch after punch onto Hades' body before grabbing the lemon juice and splashing it liberally onto his body and the cuts I already placed on him.

One by one, the officers of the Phantom Bastards step up to take their shots on Hades. As soon as we're done, my dad pours the cheap bottle of liquor we have down here over Hades' entire body before grabbing the blowtorch and lighting it up. Hades pisses himself and begins to scream in earnest before my dad even gets close to his body. I'm sure he's seen this done a time or two.

"You wanna fuck with the Phantom Bastards and lay hands on our ol' ladies?" my dad questions. "Feel our wrath and we'll see you in fuckin' hell!"

Without hesitation, my dad lights the fucker on fire. The men who haven't covered their faces already, are now covering their noses and trying not to breathe in the acrid smell of burning flesh.

Hades is screaming as the flames lick up and down his body. They don't fade out until he dies from the wounds inflicted on his beaten and battered body. Now, we have more work in front of us since we have his phone. We'll have to check out what he's got in it and then make a plan from there.

"Church in one hour. Get a drink or whatever you gotta do and take a shower before headin' in," my dad tells us all as we make our way out of the basement.

The Prospects will take care of the mess and bury the body so he won't be found. We don't need anyone finding him and pointing the finger at us. No one will know unless we have a sit down with Terror or whoever else is currently in charge of Devils Rule. My dad will only let that slip out if the man in charge pushes his buttons too much. We know better than to admit to anything like that.

Chapter Twenty-Eight

Sam

WE GOT TO the Wild Kings MC clubhouse yesterday. Even though I got to hear Playboy's voice last night and this morning, I'm missing him more than I ever thought I would. And, I'm worried as hell about him because I know what they're doing is dangerous and could lead to him being hurt or worse. It could happen to any single one of the men I have come to think of as family.

Skylar and the rest of the women have been trying to keep us busy though. Last night, we had a large dinner when we got there. Then we spent time getting settled since none of us know how long we're going to be here. Today, we're hanging out and going to cook and bake in a little bit for an impromptu cookout.

The house bunnies are giving everyone a wide berth. Especially the club girls from the Wild Kings. While they don't mind staking a claim at our clubhouse, they don't want to piss anyone off here. Well, most of them don't. Some of the bolder ones don't give a fuck if the man is single or has an ol' lady. Kareena, one of the newest house bunnies, is bold as fuck and is about to get bitch slapped by Bailey.

"I'm telling you guys, if that bitch doesn't get the fuck away from my man, she's going to lose every single finger," Bailey growls out as we sit together at two tables the men pushed together.

I watch as Kareena steps in between Grim's legs as he sits at the bar, talking to Joker, Cage, and Tank. He's been pushing her away and I know he's about to again when Bailey jumps up from her chair.

"Uh, oh!" Skylar says, sitting next to me and watching her sister-in-law head for her ol' man and husband.

We watch as Bailey walks up to the bar and bumps Kareena out of her way with her hips before stepping in between her husband's legs. She leans in and kisses him like her life depends on it. At the same time, I keep my eyes on the house bunny. She's pissed as hell and I know is about to open her stupid ass mouth.

"Bitch, I don't know who you think you are. Get the fuck away from him," Kareena yells as everyone in the common room shut up and wait to see what's going to happen.

"Skank, I don't know who the fuck you think you're talking to. See this rag on my back? It means the man you had your nasty, disease-infested hands on, is *my* fucking man. I suggest you back the fuck off and go back with the rest of the skanks," Bailey says, keeping her voice low.

"You can't satisfy him. That's why he wasn't pushing me away," Kareena says, digging her own hole deeper and deeper.

"The fuck you say?" Grim growls out.

"Baby, I got this bitch. Cause you know I keep you extremely satisfied. Just like I did this morning," Bailey retorts, turning her attention back to Kareena. "Now, I know you're one of the newer house bunnies, so I'm gonna give you a little lesson. In this clubhouse, I'm the Queen bitch. You listen to me while you're here and don't *ever* touch a man who's taken. If I see it again, you'll be out on your ass and I'll take it up with Slim."

"You can't tell me shit," Kareena says. "As you said, I'm not from here and I don't have to listen to you at all."

Bailey loses her shit. She rears back and punches Kareena dead in the face. Kareena immediately begins to shriek, cry, and cover her nose as it begins to bleed.

"You better watch your back," Kareena says as one of the other women come over to get her.

"Leave her alone," Grim bellows out. "Bitch, you're no longer welcome here. You don't come in here and threaten my ol' lady after she tells you the rules. Which you heard last night. So, I'm gonna call Slim and I know you'll no longer be welcome in his clubhouse either. We don't tolerate that shit."

For a minute, Kareena stands there staring at Grim like she has no clue what he's just said to her. When Tank and Cage go to step closer to her, she takes off. Only instead of going to the door to leave, she heads to the hallway leading to the rooms we're staying in. Kareena doesn't make it too far. One of the other men, a Prospect, grabs her by the arm and leads her from the clubhouse. She's bitching and screaming the entire time.

Well, shit. This isn't how I wanted our stay here to start. I feel like this is all my fault and I just want to disappear into the ground.

"Sam, don't. This isn't on you," Grim says, seeing the look on my face. "Your men are takin' care of shit and we're keepin' an eye on you until it's done. That bitch was gonna pull shit no matter where you were."

I nod my head at him and place my hands under the table, wringing them in my lap. Skylar places a comforting hand on my shoulder before getting up.

"Alright, ladies, why don't we start making food while the guys go start the grills up?" she asks, trying to get everything back to normal. "Sam, you stay here and I'll bring you out something to eat."

"No. I'd rather be in the kitchen with you guys," I answer as Caleb and the rest of the kids run into the common room.

"Mama!" he yells out, heading straight for me. "Look what I found."

Caleb stops just before me and holds his hand out to show me a worm. It's the longest one I've ever seen and it's squirming around on his hand. While I'm grossed out by it, he's so proud.

"That's cool. Where did you find it?" I ask, feigning interest.

"Out by the playground," he answers, a large smile on his face. "I wish Playboy and Papi could see it."

My little boy's face drops and I can see the sadness on his face. It's only been a day and we both miss him so much. There's nothing I can do to take this pain away from him.

"Me too, buddy," I tell him, my own face mirroring his.

Tank comes over with his boys and stands behind Caleb with a smile on his face.

"What you got there, buddy?" he asks, as Caleb turns his attention to the big man.

"A worm," he proudly answers, showing Tank his prize.

"Let's go out and see if we can find more," Tank says, shooting me a wink while turning the boys to head back outside.

Once the boys and Tank are out of the common room, we all burst into laughter. That's the last thing I expected to see when they all came running inside. On the one hand, Caleb is excited because he's with his cousins and he's met the other kids in the Wild Kings family. But on the other one, he's sad because he's missing Playboy and the rest of the guys from home.

While everyone else is still chuckling over boys and the things they find when playing outside. I stop laughing and look down at the bottled water sitting in front of me. My eyes fill with tears as I think of Playboy and what he's doing right now. This is even harder than when I left Benton Falls on my own because Playboy is out of jail and I know he's about to do something dangerous.

"Hey, you okay?" Keira asks, walking up and sitting down next to me.

"No. I miss Playboy so much. And Caleb does too. I can't do anything to make it better for him," I answer her honestly.

"I know, honey. But, it will be over soon and then you'll be back home. And, you have to look forward to having these beautiful babies soon," she says, smiling up at me.

I nod my head at her. We sit in silence for a minute before a mischievous smile fills her face. I'm not sure I'm going to like what she's about to say.

"So, Kim tells me you designed my new cover?" she asks.

"I did. I hope you like it. It's my first one ever," I say in response.

"I absolutely love it!" she says, pulling out her phone and showing me it's saved in her photos.

"Did you want me to change anything on it?" I ask her.

"Not at all. You captured what I wanted on it perfectly," Keira tells me. "Now, I think it's time we reveal this bad boy to the rest of the girls and see what they think."

"Oh, um, well, I'm not sure about that," I tell her, my nerves kicking up at the thought of others seeing it.

"They don't know who my designer is," Keira says. "But, I think that may change right now."

Keira and Cage help me out of the chair and I slowly follow her to the kitchen. Skylar is making sandwiches while the rest of the women are pulling various ingredients out of the refrigerator and cupboards to make salads and different side dishes for the cookout today.

"Ladies, I have something to show you," Keira says, once I've been sat at a table and a bowl is placed in front of me.

"What's that?" Whitney asks.

Keira pulls her phone out of her pocket once again and clicks on the gallery app to pull up her photos. Once she has the cover I designed on the screen, she turns it around to show the rest of the women standing around in the enormous kitchen. They all 'ooh' and 'ahh' over it before Melody speaks up.

"That's a fucking gorgeous cover, Keira," she says as my cheeks fill with a blush.

If the women don't know yet who designed the cover, they will if they take one look at my flaming red face. I can't believe they actually like it.

"Well, I'd like to fill you in on a little secret. I've talked to my designers and they've given me the okay to let you all know who they are," Keira says. "Well, kind of. I'd like to introduce you to them."

Keira walks over to the table I'm sitting at and Kim joins us there. For what feels like forever, no one says a word. The ol' ladies just stare at us in shocked silence.

"Are you fucking kidding me?" Bailey finally asks.

"Not at all. Kim's been the main one designing them but Sam did the one I just showed you. It's her first-ever cover design and I think it's kick-ass," Keira tells them.

"It definitely is," Kim agrees wholeheartedly.

"Thank you," I respond with my head down.

"Sam, Kim, you both have real talent and I can't believe it's been you all this time," Skylar says, bringing me over a plate with a sandwich on it.

We all sit down to eat while the Prospects come in and grab the trays of sandwiches to take outside to the men and kids. They'll make sure the kids take a break from playing and eat. A second Prospect comes in to grab drinks, chips, and a few snacks for the kids.

Once we're done eating, we begin to chop vegetables, boil eggs, pasta, potatoes, and mix up brownies, cake, and other delicious looking desserts. We talk, laugh, and just enjoy our time together. We'll have to start doing this more when we get home because this is the most fun I've had in a long time. And, it's nice to see women from two different clubs getting along so good without the normal jealousy and all that other shit usually associated with women when they get together; we're just a bunch of women content to be with one another.

My mind never strays from Playboy, though. I can't stop thinking about him and what's going on with him right now. If I could've talked him out of dealing with this shit, I would have. But I know he wouldn't be the man I love if he wasn't taking care of things and making sure Benton Falls is safe for the people of the town and his family members. None of the men in Phantom Bastards would.

Chapter Twenty-Nine

Playboy

TODAY, SLIM AND I meet with Terror. We're meeting on neutral ground and it's only going to be him and one other man since he no longer has access to his Vice President. Not that we're going to tell him where Hades is now. And, it's not like he's going to see the rest of our men there. They've already left and gotten into place so no one else will find them. If anything happens, our guys will have our backs and won't let us die without a fight.

We're meeting in an empty field on the outskirts of town. It's not far from where Terror and his band of pussies are staying. Fox has already looked at the place where meeting Terror and his other man and scouted the best spots to hide. We've gone over every detail with a fine-tooth comb and now it's almost time for us to leave here and head out.

"You ready, son?" my dad asks me, coming out of his office.

"Yeah. Let's get this done so the women and kids can come home," I answer him.

We head out of the clubhouse and make our way to our bikes. I straddle mine and wish I could talk to Sam before we leave. I've got a gut feeling today isn't going to go how we plan on it going. Knowing we have the rest of our men at our backs isn't making the feeling lessen either.

"You good?" my dad asks before we turn our bikes on.

"Just got a gut feelin'," I respond.

"In and out," he says, finally firing up his bike as I follow suit.

It takes us almost a half hour to get to the designated meeting spot. Once we're there, I hear the rumble of more bikes coming in. More than two bikes like it's supposed to be from Terror and his merry band of bitches. What the actual fuck?

Turning my head, I see him riding in with a total of ten bikes. Yeah, he can't stick to the game plan because he knows he should fear us. So, he's trying to show he's the big man by bringing more than just one other guy. I guess it's a good thing we planned for this and our men are placed throughout the area. They'll never know what hit them.

"Slim, good to see you follow directions," a man says, getting off his bike and walking toward us.

"You must be terror. Not surprised to see you don't stick to your word," Slim says; not in dad mode right now, he's my President.

"Why should I?" Terror asks.

"Because a man who doesn't stick to his word isn't a fuckin' man in my book," Slim answers.

"The fuck you just say to me?" Terror questions as his men move closer to us and pulling their weapons on us.

"You heard me the first time. Now, I don't want to be out here all day. What the fuck do you want?" Slim asks him.

"It's simple. I want your territory and your contact in the cartel," Terror responds.

"You think I'm gonna give that to you, why?" he asks.

"Because you're too old to run a club and everyone else in the club are too fucking pussy whipped. They only care about the women and kids. No way to be when you're in a club," he answers.

"So, you think I'm too old and we're all pussy whipped because we got love and respect for our women? Women who support us, take care of us, give us beautiful kids who will continue the club, and have our backs more than anyone else on Earth. You've got it all twisted," Slim tells him, getting in his face to show him exactly what he thinks of Terror's train of thought.

"That's why this dumbfuck lost his shit when we went after his woman?" another man questions. "Yeah, we saw it."

"Fuck you, bitch," I spit out, looking at the man closer. "It seems you're the one who likes to put his hands on property that's not yours. You come near my ol' lady again and I'll gut you where you stand."

"You're right, I did. And, it's only a matter of time before that bitch is mine," Rancor says, trying to taunt me because they think we're outnumbered.

"Now, Terror, you know my boys and me aren't givin' up shit. So, what's this really about?" Slim asks, turning his attention back to the so-called President.

"I just told you what it's about. Why the fuck would I put in the work to make something happen when it's already all set up for me," Terror says.

"And what makes you think the cartel is goin' to work with you fuckwads?" I ask. "He can't stand so-called men like you."

"Slim, you better get your boy on a fucking leash before I put a bullet in his fucking head," Terror threatens me.

"Fuckin' try it," I growl out.

Terror raises his gun and points it directly at my head. I take a step toward him and show I'm not afraid of his fucking ass. These men are just playing at being men and I know he's not man enough to pull the damn trigger.

I never once take my eyes from his as everyone surrounding us don't move or breathe at this moment. As I stare into his eyes, I can see the fear Terror is trying to hide. He knows he's going to lose and it's just a matter of time before he's sent to the reaper curtesy of the Phantom Bastards. A smile breaks out on my face as I walk until the gun is pressed up against my skin. Terror knows I have his fucking number and he's pissed as hell about it.

"You're fucking crazy," Terror finally says while lowering his gun. "You have twenty-four hours to make the right decision or we're going to take everything you love away. Starting with making a trip to Clifton Falls for your women.

Yeah, we know you shipped them all out, dumb fuckers."

"I'll call you tomorrow then," Slim says, as Terror turns his back on us.

He's really not a smart man to turn his back on my dad after just pissing him the hell off. He may not be showing how pissed he is right now, but my dad is ready to snap Terror's neck with his bare hands. Terror is going to meet his maker before he gets close to our women.

"Let's head back. We need to get ahold of a few people before tomorrow," my dad says as we walk the few steps to our bikes. "And don't ever pull a fuckin' stunt like that again."

"He's scared shitless, dad. If he weren't, I wouldn't have done it," I respond, putting my helmet on and straddling my bike.

"Don't give a fuck. Never. Again," he tells me again, turning on his bike so I can't respond to him.

We pull out and make our way back to the clubhouse. The rest of the guys will meet us there and then we'll formulate a game plan. I'm tired of dealing with these pussies.

I want my woman and son home. And, I want to be able to see her belly growing with our children and feel them move in her. These are the things I'm missing out on. And I miss Caleb and his crazy antics. I can't wait for them to come back to me so I can wrap them in my arms and hold them close.

Dad and I are sitting at the bar when the rest of the guys walk through the door. It took them a lot longer because they had to walk to the hidden van from their spots and then drive back. They all join us and the Prospects run behind the bar to start filling drinks and get them what they want so we can talk.

"Goin' to church?" Stryker asks.

"Nope. Gonna talk right here. No one's here to hear us. Fox, do your thing," my dad replies.

Fox heads to his room and comes back a few minutes later with some device in his hand. While we finish our drinks, he makes his way around the entire room to make sure there's no bugs planted in here before we start talking. The second he's done, he smashes five bugs that were placed around the room and then places a second device on the top of the bar. Once he hits a button, he looks at my dad.

"All clear now," he states.

"What's that?" I ask him.

"It's a signal jammer. No one will hear anythin' if I missed one or there's somethin' else in here that can't be picked up by this," Fox answers, holding up the first device in his hands.

"They know the women and kids are in Clifton Falls. I'm not gonna bring Grim and his guys into this war when they're not a part of it," my dad says, picking his beer up to his mouth. "I'm callin' for them to come home. No sense in them bein' there if Terror and his pussies know they're there."

"Want me to call Grim?" I ask him, already pulling out my phone.

"Yeah. They're stayin' in the clubhouse so they're all together. No one is stayin' in their homes on the compound," my dad says as I walk away. "I'll call our contacts tomorrow when we've had some time to think about our next move. I want all ideas and plans ready in an hour."

I place the call to Grim and let him know the women and kids need to come home. What he tells me, has me pissed even more than our meeting with Terror and is bitches.

"Dad, need to talk," I say once I'm off the phone. "Seems Kareena, the new house bunny, started shit with Bailey and Grim threw her out of the clubhouse. Went so far as to threaten her after Bailey punched her for not listenin' and puttin' her hands all over Grim."

"Don't need that fuckin' bitch here then. Didn't like or trust her from the beginnin'," he answers.

Nodding my head, I agree with him. Her timing here just doesn't make sense. She showed up just before the Devils Rule made a move and we knew they were in town. I've been keeping an eye on her, but I'm not always here. So, she can kick feet and get the fuck out. She's not hitching a ride back with our women. Not to mention that no one should know where our women and kids were taken. Fucking bitch!

"Grim, Tank, Cage, and Rage are gonna head out in less than a half-hour. They're only givin' the women time to get their shit around so they can head out," I inform my dad.

"Got it. Make sure shit's ready. Prospects, make sure everythin' is stocked. I want two of you goin' out to get whatever we need. Valor, you go with them," he says, fully in President mode right now.

For the next hour, I go into my room and make sure everything is ready for when Sam and Caleb come home. I change the bed, clean up the room, make sure extra pillows are on the bed for Sam, and make sure Caleb's things are ready too. He's going from being surrounded by kids, to not having very many around. It's going to suck, but we have no choice in the matter right now.

Chapter Thirty

Sam

WE WERE ALL sitting outside around one of the fire pits when Grim gets a call and takes off from our circle. He doesn't look at anyone, but Tank and Cage follow him and make sure no one else gets close. I'm not sure what's going on as my heart begins to race and I can't take my eyes off him.

"Everything will be okay," Shy says, leaning over closer to me.

I nod my head to let her know I heard her, but still don't move a muscle. My attention is firmly on Grim and the facial expressions he's making. Or rather the lack of emotions or expressions on his face. I'm not sure if this is a good thing or bad thing right now.

My fear level ratchets up several notches as I try to calm myself down for the babies I'm carrying and the kids running around the yard. It's not working, though, as I sense the other women moving around me to close in on me and make sure I'm okay while we wait to find out what's going on.

The only time I take my eyes off Grim, who's still on the phone, is to look at Caleb playing with the rest of the kids. When I notice them surrounding my son, I take a shuddering breath and slowly release it, turning my attention back to the man on the phone who knows something is going on with my man and the rest of the men in the club.

Finally, Grim's off the phone and he takes a minute before talking to his men surrounding him. At some point, every member of the Wild Kings surrounded their President and now they're having a conversation while I'm sitting here and dying to know what's going on.

After several more minutes, Grim and his men walk back over toward us. His eyes bore into mine and the fear I was feeling before skyrockets. The only thoughts running through my head is something happened to Playboy. Dread fills me and I can fill myself slinking back into the chair I'm sitting in.

"No," I begin to say as tears silently fall down my face.

"Sam, sweetheart, you need to calm down. Playboy's okay. I'm just pissed as fuck right now and I'm sorry for scarin' you," Grim begins. "That was Playboy on the phone. You ladies need to pack up your things and get the kids around. We head out in less than a half-hour."

"W-w-what?" I ask, not understanding what's going on right now.

"The assholes who already put their hands on you once, know where you are," Grim informs us. "They want you back home. So, we're going to head out as soon as you're ready to leave. I'll have Sky and Bailey get your things around while you go to the bathroom and whatever else you need to do. We're goin' to try to ride straight through."

"Is it safe to go back?" Jennifer asks as Gwen sits down right in front of me.

"You'll have to stay in the clubhouse. Your men won't let anythin' happen to you. They just don't want to get us mixed up in the same shit as they're dealin' with," Grim responds.

We all nod our heads as my heart starts to come back under control and my breathing isn't as labored as it was. The only thing I know for sure is Playboy is okay and I'm hoping the rest of the men are too. Grim didn't say anyone didn't get hurt, he just said Playboy's okay; it's not the same thing.

Grim and Cage help me up from the chair as everyone else leaves to pack their things up. Caleb runs over to me.

"Mama, where we going?" he asks.

"Well, buddy, we're going home. Skylar and Bailey are packing our things up so we can leave," I answer him as we walk inside the clubhouse.

"Yay!" he says excitedly.

"Why don't you spend a little more time with your cousins and stay close so you're here when it's time to go," I tell him.

Caleb nods his head and runs back off to find Tank and Maddie's triplets and the rest of the boys. I know he's going to miss them, but I'd rather be home with my man right now. We'll just have to make visits a more regular thing from now on as the kids get older and head off into the world on their own. Not that I'm looking forward to that at all.

We're all loaded up and almost home. I think we have a little over an hour left until we're back. It's enough that we have Grim, Tank, Rage, and Cage from the Wild Kings with us and now I hear the rumble of several more motorcycles coming up on us. As I look out the window, I see men from the Phantom Bastards mixing in with them and surrounding the three SUVs we're currently in.

"Mama, it's Daddy," Caleb says, rubbing the sleep from his eyes.

"How do you know?" Gwen asks him.

"Because he's right here," he says, pointing out the window.

I look and can barely make out his blonde hair sticking out from under the helmet. Caleb is right, Playboy is riding next to his window.

"You're really smart, buddy," Gwen tells him.

Instead of going to sleep like he was going to, Caleb now has his eyes glued to the window watching his Daddy. The only thing that would make it better is if Slim was here too. And he might be, but in a different spot. Maybe closer to the SUV Shy's riding in with their kids.

"You're not gonna sleep?" Gwen asks Caleb as they sit in the back of the SUV.

"Nope. Gonna watch my Daddy," he answers matter-of-factly.

"Well, okay then," Gwen responds to him laughter filling her voice.

"Look, it's Uncle Killer," Caleb says, pointing out the other side of the SUV.

Turning our heads, we see Killer riding on the opposite side of Playboy. I can feel the shift in Gwen as she realizes the man she's in love with is riding next to us. She sinks back into the seat and as I look at her, I see the sadness and desperation on her face. Gwen is in love with a man who loves her and won't follow his heart. I don't know what I can do to help her.

I pull out my Kindle and begin to read a book. It's an MC book and I hope the rest of the ride passes by quickly. I'm getting uncomfortable and I'm more than ready to be in bed where I can lay down and stretch out a little bit. And, I want to curl up next to Playboy and make sure for myself he's truly okay.

"Mama, we're home," Caleb says, his voice laced with sleep.

Looking up from my book, I see that we're pulling up to the clubhouse. I put the Kindle in my purse and sit up a little straighter in the seat. Tank pulls up to the door and I know it's because of me, especially when he doesn't leave much room between the SUV and Slim's bike.

As we're unloading from the SUV, Slim comes and stands in the doorway of the clubhouse.

"Papi!" Caleb shouts and jumps out of the SUV to run to his Papi.

Slim scoops him up in his arms and hugs him close for a few minutes while the rest of us get out and make our way to him. When Shy gets up to him with Kinsliegh and Rayven, Slim sets Caleb down on the ground so he can run over to Playboy. I watch as Slim pulls his wife and daughters into his arms and leads them inside. They're perfect for one another.

"Hey baby," Playboy says, walking up and pulling me into his arms. "I missed you so fuckin' much."

"I missed you too," I say before he leans down and kisses me soundly.

"Let's get inside and to bed," he says, leading me inside.

"I'm ready for bed," I tell him honestly. "It's been a long day."

"I know, baby."

Playboy and I bypass everyone as Tank and Caleb follow us to the bedrooms. Tank sets our bags down once we get inside our room and does that whole man hug thing with his brother-in-law before saying goodbye and leaving. Caleb jumps on our bed and thinks it's playtime because we're back home and he hasn't spent any time with Playboy for a few days.

"It's time for bed, Caleb," Playboy tells him.

"No, I don't want to go to bed. I want to stay with you," he responds, sitting down in the middle of the bed and beginning to cry.

Playboy looks at me helplessly and doesn't know what to do. I shrug my shoulders already knowing what he's going to do; Caleb will be in bed with us.

"Just tonight, you can sleep in here," Playboy says, seeing me not giving him any help.

Caleb looks up and I lean over the bag to get him a pair of pajamas he can change into. Once I have his things out, he heads into the bathroom and shuts the door behind him. I grab a tee-shirt and pair of pajama pants while he's changing so I can go in after him.

Playboy pulls me back into his arms and one of his hands falls to rest on my expanding belly. After placing a soft kiss on my lips, he kneels on the floor and lifts my shirt up. He places another kiss on my stomach and I feel the babies move as he looks up at me. A smile lights up his face and it's the same expression of wonder and awe he gets every single time he feels them move in my stomach.

"This will all be over with soon," he assures me. "How are you feelin'?"

"I'm tired and feel like I'm the size of a house. Or the clubhouse at this point," I respond.

Before we can say anything else, Caleb is rushing from the bathroom in his pajamas and jumping on the bed. I laugh at him and make my way in to get changed and brush my teeth, seeing Caleb's toothbrush on the counter, knowing he already took care of his teeth.

By the time I finish getting ready for bed, Playboy and Caleb are relaxing in bed with a movie on the TV. It's one of Caleb's favorites and I know he'll crash out soon with it playing softly in the background.

I climb in bed on the other side of our son and Playboy helps me get the pillows around me. Once I'm settled, he pulls the blankets up around us and wraps an arm around Caleb and me. I can't stay awake any longer as my eyes flutter closed and sleep claims me.

Chapter Thirty-One

Playboy

IT'S FIRST THING in the morning and I'd rather still be in bed with Sam and Caleb. Well, with Caleb awake because he likes to kick and hit in his sleep. I'm sore as hell, but at least my family is home and I got to sleep with them wrapped in my arms.

We're all gathered in church so dad can call Butcher and let him know what's going on before calling Jose. Jose needs to know what's going on and that this Terror bitch wants him to work for his club. Because essentially, that's what he wants. He may word it as he wants to work with the cartel, but that's not how he means it. Terror honestly thinks he can make the cartel his bitch and that's not how this works. Especially not with Jose.

"Yeah?" Butcher asks, answering his phone.

"Butcher, got some shit goin' down here and want to give you a heads up," my dad says.

"What's goin' on?" he asks as I hear the noise in the background begin to fade.

"Got a club, Devils Rule, tryin' to move in on our territory. They think they're goin' to take our shit, work with the cartel, and then take our women and kids. They've already put hands on Playboy's ol' lady and she's heavily pregnant with his babies," my dad informs the other President.

"The fuck?" he questions. "Who does this bitch think he is?"

"He's a bitch leadin' a bunch of pussies," I tell Butcher.

"Must be if he's puttin' hands on a woman and a pregnant one at that," Butcher says. "What do you need from us?"

"Nothin' right now. At this point, it's just a matter of givin' you a heads up. Need to call the cartel leader now and inform him of this bitch because he wants to make him their bitch," my dad says.

Butcher begins laughing his ass off as my dad hangs up on him. He knows what's about to happen to Terror and his merry band of bitches. Terror is going to die. I don't give a fuck what happens to Terror as long as I get my hands on Rancor. He's going to die a slow death by my fucking hands.

"Everyone quiet now," my dad says as he pulls up another contact on his phone.

We all lean back in our chairs and those that smoke light up while we wait for Jose to answer his phone. He knows it's an emergency if my dad is calling him. Hopefully, he gets how dire this situation is and gives us a hand to take these bitches out. We don't necessarily need it, but we're not dumb enough to think he's not going to take offense to them wanting him to be their bitch.

"Yeah," Jose says, finally answering his phone.

"Jose, it's Slim. We have a problem," my dad says.

"What do you mean?" Jose asks.

"Well, we have a club, Devils Rule, and they know we have ties to you. They want our territory, business, women and kids, and to work with you. Actually, they want to make you their little bitch," he answers.

"They think we'll be their bitch?" Jose questions.

"Yeah. I think they're into runnin' skin. Young skin," my dad tells him.

"I don't give a fuck what they do. They'll never work with us," Jose says. "That's not all to the story, though."

"No. They already put hands on Playboys ol' lady and she's pregnant with his twins right now," he responds.

"They did what?" Jose asks, his voice rising several octaves.

"Put hands on her and threatened her," I say, not being able to remain silent any longer.

"Is she okay?" Jose enquires.

"Yeah. We sent them away and somehow Terror found out where they were," my dad says. "We brought them home. Supposed to give them an answer in less than six hours."

"We'll be there in two," Jose says. "You got a plan already?"

"Yeah. We'll be gettin' ready while we wait for you," my dad tells him and hangs up the phone. "Okay, you heard Jose. Get everythin' ready and make sure we're ready to head the fuck out when they get here. I want the Prospects makin' sure the landin' pad we don't have is ready when Jose lands. You know he's bringin' his helicopter here."

Dad slams the gavel on the table and we all stand up to prepare for battle. As we leave church, the ol' ladies and house bunnies are setting out food on the top of the bar. They know something is going down and they want to make sure we eat right now before we head out. Otherwise, who knows when we'll eat again.

I walk up to Sam and place a kiss on her mouth before placing a hand against her stomach for a second. The babies move against my touch and I can feel my smile. This is my favorite part of her being pregnant, feeling the babies move while they're protected in her body.

"How you doin', baby?" I ask her.

"I'm okay. Get somethin' to eat," she tells me, handing me a plate so I can get some food.

"Did you and Caleb already eat?" I ask her.

"He did. I'm not very hungry right now," she answers me.

"You're gonna eat," I say, a slight growl to my voice.

She nods her head and picks up another plate for herself. We make our way down the line of the food and fill our plates. I know I'll be eating half of her food because her eyes are definitely bigger than her stomach right now. It happens at every meal but I'm not complaining as long as she truly eats enough for her and the babies.

Everything is ready to go. Our weapons are loaded up along with extra ammo. Jose let us know he'll be here in a few minutes as we usher the women and kids back inside. We spent some time outside and now everyone needs to go back inside while Jose makes his way into the clubhouse and church.

As soon as we make sure they're in the game room with the Prospects making sure they don't leave the room, we all head out back to the open field at the back of the clubhouse. Sure enough, Jose's helicopter is landing. We wait for him to get out and then make our way over to greet him. Well, my dad and I do.

"Slim. Playboy," Jose greets us in his heavily accented voice.

"Jose," we both respond.

Walking into the clubhouse, we all head directly to church. Jose takes my seat and I lean against the wall.

"What are we gonna do?" Jose asks.

"I want to get in there and take all their asses out. Now," my dad says.

"I would normally agree," Jose says. "However, in this case, I think if these guys are complete bitches than we need to play with them a little bit."

"What are you thinkin'?" I ask from my spot against the wall.

"They're going to be calling for an answer soon. Well, you place the call to them first and let them know you've talked to me and I'll be coming into town within a few days. At that point, we'll all sit down together and have a meeting about where these relationships are going to go," Jose responds.

My dad looks around the table and I can see the men of the club all smiling and nodding in agreement. They want to show Terror and his bitches we're one step ahead of them; if not more. For now, maybe we should play Jose's way.

"Alright, I'll call now," my dad says.

He picks up a burner phone and places the call to Terror.

"The fuck you want?" Terror asks, answering his phone.

"Talked to our contact in the cartel. After he talked to the boss, he called me back. I can't give you an answer today, Terror," my dad says as we all remain deathly quiet in the room with him.

"Then it looks like we're comin' for your bitches and land," Terror says.

"Now wait a minute," my dad says quickly. "The boss wants to come here and have a sit down with you and us. If you don't give him this, then there's no deal and he won't *ever* work with you."

Terror is silent for a few minutes. He's thinking over what my dad told him and trying to find a way to make this work the way he wants it to. It's not going to happen, but he's going to try to find a way.

"If you're fucking me over on this Slim, I'm going to kill your wife in front of you after making her choke on my cock. I'll destroy everything you love before killing you slower than fuck," Terror says as we all grind our teeth and try not to say a single word.

"I'm not fuckin' you over, Terror," my dad says, completely ignoring anything about Shy because he's so fucking pissed right now.

"You have two days to get this fucking cartel boss here. I'm running this show, not you and certainly not some fucking cartel bitch," Terror says, digging his grave faster as Jose looks on with rage and straight venom filling his eyes.

"I'll be in touch," my dad says, hanging up the phone on him.

We all watch as he picks up the phone and throws it against the closest wall to him. The phone shatters into a million pieces and we won't have to worry about using that phone again. At the same time, Jose stands from his chair.

"So, I'm nothing but a bitch?" he questions. "This Terror man is going to die by my hands and my hands only. We have two days to come up with a game plan. I'll have my men come in if you have room for us to stay."

"We'll put you guys in our houses here since we have the ol' ladies and kids in the clubhouse. We want everyone together so no one wanders off on their own," my dad answers. "You can stay in my home."

"Gracias," Jose says. "I'm goin' to make some calls and my men will arrive within a few hours under cover of darkness."

"Oh, you should probably know, the Wild Kings and Satan's Anarchy clubs will be here tomorrow. The ol' ladies want to throw my ol' lady a baby shower. And then there's goin' to be a weddin'," I alert Jose.

"May I join the wedding with my men?" he asks, a smile on his face.

"You may," I respond. "Are you sure you want to attend?"

"Yes. I love a wedding," Jose tells me. "We will not disturb your party or wedding while we prepare. Fox, can I see what you have already?"

Fox nods and stands from his chair after getting a nod from my father. Jose follows him out and they head to Fox's room. He has a backup room when Kim is here, so she doesn't know anything that's going on. The system in his room is shut down and he uses the other place in the back hallway.

"Now, I want everyone pitchin' in to make sure the houses are ready for the cartel men. When that's done, finish gettin' ready for the weddin'. I want everythin' perfect for Sam," my dad says, dismissing everyone as he slams the gavel down.

I go in search of Sam. The only thing on my mind right now is sinking balls deep into her warm, wet pussy. It's been way too long and I need to keep her busy, so she doesn't suspect anything about the baby shower or wedding tomorrow. As I wander into the common room, I don't see her anywhere. But, Caleb is sitting with Shy and Gwen.

"Where's Sam?" I ask, walking up to the table they're sitting at.

"She went to lay down. She's not feeling good, Playboy. I'm not sure what's wrong," Shy tells me.

I turn on my heel after asking her to watch Caleb for a while. Opening the door to the bedroom, I see Sam curled up around two pillows in our bed. Tears are streaking down her cheeks and I'm instantly by her side.

"What's wrong, baby?" I ask her, brushing her hair off her forehead.

"I'm so uncomfortable, it's not funny. No matter what I do, I can't get relaxed right now. And sleep is almost nonexistent," she answers me.

"Okay. Move over to the middle of the bed," I tell her, not caring that my dick isn't going to get his release right now.

After helping Sam slide into the middle of the bed, I climb into bed behind her and begin to rub her back with the heel of my hand. I use just enough pressure to help relieve the pain and tension in her aching back so she can try to take a nap. Sleep and rest are the most important things for her right now.

Once she's sound asleep, I place a kiss on her head, cover her up, and leave the room to get something to eat and bring Caleb in with me. There's way too much going on right now for him to be out and about. Plus, I don't want to be away from Sam for too long in case she wakes up in pain. She's almost seven and a half months pregnant now and only has a month or so left because we were warned she would more than likely go into labor early.

Caleb and I grab our dinner of pizza, wings, and garlic bread before making our way back into the room. Shy made sure to put some up for Sam before anyone else got their food so she can eat when she wakes up. Otherwise, all these heathens I call family will eat the food and she'll have missed out. We never know what she's going to crave and I don't want to send the Prospects out in the middle of the night right now. Or go out myself.

As soon as I have Caleb settled on the couch in our room, I gently climb back into bed and sit next to Sam. I turn on a movie my son loves to watch as we eat our dinner in silence. He keeps glancing over at his mom to make sure he's okay, so I know he's going to be sleeping in here with us again tonight. Only he'll be on the couch so she can rest comfortably. This is how the rest of my night goes as the rest of the club prepares Sam's surprises for tomorrow.

Chapter Thirty-Two

Sam

WAKING UP THIS afternoon, I feel slightly better than I have in the last few days. While I'm still uncomfortable, Playboy rubbed my back most of the night. I feel horrible for keeping him up most the night, but I'm not sure what else I can do about it. It's not like I didn't try to get him to go to sleep because I did. Playboy is just stubborn and refused to listen to me.

Now, I'm up and have had my shower, which Playboy joined me for. I swear, the closer I get to my due date, the more he doesn't want to let me out of his sight. I'm honestly surprised he let me go to Clifton Falls even though they're trying to take down this other club. Who knows what could've happened while I was there?

"What are you doing today?" I ask him as I slip on the white summer dress he picked out for me to wear today.

"I think we're havin' a cookout at some point today. Not really sure what else is goin' on. I have to get with Dad," he answers, not quite looking me in the eye as he does.

"Oh. I should get downstairs and help the ol' ladies out then," I say, brushing my hair and putting it up in a messy bun.

I hate my hair is so short I can't keep it up once I secure it. It's always slipping down and I have to put it back up a million times a day. But, I don't like having long hair either. So, I do what I have to do and continuously mess with it. Playboy laughs at me when I do it too.

Playboy said a cookout at some point today, but I already smell delicious aromas penetrating the air. My mouth is watering, even though I'm not hungry. If I didn't get to help the ol' ladies, I'm going to be upset because that's one thing I can do while sitting down so my man doesn't have a damn fit because I'm moving around too much or standing for long periods on my feet.

"The first thing you're goin' to do is eat. Caleb is already down eatin' his breakfast and I'm not lettin' you do a damn thing until you have food in your body," he informs me as he pulls on his shirt before reaching for his cut.

"Oh. Well, I guess I can do that," I tell him, not feeling overly hungry right now.

"It's almost over with, baby. Then we'll be holdin' our sons in our arms and you'll feel normal again. I'm sorry you're so uncomfortable," he tells me, pulling me into his arms and placing a kiss on the top of my head.

"I know. It's just hot and I'm uncomfortable, so it's making me cranky. I love you," I say, looking up into his eyes.

"I love you too. Now let's go feed our sons," Playboy says, leaving the room with his arm wrapped around me.

We head into the common room and my jaw about hits the floor. Blue balloons, streamers, plates, napkins, and silverware are everywhere. There's a huge banner saying, 'It's a boy' is hanging right over the door to go outside. A comfortable chair is sitting at one table as I look around.

There's a table in the corner that's loaded down with presents to the point more are sitting on the floor surrounding it. I've never seen so many gifts in one area in my entire life. A second table is close to it with a cake and several other plates and silverware on it.

"What's going on?" I ask, looking up at Playboy.

"The girls are throwin' you a baby shower. We thought everyone could use this right now," he answers me.

"I can't believe they did this," I say.

Before Playboy can respond, the common room becomes filled with people. It's not just the men and women from the Phantom Bastards here; it's men and women from the Phantom Bastards, the Wild Kings, and Satan's Anarchy. Tears fill my eyes as I look around the room at everyone here to celebrate Playboy and I have bringing new members into the family.

"I don't know what to say," I tell the room.

"Nothing for you to say," Hadliegh says, walking through the mass of people. "You're in this ginormous, rowdy, dysfunctional family and it's time you realize it."

Playboy leads me to the chair as Shy and Slim walk over to us. Shy has a full plate in her hand while Slim has one with even more food on it. They smile as I get comfortable, and Playboy takes a seat next to me.

"How are you feelin'?" Slim asks me.

"Uncomfortable as hell, but it's almost over," I answer him. "Thank you for this."

"No thanks necessary, honey. You're growin' my grandsons in you and we want you to know that your entire family is loved and a part of our family. Forever," he returns. "We're gonna eat and then you guys can open your gifts. Well, all but one that's already been set up in the nursery."

"Oh, um, okay," I respond because I have no clue what would already need to be in the nursery.

About the only thing we've gotten accomplished is painting the walls a light blue so Boy Scout could go in behind us. I don't even know what he's done to the walls since Playboy painted it. It's off-limits to me and I haven't even attempted to look— not to say I haven't wanted to.

Playboy and I are joined by Tank, Maddie, Shy, Slim, Grim, and Skylar as they bring in their own plates of food. We talk and laugh until I realize none of the kids are inside. As I look at Playboy, he must already know what I'm going to say.

"They're all outside with the Prospects and stayin' close to the clubhouse," he informs me.

"Okay," I respond, going back to my food.

I've got chicken, pasta salad, salt potatoes, a roll, and a bowl of chips in front of me. No, I'm not going to eat it all; I never do. However, once I started eating, I realized I was hungrier than I thought I was. I'll make a good dent in all this food and then Playboy will finish the rest of it for me.

We've eaten our fill and I've laid eyes on Caleb as the Prospects brought all the kids in once they were done eating. Now, the guys are bringing presents over to us so we can begin to open them. Caleb is excited as hell even though none of them are for him. He'll still be allowed to help us out because there's way too many things for Playboy and me to open ourselves.

It still takes us an hour to open everything up with Playboy, Caleb, and myself working on them. We've gotten everything from clothes, small toys, diapers, bottles, wipes, lotion, bath stuff, bathtubs, and anything else you could even begin to imagine a baby could need. Tears have been filling my eyes since we started because I never once expected this.

Playboy hasn't left my side since we came downstairs. He's made sure I have food, drinks, and has helped me up to use the restroom. Caleb is now at my side and we're surrounded by our entire family consisting of three different clubs.

"Mama, look at all this stuff," Caleb says as his eyes go wide. "It's a lot."

"Yes, it is," I reply as those closest to us laugh with us.

"You've got two more gifts and that's it," Bailey says, walking up with a large box in her hand.

She sets it down in front of me and I look to Playboy. He nods his head and I begin to unwrap the box. Nestled inside among the tissue paper are two little matching outfits. There's little pair of jeans, white onesies proclaiming them future Phantom Bastard Prospects, little leather vest like the cuts the men wear with the Prospect patch on them, and little black bandanas like the one Playboy usually wears around his face when he's out riding.

"These are so precious," I say, tears streaming down my face as I look up at Bailey. "Thank you so much."

"You're welcome, honey," Bailey answers. "You know, my mom started this tradition when she was alive and since losing her, I've been keeping up with it. The only difference is I go to the other clubs and try to make sure I get one for every new baby that comes into the family."

There's not a dry eye on the women as Bailey talks about something her mom started so long ago. Now, Bailey keeps her memory alive in continuing with the tradition. It's special and even after the boys outgrown these outfits, I'll be saving them to ensure they never get damaged or lost.

Before I can blink, Playboy is standing next to me. As I go to ask him what's going on, he drops to a knee and pulls a box from the inside of his cut. I gasp and tears fill my eyes. Again, this is the last thing I expected with everything that's been going on with this new club in town.

"Sam, you have been to hell and back and you're still here to live your life. You've let not only me but the rest of the club and ol' ladies in your life and Caleb's life. I love you with all my heart and there's no one else who can gain access now that you own it. You're givin' me two new little boys and I want to know if you'd do me the honor of spendin' the rest of your life with me. Will you marry me?" he asks as he opens the box he's holding.

"Yes!" I yell out so everyone can hear as tears stream down my face and I hold my hand out to him.

Looking down, I see a stunning platinum band on my finger with a diamond in the middle of light blue stones that go down along the band as well. It's not too big and it fits perfectly.

Playboy leans up and kisses me. He lets his lips linger against mine and I can feel the smile on his face as he remains connected to me. I can't help but smile in return.

"Are you ready?" he asks as he finally pulls from my lips.

"Ready for what, baby?" I ask him.

"To get married?" Playboy asks like it's the most normal thing in the world to get engaged and married in the same day.

"Nothing has been planned or done for it," I tell him, letting him see the shock on my faces.

"Everythin' is ready, baby. Just waitin' on your to say yes," he informs me.

"You're crazy! But that's why I love you," I say on a laugh. "Let's do this."

Playboy helps me up from the chair where Bailcy, Skylar, Maddic, Shy, Hadlicgh, Gwcn, and Callie are waiting. The rest of the ol' ladies have disappeared and I'm sure they're putting the finishing touches on the wedding. I didn't even know this could be done legally.

"Go with the girls. I'll see you in a few minutes," he says, placing another lingering kiss on my lips.

As soon as he's done kissing me until I can't think anymore, Shy and Hadliegh lead me to our room. We enter and I see they already have the make-up and curling iron ready to go.

"This is why Playboy picked out a white dress for me to wear today, isn't it?" I ask them.

"It is," Shy says. "I picked it up yesterday when we went out.

Tears fill my eyes as I realize they helped Playboy do this. And, there's more than likely only one reason why he's doing this for us right now; he's worried something is going to happen to him. That he's not going to come home to me and he wants to protect us.

"No crying," Hadliegh says. "I don't know what's going on, but he's coming home. They all are."

I nod my head as they get to work. Shy informs me we only have ten minutes before he's expecting me out there.

"You realize I don't even have a maid of honor or anything?" I ask them.

"So choose one," Hadliegh tells me, not letting me think of anything to get out of marrying Playboy right now.

"Gwen, would you?" I ask her, knowing I'm the closest to her.

"Yes, I would," she answers with tears in her own eyes.

Gwen is wearing a pretty black dress. It's strapless and falls to just above her knees. Her golden skin is shown off in it and I know Killer is going to lose his shit because she sure as hell wasn't wearing this for the baby shower. Gwen's make-up is light and accentuates her golden eyes. She's beautiful with an air of innocence surrounding her and there's no way anyone can deny it.

Hadliegh does my hair while Shy does my make-up. Skylar, Bailey, Maddie, and Callie emerge from the bathroom wearing similar dresses to Gwen. Their hair and make-up is done by the time I'm ready. Shy and Hadliegh are the last two to get ready as they change into dresses and take care of their hair and faces. Each woman is stunning and I can't wait to see the men. My only hope is they aren't dressed in suits or anything; that's not who they are and I don't want them to change.

"Are you all in the wedding?" I ask them.

"Yeah," Skylar answers me. "Playboy wants it to be a family affair, so there's men and women from each club in the wedding party. Are you okay with that?"

"I couldn't be happier about it. Thank you all so much. For everything you've done with the wedding and baby shower today," I tell them.

"You're welcome," Hadliegh says, walking up to me. "Two more surprises for you."

The second Hadliegh finishes talking, there's a knock on the door. When Shy opens the door, Tank is standing before us. He's got a smile on his face as he looks at all the women standing before him.

"You ladies ready to go?" he asks, stepping in to kiss Maddie.

"Yep. Just finished up," she answers him.

All the women head out and make their way to the back door. Tank is the only one to remain. I look up at him with confusion on my face.

"I'm the lucky fucker walkin' you down the aisle to your man," he says, giving me a wink.

"Thank you. I didn't even think of that," I respond as he leads me from the room and toward the back door.

As we step up, I see Caleb standing there with a little leather vest on over his white tee-shirt. He's got a pair of new jeans on and boots on his feet. Caleb has a pillow in his hands with our wedding bands on them. Shy is standing next to him with Kinsliegh in her arms. She's got a basket of red rose petals in her hand and tears fill my eyes. This is truly a family event when I've never really had a family to call my own. Now, it seems I do in the form of three clubs and the men and women in them.

I soon hear *Love Me* by Aaron Lewis playing through the speakers. This song fits us perfectly as I listen to the words again. We both fought our feelings for so long and even now, we have a hard time loving one another. Not that we don't want to; I've just never had it shown to me, so it's harder for me. It's a favorite of mine and Playboy has had to listen to it more than enough.

One by one, all the women walk out of the clubhouse and down the yard behind it. I glimpse Playboy standing at the front. He's wearing a pair of jeans, a black tee-shirt, his cut, and a black bandana on his head. His hair is showing under the bandana and the way it's laying, I know he's got it pulled back in a low ponytail. Playboy knows I love it when he looks like this. It's my favorite look besides when we're having sex and his hair is hanging around him while his eyes penetrate mine and a look of bliss covers his sexy face.

Finally, it's our time to leave the clubhouse and as we do, I take a deep breath. The second we step through the door, all eyes swing to us and I can feel the blush creeping up my face. Tank leads me to Playboy, who's not all that far away because of how pregnant I am.

What takes us minutes feels as if it takes hours to get to my man. The smile on his face lights my way toward him and I can't take my eyes off his sexy face. I don't even realize Slim's standing up to marry us until Tank leaves my side after placing a kiss on my cheek to a growling Playboy.

Each man standing up with Playboy matches up with their ol' lady standing up for me. I love we're combining all the clubs in our day even though I seem to be the last one to know. Today is turning out to be an amazing day and I'm happy it's happening before our sons are born, so other than Caleb, we all have the same name. And I know it's just a matter of time before Caleb has the same last name as us.

"This is gonna be short and sweet," Slim says, launching into the ceremony.

Honestly, my only focus is on Playboy as Slim talks to the crowd behind us. It's not until it's time for us to say our vows that I look around for the first time. There's a path of blood-red rose petals we walked across, wildflowers hang from Sheppard's hooks on the outside of the chairs, and there's an arch behind Slim covered in wildflowers.

"Sam, you came into my life completely unexpected and now I can't imagine a day without you by my side. When we were apart, you were always on my mind and I couldn't get rid of you. Not that I'd ever want to. Caleb is my son and he's always on my mind too. We're about to add two new members to our family and I can't wait for the day we can hold them in our arms and watch them learn and grow, moldin' them into the kind of men we want them to be. I love you more every single second of every day and that won't ever change," Playboy says.

"Playboy, when I came here, I was afraid of my own shadow. You helped me overcome that, helped our handsome son get over his lack of talking, and are making me a mother twice over. Without you, I don't know where we'd be and I'll never be able to thank you for that or giving us a family we never had before. I love you, always and it only grows on a daily basis. You're teaching me how to love and let someone in to love me back," I tell him, tears rolling silently down my face as his eyes glisten as well.

"Sam, do you take Playboy to be your husband?" Slim asks as I take the ring from Caleb's little hand.

"I do," I respond.

"Playboy, do you take Sam to be your wife?" he asks his son.

"I fuckin' do," Playboy says as laughter rings out around us.

Once the rings are in place on our fingers, we join hands and Slim places his hand over them.

"I now pronounce you husband and wife. Son, you may kiss your beautiful bride," Slim says as catcalls, whistles, and cheering erupts and quickly fades into the background.

Playboy pulls me into his body and our lips part so he can deepen the kiss in front of all our family and friends.

When we finally break apart, Playboy leads me from our wedding place to a chair. Once I'm seated, he slides one over to me and parks his ass while everyone else mingles and music starts playing.

"We're out here long enough for somethin' to eat and then we're inside. Shy and Dad will have Caleb tonight," he informs me, placing a gentle kiss against my lips.

True to his word, Playboy ushered me inside as soon as we were done eating. He leads me to our room, and as soon as the door's shut behind him, he's on me. Playboy strips me out of my dress and quickly removes his clothes. While he's standing before me completely naked, I'm wearing my bra and panties still.

I'm more than ready for him to take me. The entire time we were waiting for our food, then eating, and talking to our family, he had his hands all over me. If his hands weren't on me, he was kissing me somewhere on my body. I've been turned on and wanting him for over an hour now, and I can't wait much longer for him.

"If you don't want to lose them permanently, take them off," Playboy grits out.

He reaches behind me and undoes the hooks holding my bra in place. I drop my arms and let it fall to the floor before lowering my panties. Once they can fall by themselves, I let them. As soon as I step out of them, I sit on the bed and wait for what my husband is going to want to do next.

"Hands and knees, baby," he tells me, his voice low and husky with want. "This time will be fast and hard. Later, I'll be slow and gentle."

"Anything, babe. I just need you now," I tell him, starting to pant in anticipation of him filling me.

Playboy does as I ask and slides into me after sliding his fingers through my folds to make sure I'm wet and ready for him. He doesn't stop until he's balls deep in me. After letting me adjust for a second, Playboy begins to pull out of my body before slamming back in as hard as he dares with me being almost eight months pregnant now.

Once he finds his rhythm, Playboy leans over and begins to place kisses down my back. He removes one of his hands from the bed beside me and begins to tweak one of my nipples. I let my head drop and let out a long moan. Playboy pauses long enough to place a pillow under my stomach, so it's not pulling on me and then resumes his tempo as if he's never missed a beat.

"I'm close, baby. You need to get there," he grits out from clenched teeth.

Instead of answering, I start meeting him thrust for thrust. He moves his hand from my tit down to my clit. Playboy begins to pinch and pull on it as his tempo picks up just a bit. Even with his pace increasing, Playboy doesn't move in and out any harder than he already is.

With him manipulating my clit, I can feel my body coiling tighter and tighter, and my release begins to pull me to the edge of the cliff. The next time he pinches my clit between his fingers, my release crashes over me, and I can't stop the scream erupting from me.

"Griffin!" I yell out as my orgasm crashes over me.

My body tightens and shudders beneath him. I pull Playboy over the edge with me. His own body tightens and stills inside me.

"Sam!" he shouts out.

Playboy slowly glides in and out of me, prolonging both of our orgasms. When he finally slides from my body, I watch with hooded eyes as he walks naked into the bathroom. He cleans up and then brings a washcloth back to clean me up. Once I'm clean, he climbs into bed with me and pulls my back to his front. He rubs his hands up and down my stomach as our breathing comes back to normal. My eyes slide shut, and sleep instantly claims me with my husband's arms around me.

Chapter Thirty-Three

Playboy

YESTERDAY WAS THE best day of my life up to this point. I got to marry the love of my life. After ravishing her body, and Sam taking a nap, we went back outside with our family and friends. Jose joined the party and met Sam. He handed me an envelope filled with money as a wedding gift for us. When I tried to hand it back, he told me to do something special for my family.

I danced with Sam as *Outlaw In Me* by Brantley Gilbert played. Not a traditional wedding song, but we're not a traditional couple. After dancing with my wife, we cut the cake and then went back inside while the rest of the clubs partied and did what they do the rest of the night. My time was spent buried in my wife throughout the entire night.

Although the best part of the night was when I took her home after dancing with her. It was my dad's one concession to us getting married; we stay in the house on our wedding night. I showed Sam the nursery, and she fell in love with it.

Painted on the walls are a group of motorcycles. The riders are all wearing Phantom Bastards cuts and bandanas covering their heads. The road is stretched out before them and trees are painted on one side of the road. What really got her was that all the riders were bears instead of people.

When her gaze landed on the nursery room furniture, there was no stopping the tears. Pops brought up his normal set of furniture. So, there's two cribs, toy boxes, and two rocking chairs. The Phantom Bastards colors are on all of them, and teddy bears are carved into the wood as well. It's the same thing he does for any new baby into the family.

Today, the feel around the clubhouse is much different, though. It's the day we go to war with Terror and his pussies; the day I make Rancor pay for touching what's mine. I won't rest until he's buried in the depths of hell. None of us will rest until Terror, and every last man wearing a Devils Rule cut is burning in hell.

"Church in session," my dad says, slamming down the gavel as we're in our last meeting before heading out.

"What's goin' on today?" I ask, leaning up against the wall again so Jose can have my chair.

"Again, you guys are going to go ahead. Playboy, Jose, and I will show up together. I want you all closer than last time, so we can take them the fuck out. We go in, act like Jose wants to talk about workin' with them. When I hold my hand up, I want all hell to break loose," my dad answers. "We've gone over and over this plan more than once in the last few days. Fox, you've been over the maps with Jose's guys, and everyone knows what you're supposed to do. Any questions."

"Not a question," I begin, looking at every man in the room. "Rancor is mine. He put his hands on my ol' lady, and he dies by my hand and my hand only."

"Terror is mine. He called me a bitch without saying the words," Jose adds in.

My dad nods his head in understanding. Every single guy in the Phantom Bastards knows Rancor is mine after what he did to Sam. She's my woman, and he dared to put his hands on her knowing she belonged to me. And I know Jose has his reasons for wanting to put Terror to ground, and I don't blame him one single bit.

"Alright, the arsenal and ammo are loaded in the van already. You guys head out, and then we'll be behind you shortly. Get into position and make sure you're out of sight. I don't want the van to be spotted either. Hide is as good as the last time," my dad says before slamming the gavel on the table once more.

The men leaving first all head out. They don't stop at the bar to have a drink like normal after church. Instead, they all head to the van and climb in except for Killer. He'll ride his bike because if any of the fuckers want to escape, he'll chase them down on his bike.

Jose, my dad, and I stay in our meeting room. We don't really talk or anything else as we sit in the room around the table. I'm mentally preparing for the upcoming battle, and I know this is what my dad is more than likely doing right now too. I'm not sure what Jose's doing; it's not my problem as he sits in silence, twirling his bracelet around his wrist. That's honestly the only sound in the room as we all think about what we're about to do.

It's never an easy choice to take out someone, let alone kill an entire club of men. These men are blindly following Terror into drug use, rape, beating up people for no reason, taking from others because Terror doesn't want to put in the work it takes to run a club. Or to live his life. He wants to coast through on someone else's dime, and effort put in. That's not a life; that's taking advantage and using people for your gain.

"It's time," my dad finally says, pulling us out of our heads.

The three of us stand up, and we head out of the meeting room. Sam is sitting in the common room with Gwen and Kim. Caleb is sitting on the floor next to her, playing with some motorcycles. She looks up as we enter the room, and I can see her eyes filling with tears already. I want to comfort her, but the most I can do right now is kiss her goodbye.

"I love you," she tells me with a watery smile as I approach.

"I love you too, wife," I return, a small smile on my face.

Leaning down over her, I place a kiss on her lips and linger for just a second. I don't have time for much else before heading out to meet with the Devils bitches. As soon as I break our lips apart, I lean further down and place a soft kiss on her stomach to tell our sons goodbye. Caleb stands up, and I hug him and kiss the top of his head before turning and leaving the clubhouse behind.

Without turning back, I let the door slam shut behind me and continue making my feet move to my bike. Dad is already on his bike, and Jose is just getting into his car by the time I straddle my bike. I tie the black bandana around my face and put my helmet on. As soon as I'm ready, we start our bikes and leave the clubhouse behind. I still don't look back because I know if I do, I'll turn around and pull my wife in my arms so I can give her one more kiss, hold her tight to my body for a minute longer, and hold Caleb close to me.

Instead, I ride next to my father as he goes from being my dad to being Slim, the President of the Phantom Bastards MC. It's almost scary how he can go from President of the club who's ruthless, only looks out for the men and women in the club, and does whatever he can to try to straddle the line of good and evil. When he's my dad, he's caring, loving, not ruthless at all, and shows emotions not many people get to see from him. He's the man who taught me you can have feelings, but also have a ruthlessness to you when it comes to the club.

Before I can think of much else, we're pulling up to the meet, and once again, Terror isn't here. Dad and I park our bikes just off the dirt path and shut the engines off. Jose's car pulls up behind us, and I know he's going to sit in there until Terror shows up.

I try not to glance around to alert anyone to the rest of our guys in different locations surrounding the area. We have at least two snipers here today, and that's just the men of the Phantom Bastards. I'm not sure how many more snipers are here from Jose's crew. At this point, I don't give a shit. The only thing I want right now is for Terror and the bitches to show up so we can take them the fuck out once and for all.

Finally, I hear the bikes pulling up the dirt road, and the adrenaline starts pumping through my veins. It's showtime, and my trigger finger is getting twitchy. So, I shove my hands in the pockets of my jeans before I do something stupid as fuck. That's not going to happen until later. I give it ten minutes before the first shot rings out. Terror isn't smart enough to keep his mouth shut and let Jose do the talking in the beginning.

Terror pulls up, and he has all his men with him once again. A smile wants to show on my face, but I think of Rancor putting his hands on my woman, and the urge quickly disappears as I search for him. He's the last man to get off his bike. I watch as he spits on the ground and searches for me. It's not like I'm hard to fucking spot with only three of us standing here since Jose has gotten out of his car and joined us.

"So, this is your contact with the cartel?" Terror asks.

"Yep," my dad answers in a clipped tone. "This is Jo . . ."

"I don't want to fucking talk to you," Terror cuts in, pissing my dad off even more as his face turns red.

Jose doesn't say a word for a minute, and I know he's trying to compose himself. There's a vein jumping not only in his forehead but in his neck as well. This shit is about to jump off, and Terror has no fucking clue. Sucks to be him and the rest of the Devils Rule bitch ass pussies.

"Jose," he finally says, holding his hand out for Terror to shake.

Instead of shaking Jose's hand, Terror spits on the ground at his feet. Jose quickly raises his hand, and I reach behind me to pull my gun from my back. Gunfire erupts, and I watch as Rancor tries to get to his bike. I fire on him and hit him in the leg. Jose goes for Terror as my dad pulls his gun and starts returning fire.

I move directly for Rancor; he's the only one I'm focused on as chaos erupts around me. Rancor is on the ground, and I stand over him. For a minute, everything around me fades as I remember the bruises and cut on the back of Sam's head when she came back from the store that day, he put his hands on her.

"Don't kill me," Rancor pleads like the bitch he is. "This is all on Terror."

Not only is Rancor a bitch, but he's also a snitch too. I don't like a man who's either. This goes to show there's no loyalty in Devils Rule, and each man is out for himself. This isn't a fucking club; it's a band of pussies pretending their badasses because they beat on women to submit to them and steal from real men killing anyone who doesn't follow their orders. Fuck these assholes and the bikes they rode in on.

I point my gun at Rancor's head and pull the trigger. There's an uneasy feeling in my gut as I turn from the man I just killed, and look for my father. He's standing next to Jose, and his gun is raised to take out the few remaining assholes we came here to kill. As I go to walk to his side, I see something out of the corner of my eye. Turning in the opposite direction, I go to see what it is.

Behind a bike is a young man. He can't be more than seventeen years old. He's cowering behind the bikes, and I can see the pain and fear in his eyes.

"Who are you?" I ask, raising my gun in his direction because I still don't trust him.

"I-I-I'm Ryan," he answers, his voice quivering as he stares at the barrel of my gun.

"Why are you here?" I ask him, not lowering the gun.

"Terror is my brother and forced me to come with them today," he tells me.

"You don't want to be here?" I question him.

Ryan shakes his head. The fear in his eyes isn't from the gunfire or being here— it's from Terror.

"Stand up," I tell him.

He does as I tell him and stands before me, his eyes never leaving mine. I lift up his shirt and see bruising littering his body. He's got a black eye, and there's bruising on his arm too.

"You a drug user or anythin'?" I ask, going with my gut on him.

"Never touch the stuff because I see what it's done to my brother. He's changed and not for the good," Ryan answers.

"How old are you?"

"I'll be eighteen in two days," he tells me.

"Come with me. And watch your fuckin' back," I warn him.

As we walk up to my dad, Jose is about to lose his shit on Terror, who's the only one still alive. The gunfire has ceased, and Terror is still looking like he's the king of the world. This man really has no fucking clue, but he's about to.

"What did you find, Playboy?" my dad asks me.

"This bitches brother. Seems to me Terror likes to hit him," I say, lifting his shirt to show my dad and Jose the bruises covering his body.

"I see. Son, you no longer have to worry about this happenin'," my dad says. "You wanna come home with us?"

Ryan doesn't even look at his brother as he nods his head and steps behind me.

"You dumb fucker. I took you in when I didn't have to and let you live with me rent-free," Terror shouts at his brother.

"Yeah, and he was beaten for probably every bad mood you were in. He'll learn what a man truly is now. Not a worthless piece of shit like you," I tell him, cocking my arm back and letting it fly to punch him in the face.

I land a few more punches before Jose, and my dad pulls me from him. Terror is Jose's to kill, and I need to remember that.

"I'm sorry, Jose," I apologize to the cartel king.

"I get it," he responds. "Now, let's get him taken care of so we can get the fuck outta here."

Jose pulls his gun out finally and shoots Terror between the eyes. We all wish we could take our time and torture these fuckers, but we just don't.

"Dad, I think we need to get out of here," I tell him, the feeling in my gut not going away with all these men dead before us.

"What's wrong?" he asks, looking at me.

"I don't know, gut feelin'," I respond.

"Get outta here. Go find out what's going on. Slim, I'll be in touch. Thank you for the heads up in this," Jose tells us.

My dad and I run to our bikes. Ryan waits for us to get on before he looks around. He's not sure what to do right now, and I can't honestly say I blame him.

"What's wrong, son?" my dad asks.

"I don't know what to do now," Ryan states.

"Can you ride?" I ask him.

Ryan nods his head at me but doesn't say a word. I guess Terror never let him talk. That's about to change if I have anything to do with it. Hell, if the club has anything to do with it.

"Pick whatever bike you want, and let's roll," I tell him.

Ryan goes over to get on Terror's bike. It's honestly the best one of the bunch. The bike is all matte black with only chrome accents. I watch closely as Ryan gets on it and starts it up after putting a helmet on. Nodding to him, I let my dad roll out first while Ryan and I head out behind him. At least the kid has ridden in some sort of formation before as he rides perfectly by my side.

The only thing I can think of is Sam right now. Something isn't right with her, and I know it in my gut. Whatever is going on has to do with her specifically.

Hang on, I'm coming, baby. I think to myself as we race toward the clubhouse. I don't even give a shit about the blood spatters on me or anything else. Not right now.

Chapter Thirty-Four

Sam

PLAYBOY AND THE guys have been gone just about an hour when all hell breaks loose at the clubhouse. I'm sitting with Gwen, Kim, and Shy when the first contraction hits. I don't even say a word to them as I silently breathe through it, hoping it's just a Braxton hicks contraction.

"Can someone help me up?" I ask once it's gone.

"What's going on?" Shy asks, standing up with Gwen to help me.

"I have to go to the bathroom," I reply.

The second I stand up, my water breaks, and it lands in a puddle on the floor directly under me. We all look down as one and Shy goes into protective mama bear mode. She's giving out orders since only the women are here right now.

"Have you been having contractions?" she asks me once the rest of the women have left to do what she's ordered them to do.

"I've only felt one. It was right before my water broke, and I thought it was a Braxton Hicks. Shy, it's too early," I tell her, fear beginning to fill me as my senses come back.

"It's okay, honey. We're gonna get you to the hospital. Kim is calling Doctor Sanchez now so she can meet us there. Gwen is trying to call Slim and Playboy," she informs me.

Caleb comes running up to us with tears in his eyes. He doesn't understand what's going on right now, and I go to comfort him as another contraction hits.

"Mama!" he cries out as I double over in pain.

"Mommy's okay," Shy says, pulling him into her side. "We're gonna go get her cleaned up and then take her to the hospital."

Caleb nods his head, but the tears don't stop. He follows us as we move toward the bedroom once the contraction has left me. My son doesn't take his eyes off me until we get inside the door, and it's time for me to put some dry clothes on.

"Buddy, can you help me put this in the SUV?" Gwen asks him, pulling my bag out of the closet. "You can help me call Daddy and Papi too."

"Yeah," he says, sniffling as Shy gets me out a dress and clean pair of panties.

As soon as Gwen and Caleb are gone, she shuts the door and helps me change. It's takes longer than I'd like to admit because I'm having contractions and we have to keep stopping. This is going a lot quicker than I remember it being with Caleb. All it's honestly doing is making my fear level spike because I'm early, and it's going faster. Not to mention Playboy isn't here and he should be.

I know he's taking care of business, and we had no clue I'd go into labor this early. We were told to expect it to happen before I made it to forty weeks since I'm having twins. However, I'm only thirty-five weeks pregnant, and it's way too soon for me to have our sons. My only concern is for them at this moment, and I don't want my fear to have a negative impact on them.

"Sam, calm down, honey," Shy tells me, helping me up from the bed once my panties are in place.

Shy has seen more of me than I ever thought she would. But, we're all women here, and it's not like she doesn't have the same parts as I do. I get up with the help of Kim and her, and we head out of the clubhouse.

"Where did Jennifer go?" I ask, not seeing her around us.

"She's staying here with the kids. Caleb is the only one coming with us because I know he won't stay here with her," Kim tells me.

"Okay. Thank you all for everything," I tell them, getting up in the SUV as another contraction hits me.

"No thanks needed," Shy tells me as she closes my door and races around the front of the vehicle. "Did you get a hold of her doctor?"

"Yes, she's going to meet us there," Kim answers.

I nod my head as Shy pulls out of the clubhouse and leaves. She's racing through town to get me to the hospital before we end up delivering these babies in the SUV with Caleb here. That's the last thing I want to do because it will scar my poor son for the rest of his life.

"Anyone get a hold of Playboy?" I ask as tears start falling down my face.

"Not yet, honey," Gwen answers. "I'm still trying, and so isn't Kim. Caleb's helping us."

Nodding my head, I grab the edge of the seat as another contraction starts. These hurt so damn bad, and that's something else I don't remember about having Caleb. I'm sure they hurt just as bad, but I blocked it out. I think every single woman who's gone through childbirth blocks the pain out while they're pregnant again.

Shy pulls into the hospital, screeching to a halt just outside the emergency room doors. Doctor Sanchez is waiting for me with a wheelchair. She opens my door, and Kim helps her get me into the waiting chair before wheeling me inside. I can hear Caleb screaming for me as he's still in the SUV with Shy and Gwen so she can park in a spot before coming in. My heart is breaking for him because he's in pain, and I can't help him right now.

"How far apart are the contractions?" Doctor Sanchez asks me.

"They're about five minutes apart," Kim answers for me. "She's panicking because her husband isn't here, and it's too early for the boys to be born."

"Sam, I need you to relax for me. We knew it was a possibility the babies would be early. This isn't as bad as you're thinking," Doctor Sanchez tells me. "You got married?"

I nod my head as another contraction hits. Kim holds my hand and lets me squeeze the shit out of her. She smiles at me and gives me encouraging words until the contraction is finally over with.

Doctor Sanchez's distraction isn't helping as the contraction hits right after her question.

When we get to the maternity ward, Doctor Sanchez grabs some nurses and brings them in the room with us. From there, it's a whirlwind of activity as I'm changed into a gown, put in bed, and the monitor is strapped around me to monitor everything going on.

Once I'm settled, Gwen, Shy, and Caleb come into the room. Caleb gets up in the bed with me and rests his head on my shoulder and his hand on my belly above the monitor.

"You okay, mama?" he asks, his eyes still filled with tears.

"Yes, buddy. Your brothers have decided they want their birthday to be today," I tell him, trying to make him understand.

"My brothers are coming?" he asks, excitement replacing his fear.

"Yes, they are," I respond to him.

Caleb leans down over my stomach and is careful not to touch anything.

"I'm your brother. I want to meet you now," he says, talking to his brothers still in my stomach. "I love you."

"Caleb, why don't you come to the cafeteria with me?" Gwen asks him, trying to get him out of the room as the doctor comes back in.

He nods his head and jumps down off the side of the bed. He and Gwen leave the room to go to the cafeteria. Doctor Sanchez does her thing and exams me. After a minute, she takes off her gloves and looks at me.

"This is going quick, Sam," she says. "You're already about six centimeters dilated. If you're going to want an epidural, we gotta do it now."

"Yes, please," I tell her.

"Okay. I'll send it in right now," she tells me, leaving the room after assuring me she'll be back in a little bit.

Nodding my head, I lay back and wait to get the epidural. The only thing I'm thinking about is Playboy missing the birth of our children. Shy is at my side when her phone rings. She's tried calling the men too since getting here.

"Hello, Playboy?" she asks. "You need to get to the hospital. Now. Sam's in labor and the doctor says it's gonna go fast. How far away are you?"

She listens for a few minutes, and I can't peel my eyes from her until another contraction hits. I scream out in pain as this one is stronger than the ones I've been having. She's still on the phone, and I know my husband is hearing me scream out in pain. This is not a good thing with him on his bike.

"She's okay. Just having a contraction. Get here as soon as you can," she says into her phone before hanging up.

"Where is he?" I ask her, laying back against the bed.

"Just leaving the clubhouse. They went there looking for us. I'm not sure why his calls weren't going through," she answers.

Before we can do anything else, the man giving me my epidural comes in the room, and they all help me get into position for him to do his job. I honestly have no clue what to expect because I've never had one before. Caleb, I did a natural childbirth, but there's no way I'm going to do that this time. Not if I'm already in this much pain.

He does his thing, and soon I'm lying back in the bed on my side. The contractions are still coming, and they feel like they're ripping me in half. At the same time, Caleb and Gwen come back into the room. My son has a large smile on his face, and I know he's got something to tell me.

"Daddy and Papi are here!" he says excitedly.

I don't get a chance to respond as Playboy and Slim walk in the room at that very second. Playboy rushes to my side and leans over me. He kisses me and places a hand on my stomach, and I can see his apology in his eyes before he says a single word.

"I'm so sorry, baby," he says, resting his forehead against mine. "Are you okay?"

"I'm okay. The epidural is in, and I don't think it's going to be much longer," I tell him.

"Honey, we'll be out in the waitin' room with the rest of the family," Slim says, kissing the top of my head. "Caleb, you comin' with me?"

"Yeah, Papi," he answers him. "Love you, Mama, and babies."

Soon, it's just Playboy, and I left in the room. He sits on the edge of the bed next to me. For the next little while, we just sit together and talk. Playboy helps me through every contraction, and it does help to have him by my side.

"Give me one more push, Sam," Doctor Sanchez says as I push to deliver our first son.

Playboy is holding my leg up on one side, and a nurse is holding up my leg on the other side. I flop back on the bed as the pressure I've been feeling is suddenly gone. It's not long before I hear our son's cry. His cry is loud and angry as one of the nurses whisks him away.

Before I can concentrate on the first baby, another contraction rips through me. Sweat is pouring off me, and the nurse is mopping it up as fast as it's coming. Or at least she's trying to.

"One more time, baby," Playboy tells me, kissing me on the top of my head. "You're doin' so good. I'm so proud of you, baby."

"Ahh!" I scream out as I push again. "I can't do this."

"Yes, you can. You're stronger than you know," my husband tells me. "A few more pushes, and our other baby will be here.

I nod my head at him and get ready to push again. As I feel the contraction hit me, I push again. The next contraction hits and I push again. It takes three more pushes, and our second son is born. He lets out an angry wail, the same as his older brother.

Tears fall down my cheeks, and I collapse against the bed completely spent.

"I love you so much, baby. You have just given me the greatest gift of my entire life," Playboy tells me, kissing me.

"Thank you," I tell him, leaning into his body. "You've given me so many gifts, and I'll never be able to thank you for anything."

"Mom, Dad," Doctor Sanchez says. "You have two healthy boys. They don't seem to be having any issues right now with them being early. We'll keep an eye on them, though. For now, we usually suggest you both hold them against your bare skin. It helps them regulate their body temperature. Are you ready to meet your sons?"

"We are," I answer, wiping my tears away.

Two nurses walk over with our sons in their arms. I receive one of our little boys while Playboy gets his other son. He sits down on the bed next to me as we gaze at our precious bundles of joy.

As I'm looking at our sons, I realize one thing. They are completely identical. Already I can see they're identical twins and not fraternal. I look up at the doctor and see her smiling down at us.

"How didn't we know they're identical?" I ask her.

"What?" Playboy asks me.

"They are identical," Doctor Sanchez says. "I'm not sure why the tech never told us that, but you can already see they're going to be exactly the same looks-wise."

"Fuck me!" Playboy says as the baby he's holding begins to cry.

"I'll leave you alone so you can try feeding them," Doctor Sanchez tells us. "Sam, you did amazing. I'll see you soon."

When she leaves the room, Playboy helps me pull down the front of my gown, and I hold our son to my chest. He latches on to my nipple, and Playboy looks down in amazement. I pull back the little hat they have on his head and see a headful of blonde hair. He's got grey eyes based on the quick look I had of them a minute ago. Playboy pulls back the little hat on the other baby, and he's also got the same blonde hair covering his head. I'll wait to see his eyes when he's hungry.

As one son eats, I carefully unwrap him and take a look at his little body. I count his ten fingers and look down to see his ten little toes. These little ones are so tiny weighing in at just under five pounds for each of them. My only concern right now is that they don't end up having to go to NICU. Playboy unwraps our other little one, and I inspect him too. They are absolutely perfect in my eyes.

"You've never been more beautiful to me than you are right now," he tells me, holding our other son cradled to his chest. "I'm goin' to lay him down between your legs so I can take my shirt off."

I nod my head and keep my attention between the two babies. Playboy sets his cut on the chair in the room and then pulls his shirt from his body. When he picks the baby back up, he cradles him to his chest without the blanket wrapped around him.

"So, do you have any name ideas?" I ask him.

We agreed to wait to name them until they were born. Part of my reasoning was in case something was wrong and the babies, or at least one of them, is a girl. I look at our children and try to think of names for them.

"What about Dylan Michael for one of them?" Playboy asks.

I think it over for a minute, and I love the name. Nodding my head, I look down at the baby still nursing. And the perfect name hits me.

"I love it. How about Carson James for this little guy? Carson really helped me out when I needed it the most," I ask him.

Playboy doesn't hesitate as he tells me he loves the name. By the time Carson is done eating, Dylan is ready for his turn. So, we switch babies, and I watch on as my husband lays Dylan down to change his diaper. He's practically a pro at doing it.

Once our sons are done eating, Playboy makes sure they both have fresh diapers on, and then we hold them against our skin for a little bit. I know Caleb and the rest of our family members are waiting to come in. Caleb is probably bugging the hell out of Slim, Shy, and everyone else to get in here.

"Playboy, go get them," I tell him, having him help me pull my gown back up to cover me.

He hands me Dylan and puts his shirt back on so he can get them. I'm staring down at our boys when the door opens once again.

"Mama!" Caleb quietly yells. "My brothers are here!"

"I know, baby. You want to be the first one to see them?" I ask him, not seeing anyone else enter the room.

"They're comin'. Givin' us just a minute for the five of us," Playboy answers my unasked question.

He brings Caleb over to the bed and lifts him to sit next to me as I have both boys in my arms. I lower my arms so he can see them, and he takes a few minutes to inspect the newest additions to our family.

"They are not cute," he finally says.

Playboy and I laugh at him. Leave it to him to think his brothers are ugly. I don't know what we're going to do with him.

"That's not very nice," I tell him, without censor in my voice.

"I'm sorry, mama. Maybe they'll get cute like me as they get older," he says, looking between Playboy and me.

I can't help it. I laugh until I have tears in my eyes. There's a light knock on the door before Shy pokes her head in the room.

"Is it safe to come in?" she asks.

"Yeah, come on in," I answer with my laughter still coming out.

"What's going on in here?" she asks, walking straight up to the side of my bed to look at the babies.

"Caleb just informed us his brothers aren't cute. But, they might grow into being cute just like him," I tell her as everyone starts laughing.

"You're too much for me sometimes, little man," Slim tells him, ruffling his hair.

I nod my head to Playboy, and he grabs one of the babies from me. After walking around the bed, he hands the baby to his dad. Slim sits down in the chair and stares at the little boy in his arms. I hand the other baby over to Shy before she walks over to him and stands next to him. Shy looks between the babies and starts laughing her ass off.

"Woman, what's wrong with you?" Slim asks her, looking at the other baby.

"Playboy and Sam are in some damn trouble," she answers her husband.

The second Slim realizes what she's talking about, a smile breaks out on his face. I lift my phone and snap a picture of the four of them. It's definitely going to be printed off and hung on the wall. This is one of the best pictures I've ever seen before.

"What's goin' on?" Stryker asks, walking over to the babies.

"They're identical twins," Slim answers him. "Son, I told you all the bullshit you put me through growin' up was goin' to come back to bite you in the ass. Looks like I was right times two."

Everyone in the room starts laughing. They're all quiet, though, so the other patients up here aren't disturbed. This is what I've always wanted; a large family that supports one another and isn't ashamed to show the love they feel for one another. At this moment, I couldn't be happier than I am right now.

"So, what are the names of my grandsons?" Slim finally asks once everyone has had a look at them.

"Slim, the baby you're holding is Carson James, and Shy is holding Dylan Michael," I tell them.

"Good, strong names," he tells me, looking at them.

Shy and Slim haven't let anyone else hold them, and I don't see them doing it anytime soon. Slim is nothing but a proud man of his grandchildren, and he won't let anyone near them if he's holding any little one. His wife is no better, honestly, and I know these boys are going to be just as spoiled as the rest of the kids in the club are. I wouldn't change anything in my life right now.

"Uh oh," Caleb says. "One is crying."

We laugh as Shy walks over with Dylan in her arms. She hands him over to me, and everyone quickly makes their exit, so I can feed the baby. Shy lingers a minute with Caleb so we can tell him goodbye.

"You be a good boy for Shy and Papi," I tell him. "We'll see you tomorrow."

"Okay, Mama. I love you and my brothers," he says, leaning in for a kiss.

"I love you too," I respond as he gently leans over enough to place a kiss on his brother's cheek.

Playboy walks over to give him a hug and kiss before leaning down further so he can kiss his other brother on the cheek.

"I love you, Daddy," he says as he takes one last look at us.

"I love you too, buddy," Playboy responds just before they walk out the door. "As soon as possible, I want to adopt him."

"I couldn't agree more," I respond as I pull my gown down and nurse Dylan.

The rest of the night, Playboy and I spend together with our sons. We feed them, change them, and hold them close to our bodies for their body temperature. I fall asleep with Carson in my arms before Playboy takes him from me and places him in the bassinet with Dylan. After making sure they're both asleep, he climbs into bed with me and curls around my body. I'm so tired, and I don't even realize it.

Epilogue

Gwen

WE'RE AT THE clubhouse for a cookout to celebrate the birth of Dylan and Carson. They're the cutest babies ever, and I can't wait until I can hold them. I've been keeping my distance because I had a cold and I don't want to get them sick. So, while I'm here celebrating with the Phantom Bastards, I'm keeping my distance from all the kids.

I've been sitting with my sister, Kim, and her man Fox for most of the day. The only time I've been alone is when they've been up to dance. Other than that, I've been with them like I am every single day. I'm kind of tired of living with them, but I have nowhere else to go, and I don't have a job yet, so I can't afford my place.

Everyone keeps telling me they want me to live my life after being with my father for so long and not getting to experience anything. I wasn't allowed to go to school, have friends, talk to any of his associates who came to the house, or anything else. Still, I'm not sure how I'm supposed to get the experience they want me to have when I still do nothing. The only friends I have are club members, and the only places I'm ever at are the clubhouse, Kim and Fox's house, or shopping with the ol' ladies of the club. The most interaction I have is with the children of the club because I'm still considered one even though I'm almost twenty years old.

I had one boyfriend my entire life. His name was Neal, and the only reason I was allowed to be with him is that he was one of my father's associates. He wasn't a nice man, and I can't honestly tell you who treated me worse; Neal or my father. It's a toss-up I don't care to think about these days because it just keeps pulling me back to that place and time in my life when I have such a hard time forgetting it.

I'm taking online classes now because there's been so much going on with the club, no one wanted me to take the chance of being without a guard. And, they couldn't spare any of the Prospects to go with me to school. So, I'm still essentially a prisoner, and I have no clue how to talk to anyone about the way I'm feeling.

"What are you thinkin' about so hard over there?" Fox asks me as Kim leaves the picnic table to get another baby fix.

"Life," I answer honestly.

"What's goin' through your head Lil' Bit?" he asks. "I know you've been feelin' some type of way lately. It's written all over your face."

"I don't know if I should talk about it," I tell him, casting my eyes down and away from him.

"Let's take a walk," he says suddenly, standing up and doesn't wait for me to follow him.

I catch up to him, and he waits for me to talk as we round the corner of the clubhouse and stop. Fox looks at me, and his brilliant blue eyes shine so bright I feel as if he can see straight into my soul. It's the only reason I find myself opening up to my sister's man.

"I appreciate everything the club did to get me away from my dad and Neal. There's nothing I wouldn't do for anyone here. But, you all keep telling me you want me to get out and experience life and everything. I want to, but it's still not happening. I go to school online, I'm either at the house with you guys or here at the clubhouse, and the main people I'm around here are the kids. I just don't understand anything," I tell him, tears filling my eyes.

"What else is goin' on in that head of yours?" he asks.

"You know what. It's not like it's a secret that I like Killer. He's nice to me, and he feels the same way as everyone else that I need to get out and experience life, but there's no way to do that. I can't date because I don't have any way to meet anyone. I'm never going to be ready to date anyone or have sex because I'm still treated like a child, and I'm almost twenty damn years old," I tell him, letting the tears pour from my face as I slide down the side of the clubhouse and sob into my knees.

"Lil' Bit, we truly do want you to do anythin' you wanna do. We're just as new to this as you are. Yeah, it's been more than enough time for you to be out on your own, workin', goin' to school, or anythin' else you wanna do. Let me talk to Kim and the guys, and we'll figure somethin' out. You good with that?" he asks me, sliding down next to me and pulling me into his arms. "You'll just have to realize you're gonna have someone on you at all times if you're on your own."

"Are you sure? You're really goin' to try to help me out?" I ask him, afraid to get my hopes up too much.

"I'll do my best. Now, why don't you go inside and clean up, so no one knows anythin' is wrong. Meet us back at the table, and we'll start talkin' to your sister about things," Fox says.

Nodding my head, I let Fox help me stand back up and make my way inside the clubhouse. I don't run into anyone as I head inside and make my way to the bathroom that's in the hallway on the way to the common room. When I step inside the room, my heart breaks, and I wish I hadn't needed to come in here.

Standing less than five feet away from me is Killer. He's leaning against the wall, his long dark hair hanging down his back in his usual ponytail with his black bandana wrapped around his head. His eyes are closed, and one of his hands are wrapped around the hair of the woman kneeling in front of him. She's giving him a blow job, and I can't stop the sob that is bubbling up inside me.

Backing out of the bathroom, I slam into someone and look to see Playboy standing there. He steadies me and looks down into my face as I back away from him. I'm sure I'm nothing more than a laughingstock to everyone here. Including Fox and my sister because of this stupid crush I have on a man I have no chance with.

"I don't feel good. Can you let my sister and Fox know I'm going home, please?" I ask, turning and running from the clubhouse.

I pull my keys from my pocket and jump in my car. That's the only thing I've been given since coming here. Fox and the guys taught me how to drive, and then my sister bought me a car. Still, I'm not supposed to drive it anywhere unless Fox or Kim are with me. Well, they can kiss my ass tonight because there's not a chance I'm going to stay at the clubhouse where everyone thinks I'm a child and nothing more than a stupid girl for liking Killer.

My phone starts ringing, and I ignore it. I won't pick it up while I'm driving. Besides, it's not like it's a long drive to get from the clubhouse to Fox and Kim's house. Maybe ten minutes at most. Once I get there, I see Kim and Fox have called me repeatedly since I left. Playboy, Sam, Slim, and Shy have also called me. Ignoring all the calls and messages they've left, I shut my phone off and make my way inside the house.

I take a shower and then get ready for bed. I'm not sure I even want to be at my sister and Fox's house right now, but I don't know if I have any other choice at the moment. Every spare penny I've gotten since being here, I've been saving up, but it's still not enough to leave here.

Tears start flowing from my eyes again. This is apparently the day I'm never going to stop crying. I thought I was done with this part of my life, but it seems as if I'm not. So many thoughts are swirling through my head, and I have no clue what to do with any of them. The only thing I can think of is getting out of this house and away from everyone for a while.

Finally, sleep claims me, and it's a restless sleep filled with dreams of everyone in the Phantom Bastards laughing at me. Killer is front and center of the group, and even my own sister is laughing at how stupid and immature I'm being.

Killer

I've been hanging out with my brothers at the clubhouse all day. We're here to celebrate two new members of the family, and I couldn't be happier. However, my eyes have been on Gwen all day long. No matter who I'm talking to or what I'm doing, my eyes never stray far from her.

Gwen is absolutely stunning and has gotten better since coming back with us. Instead of being overly skinny and malnourished, she's gained some much-needed weight and developed into the woman she is now. A woman with curves in all the right places and one who has no clue how truly stunning she really is.

Today, Gwen's wearing a long white dress. It has spaghetti straps and accentuates her chest. She's been laying out in the sun, and her skin is now a golden-brown color while her brown hair has blonde highlights in it. There's no make-up on her face as she sits at the table with her sister and Fox. The second I saw her walking through the clubhouse with Kim, my cock instantly took notice and stood to attention.

I've been hard most of the afternoon, and if I don't find relief soon, I'm going to do something I regret. I'm going to end up taking Gwen to my room here and have my way with her. I'll be no better than the rest of the men who have taken and taken from her throughout her entire life. I refuse to do that.

As Fox gets up from the table and leads Gwen from the party, I know my chance is here to escape the party to find some relief. The house bunnies aren't allowed at the cookout, but they are in the clubhouse until the kids go home. I know how to be discreet as I go inside and find one of them. It's a new one, and I don't even know her name; I don't care to know her name.

This bitch has nothing on Gwen. She's skin and bones, and her hair is a bottle job in dire need of a touch-up. She's got make-up caked on her face, and it looks to be days old. There's nothing in her eyes while Gwen's golden eyes are usually full of life and wonder as she discovers new things in the world around her. Hell, she looks like she's been ridden hard and put away wet. Right now, she's good enough to suck my cock.

I pull her into the bathroom on the first floor with me, and don't worry about anything other than getting off.

"On your knees," I growl out.

The woman tries to kiss me, and I turn my head from her. I don't kiss any of these bitches. Never know when they've last had a cock in their mouth, and that's not anything I'm interested in finding out.

"On your knees, and that's it," I say.

After pouting, she does as I ask. I unzip my jeans and pull my cock out. When her mouth covers me, I start to go soft. She's not Gwen, and I know it. I shouldn't be in here and trying to find relief with someone else. But I can't go there with Gwen.

Not yet. Eventually, I will, but she needs to get out in the world and live some sort of life. Something she has yet to begin doing, and I want to give that to her somehow.

There's only one way to not only get my cock rock hard again but to cum fast as fuck, and that's to think of Gwen. I picture her on her knees in front of me and giving me pleasure. Closing my eyes, I see Gwen in all her glory in front of me, and it's not long before I feel my balls begin to tighten and pull up close to my body.

"Fuck!" I roar out as I cum down her throat.

As my breathing calms back down, I hear a commotion in the hallway. What the fuck is going on now.

Tucking my cock back in my jeans, I zip them up and step around the woman still on her knees in front of me.

"Where are you going?" she asks.

"I'm done here," I respond, not bothering to look back at her.

Opening the bathroom door, I see Playboy, Slim, Kim, and Fox standing there. Playboy looks at me, and I can see the anger in his eyes. It intensifies as the house bunny steps up behind me and tries to place a claim on me by resting her hand on my chest. Fuck that!

"I knew you had somethin' to do with this," Playboy accuses me.

"What the fuck are you talkin' about?" I ask him thoroughly confused.

"Gwen just fuckin' took off. Backed out of there real quick and spouted some shit about not feelin' well. Now, she won't answer anyone's calls," Playboy tells me.

Before I can process what he's told me, Playboy lands a punch right in my face. I reel back and almost knock the house bunny down as I catch myself on the door frame of the bathroom.

"She saw that?" I ask, my heart breaking in my chest at her catching me in a compromising position.

"Yeah, ass face, she saw you. She's fuckin' shattered and now who knows what's goin' through her head," Playboy answers.

"Killer, when are you gonna get your shit together?" Kim asks me.

"Me? Seriously Kim?" I ask her. "We all agreed to let her live her life. I gave you my fuckin' word I wouldn't touch her until she did. What has she been able to do since bein' rescued? Not a fuckin' thing. This isn't just on me. Gwen doesn't give a fuck what I do and don't do."

"You're a fuckin' idiot," Fox tells me. "You're the only one who doesn't see Gwen is half in love with you and I just talked to her about this today. She wants to live her life and is beginnin' to resent not bein' able to. Wants to be out on her own and go to school. Now, I have no clue where she's goin' to go from here."

"Let me take care of it," I tell everyone around me.

"I think you've fuckin' done enough," Playboy yells out.

"She already thinks you want nothin' to do with her," Fox informs me. "That we must think she's stupid because you're never gonna want her, and you just proved her point."

"I want her more than any of you will *ever* know!" I yell out, slamming my fist in the wall as rage fills me.

I leave the clubhouse and straddle my bike. Fox runs after me, but he can see the look on my face. I'm not going to stop for him or anyone else. My new mission is to ensure Gwen lives her life and slowly gets used to being around me. From now on, she'll be under my fuckin' roof, and I'll make sure she gets to do what she wants. Kim, Fox, and everyone else can fuck off if they think I'm going to put her last anymore.

Leaving the clubhouse, I point my bike in the direction of Fox's house. I need to have eyes on Gwen and see if she's okay. So, when I pull up, I quietly go into the house through the back door and make my way into her room. With the moonlight streaming window, I can see fresh tear marks staining her cheeks, and my heart breaks a little more at the sight.

Gwen might be asleep, but she's not resting. So, I slide my boots off and climb in the bed behind her. It's a tight fit because she only has a full-size bed, but I'll make it work. Wrapping my arms around her, I pull Gwen's body to mine and whisper into her ear.

"I'm so fuckin' sorry you saw that. I care about you more than you know, and I'll never do it again," I whisper to her.

After laying in the dark for a long time thinking about my fuck-up, I finally fall asleep with Gwen still in my arms. I'll need to be gone before she wakes up, but for tonight, I'm giving us both what we want even if she doesn't realize it.

The End . . . for now.

Sam's Playboy Playlist

Never Say Never – The Fray

Locked Away – Hamilton

Lay Me Down – Sam Smith

Missed – Ella Henderson

Half A Man – Dean Lewis

Love Me – Aaron Lewis

Bad Boy – Brantley Gilbert

The Best of Me – Brantley Gilbert

Read Me My Rights – Brantley Gilbert

Best I Ever Had – State of Shock

Out of My Head – Theory of a Deadman

Cold – Crossfade

Can't Forget You – My Darkest Days

Pass Slowly – Seether

Bad Day – Fuel

You're Beautiful Ending – One Less Reason

Uneasy – One Less Reason

Drink My Stupid Away – Royal Bliss

Don't You Dare – Alexz Johnson

I don't Know If I Should Stay – Alexz Johnson

Outlaw In Me – Brantley Gilbert

Acknowledgements

First and foremost, I need to thank my kids. You always stand by me and give me time to write. You're my biggest fans and support me no matter what. I love you more than you'll ever know.

My PA, Melissa. Thank you for all the help and trying to keep my crazy ass on task. I appreciate the talks and everything you've done since agreeing to take me on.

Kim, thank you for being you. You're a part of my family and someone I don't know what I'd do without. I love ya lady!!

To my beta girls. Thank you for everything. You point out mistakes and get me feedback immediately. Especially if I tell you I'm on a crazy deadline. Without you, this process wouldn't work and I'm glad to be able to send you more stories now as I heal.

Courtney. You're one of my best friends, a kickass editor, and an amazing person to know. I'm glad to have you as a friend, a part of my team, and for everything you do for me.

Rebecca. I'm glad we met this year at a signing. Now look at our crazy asses. I won't forget about a certain #Chronicle that needs to be written either!

Shelly. There are no words for your amazing talent. You have been working with me, helping me, and giving me advice since the beginning of my career. Thank you for everything you have done and continue to do for me and so many others.

To the fans. Without you, I wouldn't be able to live my dream. I love putting stories out in the world for you and hearing from those of you who tell me how a story or character has reached you. I'm always available for anyone that needs an ear to listen. Thank you for your unwavering support. I love you all!

As always, I know I'm leaving someone out. To the rest of you, thank you. You have been by my side and stood by me as this year decided to kick my ass. Thank you just isn't enough. I'll find some way to repay you for everything.

About the Author

Growing up, I was constantly reading anything I could get my hands on. Even if that meant I was reading my grandma's books that weren't so age appropriate. I started out reading Judy Blume, then graduated to romance, mainly historical romance, and last year I found an amazing group of Indie authors that wrote MC books. Instantly I fell in love with these books.

For a long time, I've wanted to write. I just never had the courage to go through with actually doing it. During a book release party, I mentioned that I wanted to write and I received encouragement from an amazing author. So, I took a leap and wrote my first book. Even though this amazing journey is just starting for me, I wouldn't have even started if it weren't for a wonderful group of authors and others that I've met along the way.

I am a mother of three children. Only one girl in the bunch! My family and friends mean the world to me and I'd be lost without them. Including new friends that I've met along the way. I've lived in New York my whole life, either in Upstate or the Southern Tier. I love it during the summer, spring, and fall. But, not so much during the winter. I hate driving in snow with a passion!

When I'm not hanging out with my family/friends, reading, or writing, you can find me listening to music. I love almost all music! Or, I'm watching a NASCAR race.

I look forward to meeting new friends, even if I'm extremely shy!

Here are some links to connect with me:

Facebook:
https://www.facebook.com/ErinOsborneAuthor/

Twitter: https://twitter.com/author_osborne

My website:
http://erinosborne1013.wix.com/authorerinosborne

Spotify: https://open.spotify.com/user/emgriff07

Other Books

Wild Kings MC: Clifton Falls

Skylar's Saviors
Bailey's Saving Grace
Tank's Salvation
Melody's Temptation
Blade's Awakening
Irish's Destiny
Rage's Redemption
Pops

Wild Kings MC: Dander Falls

Darcy's Downfall
Riley's Rescue
Harley's Surrender
Shadow's Dilemma

Phantom Bastards MC

Jennifer's Choice
Slim's Second Chance
Shy's Last Stand
Sam's Playboy

Satan's Anarchy MC

Satan's Revenge
Hadleigh's Desire
Cassidy's Resurgence
Renegade's Choice
Grave's Claim

Old Ladies Club

Book 1: Wild Kings MC
Book 2: Soul Shifterz MC
Book 3: Rebel Guardians MC
Book 4: Rage Ryders MC

Legacies

Desire

<u>Wicked Angels:</u>

Knight's Unforeseen Change

<u>Anthologies:</u>

Bad to the Bone
Heart of an Alpha
Twisted Steel
Guns Blazing

Printed in Great Britain
by Amazon